A MARGIN OF ERROR

LAURA HAYDEN

PARKER
HAYDEN
MEDIA

CHAPTER 1

December 8, 2142

*D*arys Kirk had all the proper ingredients for success.

A large theater, a rapt audience chanting her name, and a small group of sycophants crowding around her in the wings.

An omnipotent voice intoned, "And the award goes to . . ."

A tympani drum started a roll of thunder. The audience released a collective gasp in anticipation.

". . . Darys Kirk!"

Everything exploded—the crowd in cheers, her group of followers in tears. Spotlights blinded her. She stumbled her way to the middle of the stage amid the screams of those celebrating her triumph. A microphone rose out of the stage and someone in a tuxedo handed her a large golden statuette.

She stared at it, and then at the sea of homogeneously cheerful faces, recognizing no one—no family, no friends. What should be one of the greatest moments of her life was nothing more than a pale imitation of a world she didn't actually enjoy and in which certainly didn't belong.

Darys opened her mouth, hesitated, then released a sigh. "Computer, what time is it?"

The omnipotent voice answered, "Eleven-forty-six and thirty-seven seconds," intoning it as if introducing the world's greatest celebrity.

"I'm bored," she complained. "Why is this always the same? Can't we do something different?"

The lights flared then a sudden guitar riff filled the air. "And now," the disembodied voice said, "singing her greatest hit, here's Dar—"

"Computer. Stop program."

The music stopped in mid-crescendo. The echoes of the orchestra faded into the background. Her glittery gown faded into a T-shirt and jeans.

A different male voice emanated from the wall speaker . "Do you wish to save your place in the program for a later return or do you prefer to terminate the program?"

Darys sighed and dropped into a nearby chair, staring up at the ceiling. Holoprograms were nothing more than the most sophisticated version of smoke and mirrors, her generation's answer to a good video. And as far as holoprograms went, this one wasn't bad, especially with the karaoke subprogram, but she found it difficult to concentrate on the impending fun and games when her attention was being drawn somewhere else.

She sighed. "Set memory marker one and then close the program."

Before the crowd could completely fade to nothing, she stood and took one last bow to her adoring public.

"Computer, what time is it?"

"It is eleven-forty-nine and sixteen seconds."

Darys turned and glared at the vidphone sitting on the

nearby table. If the instrument didn't ring in the next ten minutes and forty-four seconds, her father was going to break a sacred promise he'd made and kept since she was twelve years old.

Twelve. She sighed at the memory. That was the year she'd tested high in applied astrophysics and had been shipped off to a boarding school for a summer semester of specialized studies. It had been her first time away from home for any real length of time, and as luck would have it, she'd come down with the Scadarian flu her first week there. She was miserable and sick and she wanted to go home.

But the school was too far away for a quick visit and the best her father could manage was a long chatty phone call that Saturday night. Although she was reluctant to admit it, especially to her jaded peers, the call cheered her up immensely and made the next week a bit more bearable. He called the following Saturday and every one after that until she finished the semester and was allowed to return home to her regular school.

Years later, when she went off to college, he resumed the Saturday night calling schedule and he'd been doing it ever since.

It didn't matter where he was, where Darys was, what either of them were doing, her father always called her on Saturday nights around ten o'clock. Even if they had spent all day together and went their separate ways only hours before, Harvey Kirk always called his daughter. As she grew up and their respective lifestyles meant they spent less time with each other, the weekly call became almost one of the only absolutes in the mobile, volatile society that formed her life.

It was nice to know she was loved. He was comforting . . . but not controlling. Her father respected her privacy and she found great solace in the fact that he cared enough to make and always keep such a promise.

3

That was . . . until now.

She drummed her fingers on the table in impatience. Maybe he'd forgotten his cell. Or maybe he'd remembered his cell, but his batteries had run down. Or there was no signal. Or maybe . . .

As she created a checklist of possibilities, she realized that one concept never entered the picture, one concept about which she was perfectly clear; Harvey Kirk hadn't forgotten his only daughter.

Especially not today. Not on her birthday.

Darys snatched the vidphone and punched in his number. She flinched for a moment when his image flashed on the screen. Then she reminded herself it was only his answering system.

He wore his usual goofy smile. "Hi! You've reached Harvey Kirk's phone, but not Harvey Kirk himself. I'm sorry I can't answer your call right now. I'm probably in the shower, soap in my eye, no towel in sight . . . you know how it goes. So, leave your name and number and I'll get back to you as soon as I've dried off. And don't forget to smile!"

He beamed into the lens, and Darys found herself returning his smile as usual. She punched in the security code which allowed her to access his personal message unit. The picture flickered and Harvey reappeared, still wearing his signature smile. "Hi Darys. Don't forget that I'm starting my time-share vacation on Monday. The suspension was lifted last week and I'm itchy to get back into the stream of things." He grinned. "Time stream, that is. I'm using the regular agency, This Time Around, and my agent is Ferrin Bellanger. He'll have my itinerary if you need it."

Harvey paused to broaden his smile. "I'll talk to you on your birthday, kiddo. Love ya."

Love you, too, Dad. She punched the disconnect button. Something had gone wrong. She just knew it. Something had gone terribly wrong. "Computer, find the number for This Time Around Travel Agency."

"The number is 1-067-703-555-4291. The agency is currently closed."

"Isn't there an emergency after-hours number I can call?"

"No."

"Find me the number for Ferrin Bellanger, an employee of the agency."

"The number is 1-067-703-555-0943. Shall I attempt a connection?"

"Yes."

There was a discernible pause. "Perhaps you should review your appearance before establishing a link. Or perhaps you should attempt an audio-only link. Your appearance does not meet the minimum criteria that you have set for a level two visual communication with a business."

Darys glanced up at the mirror over her dresser, recoiling at the messy reflection that stared back at her. "Audio only."

"One moment please."

There was a pause and then Darys heard a sleepy voice. "H'llo?"

"Is this the Ferrin Bellanger who works for This Time Around?"

"Y-yes. What time is it? Oh . . . I'm sorry, the agency is closed right now. Is this an emergency?"

Darys opened her mouth to say "Yes," then stopped short of speaking. Was it truly an emergency because her father hadn't called? To her, yes. But how could she explain it to someone else?

Simple. Lie.

"Yes. It's a family emergency. My name is Darys Kirk and my father is on one of your company's time-share vacations."

She heard him swallow audibly. "K-Kirk, you say?"

"Yes. Harvey Kirk. I need to speak to him right away."

"I . . . uh . . . I mean, he . . ." There was an uncomfortable silence which made the skin prickle on the back of her neck. He finally spoke. "There's no way you can reach him right now."

"Why? Is something wrong?"

"Wr-rong?" His voice cracked like that of a thirteen-year-old boy entering puberty. "Nothing's wrong. It's just that the communication grid was taken down tonight for repair while the vacationers were going through temporal restabi-lization."

"Which means in laymen's terms . . . ?"

"It means that if you were expecting a call from your father and it didn't come, it's because the phone system is being upgraded and he couldn't get a line out of the Restabi-lization Center while he was there. He probably had to go back to his vacation before he could get a chance to call you."

"Oh . . ." It sounded reasonable enough. But it didn't explain the nervous tremor that rode the man's voice. How could you trust someone who sounded more and more like a test circuit gone bad rather than a seasoned travel agent? Since she didn't know whether she could trust him or not, she decided it was better to take action, rather than sit back and wait.

Wait? No, more like "weight," as in, time to throw her weight around a little.

She used the same haughty no-excuses tones that one of her most-feared professors in college had used with irri-tating regularity with her. "Mr. Bellanger, it is imperative I speak with my father. I'm coming down tomorrow, and I fully expect you to arrange for an emergency link to him through his temporal stabilizer."

He seemed stunned by her demands. "I don't think we can—"

"You most certainly can." Even though he couldn't see her,

she still raised her finger and shook it at the communicator lens, out of habit more than anything else. "We both know that there's an emergency communication bandwidth on the stabilizer's monitoring signal. I'm coming down there tomorrow morning at eight o'clock sharp and you're going to help me contact my father."

"But . . . tomorrow's Sunday. We don't open until noon. And—"

"Eight o'clock, Mr. Bellanger." She paused for a moment to let her demands sink in then added, "If you lack the expertise to do it yourself, then have a technician waiting for us."

"But—"

"Goodnight."

After disconnecting the call, Darys leaned back on the pillow, debating what to do next.

There was truly nothing she could do until morning to contact her father. After all, she'd probably discover the agent was right; it was nothing more than an unfortunate coincidence that the vidphones weren't accessible while he was taking a break.

She needed to distract herself . . . with something . . .

"Computer. Begin program. Resume at Marker One."

The spotlight bathed her in a circle of light, causing the tiny crystals in her gown to glow in a rainbow of colors. "This is for all the lonely girls," she said to her adoring fans. When the applause died, she took a deep breath and began to sing.

"I'm afraid you've made a mistake."

Darys watched the older of the two men scan his clipboard. His name tag read Marvin Palmretti—Manager. "We have no Harvey Kirk registered as a traveler with our agency." When he looked up, his face remained devoid of emotion. "As I recall, Mr. Kirk sustained a rather heavy penalty after his last . . . escapade. Isn't there a notation here about a suspension?" He ran his finger down the clipboard, reading the file names. "Ferrin?" He turned to the younger man who stood beside him, twisting his long fingers into a knot. "Now what were you telling me earlier about Mr. Kirk's suspension?"

Ferris Bellanger's eyebrows twitched as he punched a couple of buttons on his clipboard. He looked as wormy as he'd sounded the night before. "It says here that because of the accidental conundrum your father created in 2015, the travel industry had to cease all traffic in the Rocky Mountain hot zone for a year. Mr. Kirk was—" Bellanger paled then covered his hesitation with a patently fake cough "—banned from all temporal travel for a period no less than two years."

Darys leaned forward, trying to get a glance at the official-looking document on his board. "But those two years were up a couple of weeks ago, right?"

Palmretti shook his head, making the thin row of gray ringlets dance over his eyes. "No. Apparently, the suspension was extended. For what reason, I don't know. All I do know is that Harvey Kirk is not currently our client."

"What about Darrell Kirk? My father might have used my brother's name. Dar's in the off-world military so he never uses civilian travel agencies."

Palmretti almost sneered. "We're quite thorough when we check identification records. Even if your father tried to masquerade under a false identity, we would discover his duplicity and deny him temporal passage."

"But you said . . ." Darys glanced at Bellanger who continued to twitch. Suddenly, she realized it wasn't a tic, but his rather colorless way of winking at her. She read his silent plea easily: *Don't tell.*

The night before, he'd admitted her father was using their services. Today, he was denying it. Why the change in stories?

One simple answer: his boss.

Darys realized she'd stopped in mid-sentence and everyone expected her to finish. This was the moment of truth; did she call Bellanger down in front of his boss or did she bide her time, waiting to catch him in at a private moment? Although righteous indignation demanded that she confront the liar with his lie, something inside of her whispered for her to wait.

Play along, her instincts warned.

Monocratic authority figures were hard to bully because they were such bullies themselves. If confronted, they buried the truth beneath a ton of official documents, manifestos, and operating procedure manuals. But assistant weasels could be broken like a piñata; one strike in the right place and they spilled all their secrets.

And if that didn't work, Darys could simply wring the truth out of his pencil-thin neck.

But first, she had to get Palmretti out of the way. She plastered a crestfallen look on her face. "Uh . . . then you're saying he definitely didn't start his trip from here?"

Palmretti tapped his forefinger against the clipboard. "Absolutely not. In fact, your father has been banned from travel everywhere. No legitimate agency in the world would risk their license to transport a banned client."

His supercilious expression was almost more than she could stomach, but she continued her performance. "Then my father . . . he's . . ." She sagged theatrically against the counter, squeezing her words between sobs of award-winning caliber. "Daddy's-missing-and-I-don't-know-where-to-find-him." She launched herself at Ferrin the Ferret who grabbed her out of instinct. As much as she hated having him touch her with his sweaty palms, it was a necessary part of her act.

"Ms. K-Kirk!" he stuttered in surprise. "Please, control yourself."

"W-water," she croaked as she tightened her grip on Ferrin's arms and giving Palmretti a pleading glance. "I need to take my medication."

Palmretti made a face. She could tell he hated being forced into a subservient role, but nonetheless, he grumbled something about getting her some water and stomped out the door.

As soon as the door slid closed behind him, she pushed herself away from Ferrin Bellanger. "Okay, you little cretin, last night you said my father is your client. Today, it's a different story. I'm covering for you . . . for now, but you better tell me exactly what's going on. Now."

The blood drained from his face until he was a deathly shade of white. "Not here." He scanned the area as if afraid someone might overhear. "Not now."

She reached out as if to grab a double handful of his shirt then she smoothed down his lapels as if trying to rein in her uncontrollable temper. "You have two choices. Tell me now or tell me in front of your boss."

He twitched silently as he contemplated his decision. "Your father came here two weeks ago. He and I . . . we . . . transacted a private deal that Mr. Palmretti isn't . . . um . . . aware of. It's nothing but a quick jaunt back to visit some old friends."

"Friends?" That didn't sound right. Her father's friends lived in the here and now. They even met every week for a poker game, so he sure didn't need to travel in time in order to visit them. "What kind of friends?"

"People he met in the past." Ferrin's sunken cheeks turned dusky red as he glanced toward the door. "Even if your father wasn't under suspension, Mr. Palmretti would have frowned on such a display of . . . of sentimentality."

"I don't care about Palmretti and his likes and dislikes. Tell me what has happened to my father," she demanded.

Bellanger pulled at his collar as if it was starting to contract and cut off his air supply. "Everything was going fine until Tuesday. That's when we lost contact with your father."

The words sounded ominous. "Lost contact? What do you mean?" This time, she grabbed his sleeve, not as a veiled threat but out of sheer surprise.

Bellanger glanced at the door and lowered his voice. "His stabilizer dropped off-line two days ago, and after that, we had no way to contact him. I hoped he might reappear in the grid last night, but he never showed. Your father . . . ," he drew a deep breath which seemed far beyond the capacity of his thin body, ". . . is missing in time."

A tremor coursed through Darys, making her muscles grow watery. As her grip loosened, Bellanger stepped back, nervously brushing away the wrinkled imprint of her grasp on his sleeve.

"M-missing?" she stuttered.

"I'm afraid so."

A dozen thoughts flashed through her mind, creating unsavory scenarios, each worse than the one before.

Missing in time. Lost in time.

Lost forever.

Gone forever.

"Can't they go in and find him?" She fought her rising panic with her best weapon: anger. "Can't you find him?"

"If I do, Mr. Palmretti will figure out what's going on and I'll lose my job." He fidgeted with his clipboard, nervously dropping it. He stooped to retrieve it. "Hell, the agency could lose its license for letting a suspended traveler step within twenty feet of a functioning grid."

Muscles which had been weak suddenly grew rock hard. Her fingers curled into a fist. Anger was winning. "Let me get this straight—you plan to do nothing? You're simply going to let him stay . . . lost, merely to save your own neck?"

They heard the sound of someone approaching. All the color drained from Bellanger's face and he dropped his clip-board again. "It's Mr. Palmretti." It was Bellanger's turn to grab Darys's sleeve. "Don't say anything," he pleaded. "Meet me here tonight at midnight and we'll figure out how to find your father." He drew in a shaky breath as he eyed the door again. "Just don't say anything to Mr. P.—please."

Darys had only a moment to make her decision, a decision which might mean life or death for her father.

"Please?" Bellanger released her and began to wring his hands.

At least he was willing to help. . . . That was more than she could say of the smug Palmretti.

"Tonight. Midnight." She gave Ferrin Bellanger her fiercest glare.

The door slid open and Palmretti rushed in with a glass of water. Darys stalled for time by making a show of gulping down an imaginary pill. Palmretti uttered some useless plati-tudes about lost sheep as he ushered her out. He added a vague promise to use his contacts to see if her father had used any other travel agency.

Once outside the building and in the anonymous safety of a crowded transport tube, Darys closed her eyes. Her anger splintered into other emotions: fear fueled confusion and confusion threatened to erupt into total panic.

What if her father was truly lost forever somewhere in the past? How could she cope with that possibility—knowing he'd been relegated to exist in some archaic world, without his family, his friends, without the comforts of technology?

Logic fought through the maelstrom of emotions, only to make things worse. "Lost" was quite an efficient term, Logic whispered. Darys had lost her mother—only that was to an incurable disease, not the vagaries of temporal mechanics. And if Harvey Kirk had been lost, abandoned somewhere in the past, then, by modern reckoning, he, too, was most assuredly dead.

A new wave of emotions hit Darys as effectively as a punch in the stomach, but she struggled to contain the panic. It was okay to be sad, angry, scared, even confused. But panicking wouldn't help anyone, especially her father.

You're not in this alone, she told herself.

No matter where her father was, he wouldn't give up hope. It wasn't time to lose another parent. And knowing her father, he'd be working hard on his end to find a way back. And she'd do the same.

Darys drew a shaky breath and forced herself to try to analyze the situation. How much help could she expect to receive from the agency? Palmretti was clueless, and Bellanger was probably more concerned with saving his hide than finding her father.

Still, she reminded herself, he'd promised to meet her at midnight. Maybe together, she and Bellanger could figure out how to retrieve her father.

But if Harvey Kirk didn't step out of their time portal, there was only one option left.

CHAPTER 2

"*M*s. Kirk, I really think this is a bad idea." Ferrin Bellanger's voice cracked.

Darys ignored the man as she fumbled with the holosuit fasteners. When she finally looked up, he'd twisted his fingers into a gangly knot.

He continued. "I've done everything I can think to do to try to retrieve your father. But the biggest problem is—we don't know why we lost contact with him in the first place. If it turns out to be a localized phenomenon or a self-contained ripple, we might lose contact with you as well. I can't let you put yourself in that kind of jeopardy, too." He wore a slightly hopeful expression as if his brief flare of concern for her welfare excused his otherwise squirrely behavior.

"If I don't go in after him, who will?" She leveled him with one stare. "You aren't going to send in a crew to rescue my father, are you?"

He pulled nervously at his collar. "Like I told you earlier, I can't. Mr. Palmretti has to okay an operation like that. And if he finds out about this, he'll burn out a chip!"

"Exactly." She jabbed him in the shoulder with her forefinger. "So if you don't want me calling Mr. Palmretti to tell him he has an incompetent agent booking illegal trips on the side, you'll figure out a way so that I don't get lost in the system too." She narrowed her gaze and gave him her most threatening look. "And don't get any bright ideas about solving your own problems by making me disappear, too. I've made sure that several key people know exactly what's going on. If something happens to me, you and this company will be the top story on the six o'clock universal newsfeed."

It was a long shot, but a gamble she was willing to take. Ferrin the Ferret would respond to threats. His type always did. But ferrets could be devious if they thought they could get away with something. Darys had no intentions of giving him time to think; she played her last trump card, another carefully calculated bluff.

"And, as a precaution, I've made sure to find out exactly where your ancestors lived in 2017." She leaned forward and lowered her voice. "Did you know your great-grandfather worked as a travel agent, too? Apparently he sold some sort of cruise-ship packages. I found an extremely informative article in an old Cheyenne, Wyoming news databank which mentioned something about how he sent someone 'up the river.' If you get any bright ideas about abandoning either me or my father in the past, I'll make sure to find a Mr. Kramer P. Bellanger and . . ." she let her voice trail off.

The man took a step forward, his damp fingers entwined in a crumpled ball. "You wouldn't. . . ."

"If I discover that either my father or I have been stranded in the past, good ol' Kramer just might meet with an unfortunate accident that prevents him from fathering any children. You'll be nothing more than a 'preconceived notion,' if you catch my drift."

"You couldn't. . . ."

She offered him her coldest smile. "I could. And I will if you mess with me or my dad."

He blanched, then made an uncomfortable swallowing sound. "I'll do my very best to bring you and your father back," he whispered. "Honest."

She closed her eyes and inhaled sharply. "Then let's get going."

IT TOOK three hours for the Ferret to power up the grid which also gave Darys three hours to imagine all the possible things that could go wrong. Thanks to her father, she was a seasoned, albeit unenthusiastic time traveler. She hated the sensation of standing in the magnetic field, anticipating the propulsion to another place, another time.

But her father loved everything about time travel. He honestly enjoyed living history so much he even looked forward to having his molecules ripped apart and reassembled in the time grid where they could be transported to God-knew-where. He might have relished his little jaunts back in time, but she didn't share his love for antiquities, be it period furniture or period people. As soon as she was old enough to beg off the family time share vacation, she did. Her father had dragged her mother on vacation after vacation until she was too sick to go. Then, after she died, he took off on them by himself.

Maybe that's the problem. I should have never let him go away by himself. Especially not after last time. She sighed. Last time . . .

Margin, Colorado.

Why was her father so fascinated with that particular town and its citizens? He'd always talked about the people in the past as if they were still alive rather than entries in some dusty history book, but it got worse when he started going to Margin. In her opinion, it wasn't a healthy attitude for him to take, living in the past rather than enjoying the present and anticipating the future.

Ever since her mother died, that's when he got fanatical about his trips. Ever since her mother died . . .

Darys shook away her thoughts. Right now, her mission was to find her father. At all costs. Even if it meant going back and finding him, herself.

"When was the last time you traveled?" Bellanger asked as he set down a tray of equipment on the counter next to her.

"I stopped when I was eleven, when I was old enough to object. But I still have over thirty-six hundred hours of experience on the grid."

He gave her a critical once-over, evidently attempting to gauge her age by assessing her physical attributes, which were unavoidably revealed by the clinging holosuit. "Things have changed a little since then." He looked up from her breasts long enough to read her expression. He backpedaled quickly. "I mean . . . in terms of travel procedures."

He gave her a brief overview as he clipped various components to her holosuit. Although she hated the thought of Bellanger's sweaty hands touching her, she appreciated his tendency to play to the side of caution, giving her two backup systems for every primary one.

"This is your temporal stabilizer; it's the only system that we can't back up because the frequencies have to be unique, unduplicated." He held up a small disk suspended from a chain. "We usually give it an enhanced appearance—make it look like a timepiece or some sort of piece of jewelry appropriate to the era, but we don't have the time. Just keep this under your holosuit." He gave her a stern look. "Do I need to explain why it's important to never take off the stabilizer? Because of the urgency of this trip, I don't have time to properly process you for an extended stay in the past. Unlike your other trips as a child, this time you'll be totally dependent on the stabilizer. If you take it off, your molecules will attempt to return here. One at a time." He made a face. "The results will be . . . quite messy."

A small fissure formed in Darys's sense of resolution.

"About your holosuit," he continued, "if you haven't worn one since you were a kid, then you'll find they've changed. You don't have to do anything yourself. Your suit can adapt automatically to the fashions and climate around you."

"How . . ." She cleared her throat so that she could speak. "How quickly does it change?"

"Instantaneously at first, then it makes subtle changes as conditions warrant. Of course, you can turn it to manual if you find it necessary to override the auto function." He glanced at his watch. "Uh-oh. It's getting late and the morning crew will be here soon." He reached forward and made a final adjustment to a control cuff circling her left wrist. "Ready?"

It was such a simple, innocuous word, but it made her heart miss a beat. Her courage evaporated, and all the irrational fears she thought she'd suppressed flooded in to fill the void. She opened her mouth to speak, but found herself unable to talk. Instead, she nodded, praying for the ability to retain some semblance of being in control.

"As soon as you find your father, widen your stabilizer field to include him and hit the recall button. I'll create an emergency portal and pull you both back."

It took all her strength to keep her voice under control. "How will I know when you're on duty and can do this when nobody else is around?"

He gave her a half-hearted smile. "It's time travel. I can override usual methods."

Darys heard the words, but fear blanked her mind. "Huh?"

"Usually, if you spent a week back in time, we make sure a week in time has passed here. It's to eliminate time lag. But there are ways around it. No matter how long it takes you to find him—an hour, a day, a month—it'll be exactly a week later here. That's as soon as I can open a . . . private portal for you. We have to wait until I'm on duty alone because I can't let anybody know what I'm doing."

Her mind wandered back to one of her father's attempts to steer her away from mechtech engineering and into the wonderful world of being a travel agent. "I remember that from school—Simova's Third Law of Temporal Mechanics: 'Timeslip rates are independent of each other.'"

"Exactly." He glanced nervously at his watch again. "And time is one thing we're running out of. Activate your suit. It's been programmed to start with the appropriate early twenty-first-century regional-seasonal apparel."

"Check." Darys complied, punching the auto control and watching her gray holosuit flood with color, transforming into a garish neon-green winter jacket and pants.

"Ready?" he asked, glancing toward the door.

She swallowed hard then thought of her father. *For you, Dad.*

Darys stepped into the archway and reached up grabbed the handles to brace herself. "Do it. Next stop, January twenty-seventeen."

ONCE DARYS REMEMBERED the fundamental rules about remaining upright, the nausea slowly subsided. She released the handles of the portal and took one stumbling step forward. As one knee buckled, she reached out blindly, trying to steady herself. She might have successfully landed in another time zone, but her sense of balance was still lost in transit.

Her gloved fingers contacted a rough surface which felt eerily familiar.

A tree?

She looked around, realizing that the portal had located itself next to a stand of trees edging a wide, uncluttered slope. She didn't need to be a historian like her father to recognize this was a ski slope; the sport had recently undergone resurgence in popularity in her own time. And since this was Margin, Colorado, this had to be Margin Mountain Resort.

But there were no skiers.

Darys pulled off her snow goggles and wiped away a bead of sweat that trickled into her face. She stared at the grass-covered slope, at the flowers clumped around the base of the trees. The sun rode high in the cloudless blue sky.

She tugged at the collar of her ski suit.

Ferrin Bellanger had already made his first stupid mistake. Instead of landing in the dead of winter, she'd landed in the midst of a very hot summer. Ninety degrees in the shade. July? August?

"Warning!"

Darys flinched at the sound of the computer voice.

"Your body temperature is rising. Do you wish to place your holosuit on automatic?"

She hit the *Confirm* button on the control cuff and the suit began its slow transformation, starting at the top. The pair of snow goggles she'd pulled off faded from her hand. The garish jacket slowly metamorphosed into a loose white shirt. As the transformation worked its way down her body, Darys allowed herself a brief smile. Some things never changed. The tight ski pants transformed into a comfortable pair of faded jeans. The style was a little old-fashioned, but they were jeans, nonetheless.

"Do you want the control cuff to remain visible?"

She punched the *No* button and the cuff faded from view. *One problem down.*

She unbuttoned her sleeves and rolled them up. With a sigh, she scanned the horizon. So . . . it was summer, not winter. At least this was still Colorado. At the foot of the slope, she saw the twisting ribbon of a packed dirt road. Logic said that roads led to places and where there were places, there were usually people.

And nobody liked people better than Harvey Kirk.

More important than that, he liked an audience. She knew from experience that whenever she'd lose track of her father, she could always find him in the middle of a crowd, regaling the listeners with some outlandish tale. She headed for the road.

The air was sharp, cleaner than she imagined it could ever be without being artificially processed. Twice, she was startled by the sight of a bird, swooping out of the sky to scavenge the soil for a wormy mid-morning snack. Birds were a precious commodity in her world. Air space had gotten crowded and for their safety and continued existence, birds had been relegated to controlled aviaries. Migration season always played havoc with air traffic patterns, but people persevered for the sake of nature.

But here, she marveled, birds had no controls. She watched a flock of black birds descend on a tree by the road. Their magnificent, random squawking reminded her of an orchestra, tuning up for a concert.

But a sudden blast of noise rang out. The black cloud of birds rose quickly into the air and moved in a swarm to another stand of trees a hundred or so yards away. A second discharge echoed through the sky. After a moment's hesitation, Darys decided it was quite possibly a gunshot.

Her breath caught in her throat. Someone was shooting at those magnificent birds? The thought brought her to a standstill. But birds were a protected species; no one was allowed to take potshots at them! Not in her world. . . .

But . . . *I'm not in my world.*

A third shot split the air. Darys moved toward the source of the noise. Somewhere in the back of her mind, she remembered that twenty-first-century weapons could be used on people and well as animals, but certainly, no one would fire on—

Another shot spurred her into action.

"Stop! Don't shoot!" She ran, careful to stay in the middle of road. "Don't shoot!" Darys waved her hands as she shouted. As she rounded the corner, she heard a disgruntled voice.

"He's going to kill me," someone groaned.

Although it wasn't a cry of fear or a shout of warning, Darys dove for cover, landing in a dry ditch. If anybody was doing any killing, she wanted to be out of range. After a few silent moments, she lifted her head to peer over the fringe of grass that camouflaged her position.

A young man, a teenager, stood in the middle of the road with his arms crossed. He looked neither injured nor frightened. In fact, he looked positively disgusted. In front of him squatted a magnificent black antique car.

"Uncle Ford's gonna kill me," the young man repeated to no one in particular. He bent down, grabbed a rod that extended from the front of the vehicle, and gave it a mighty twist. The automobile shuddered, belching a cloud of gray smoke. Then something akin to the sound of a rifle shot split the air. Darys allowed herself a sigh of release. No one was shooting at anybody.

She watched him step back from the vehicle.

Anger flowed freely through his stance and his voice. "You stupid hunk of junk! I don't know why I even try to drive you. You're uncooperative, mean-spirited . . . vindictive . . ." He kicked the vehicle's thin tire and then plopped down in the dirt beside the vehicle.

"Control cuff," Darys whispered. The control pad appeared on her left wrist. "Adjust clothing. Sample subject at fifty meters."

"Override gender bias?"

He was wearing jeans. How could there be a gender bias if he was wearing jeans? "Yes," she responded. A few seconds later, she wore an outfit which duplicated the young man's, from his soft cap to his scuffed boots.

Darys pulled off her hat, stared at it then turned her wincing attention to the rest of her outfit. It was one thing to dress in the same style, but to be his fashion twin? "Does it have to be identical? Couldn't there, at least, be some . . . some color variation?"

Her leather vest morphed from black to a soft fawn color. She pulled off her hat and watched it changed from brown herringbone tweed to a red and black plaid.

That's better. She twisted her hair into a ponytail, stuffing it into the hat before jamming it on her head.

If she was going to be forced to play the role of stranger in a strange land, then the best way to ingratiate herself to the people here was to be helpful, to gain their confidence. People would be more apt to answer her questions about her missing father if she could find some low-key but comfortable niche in their society. It was a truism that was independent of time lines.

A dozen heartbeats and one deep breath later, she rose from her hiding place, stuffed her hands in her pockets, and walked toward the young man. Adopting what she hoped was a benign smile, she called out, "Having problems?"

The young man twisted his head and took a quick appraising look at her. Then he jumped up from the ground and gave Darys a rueful smile as he slapped the dust from the seat of his pants.

"It's this ol' hunk of junk. It won't start."

Although she thought she'd be too self-occupied to care, too unenthusiastic about time travel, the excitement of a first contact started to build in her, just like in the good old days. "Can I give you a hand?"

His smile broadened. "Thanks."

She imitated a teenage boy's walk as best as she could with wide, loping steps as she crossed the road to the front of the car. "Are you out of fuel?"

The boy shook his head. "Nope. My uncle gassed her up this morning. And the fuel line isn't clogged, I checked." He blushed. "At least I think that was the fuel line."

Darys leaned over the car and peered into the engine compartment, trying to identify components which bore little resemblance to the engine that powered her creaky two-year-old Hashamita Flyer. She pawed through a storeroom of memories and images, trying to remember when at fifteen she was her father's captive during a lecture on internal combustion engines. A petroleum by-product mixed with air . . .

Remembering the basics, she nodded. "Where do we start first?"

He stuck out a hand, stained with grease. "I'm Nick Callaghan."

"Dar . . . rell Kirk." She hoped he didn't notice the pause in her introduction. Certainly her younger brother wouldn't mind her stealing his name, considering the circumstances.

"Pleased to meet ya, Darrell." He stared at the engine. "I

thought my uncle already fixed the problem with the cam shaft. Maybe he hasn't gotten around to it. He's awfully busy." He offered her a proud, almost possessive smile. "He's an inventor, you know."

"Does he know anything about cars?"

Nick laughed. "More than any man I know or even hope to know. But this time, I think the problem is this gol'danged float feed carburetor."

Darys stared at the engine, trying to figure out where and what a 'gol'danged float feed carburetor' was. Luckily, the young man expressed his anger by banging his wrench against a section of the engine.

"Sometimes it works if you bang it."

She pasted on a smile; some repairs were universal, no matter their time origin. "Well, let's see what we can do."

They worked on the engine for a half hour, trying various reparations and banging it in various places with various tools. As much as Darys knew about technology in the future —certainly enough to teach a secondary level course—she knew precious little about internal combustion engines beyond her father's long-winded lecture. It was disconcerting to be an expert in an advanced field, but to be unfamiliar with some of its more basic and perhaps humble beginnings in an earlier time.

As the sun centered itself overhead and the air grew heavy with heat, the young man stripped off his hat and vest. Darys wished she could do the same, but dared not; she remembered the control cuff's warning about overriding a clothing gender bias. Not being a prized student of history and culture like her father, she had no idea what type of biases existed in the early twenty-first century—gender, race, planet of origin . . .

She strained to recall the one lecture she'd attended on "The Limitation of Women's Roles in Past Societies." If this was, indeed, a limited society, somehow she didn't think engine repair was on the approved list of activities for gentle ladies.

But, luckily, Darys didn't need an extensive knowledge of history to know what to do. She'd listened to too many of her father's travel stories not to know the basics; if you ran into an uncomfortable situation, stay in the background—keep contact with the natives on a non-personal level, observe rather than interact, and most important of all, don't try to enlighten individuals to the ways of the future.

Easier said than done.

Nick intruded into her thoughts. "Okay, try the starter again, Darrell."

Darys climbed up into the driver's seat and, after getting instruction, attempted to start the car. "Well?"

"I don't understand it. Why isn't it starting?" The boy threw himself back into the engine compartment. "Wait a minute," he said in a muffled voice. "Looky here . . ."

Darys climbed out of the car and stood next to him. "What do you see?"

"A loose wire. This may be the culprit." There was a moment of silence as he fiddled with something, presumably the wire. "Rats. It's not long enough to reattach. But maybe . . ." He straightened up, a new streak of grease marring his youthful face. "If you can reach in there and hold this wire in place, I might be able to crank it. Once we get it started, it won't matter that the wire isn't making contact."

"Sure." Darys positioned herself on the edge of the car and reached in as far as she could, trying to snag the loose wire. It dangled centimeters from her fingertips. She pulled herself out of the compartment. "I can't reach it. Sorry. What if you hold the wire and I try to crank?"

He raised a critical eyebrow. "You think you can manage it? It's not easy to use a hand crank."

Darys realized this was her chance to ingratiate herself even further into his good graces. "No problem. I've done it a million times."

His gaze narrowed. "Well . . . okay." He disappeared into the compartment. "Okay. Got it. Give it a turn."

Darys contemplated the crank, rubbed her hands together then bent over to grasp the metal handle. She gave it a mighty twist, but nothing happened.

"Again."

She lined both hands up on the handle and threw her weight into the action. The engine groaned then fell silent.

"Again," said the muffled voice. "And this time, don't stop."

Darys drew a deep breath, braced her feet and turned the crank. As instructed, she didn't let go and continued to alternately pull and push the handle, making the crank rotate several times. After a couple of grinding revolutions, the engine suddenly coughed, sputtered, then roared to life with the fury of a raging thunderstorm.

In the split second that preceded the noise, Darys had identified a key flaw in the crank's mechanical design. But in this case, having an unusually high mechanical aptitude meant nothing without proper timing. Had she figured everything out a moment sooner, she could have let go of the crank.

Unfortunately, Darys still had a death grip on the handle when the engine backfired. When the crank suddenly reversed, it threw her off her feet. As a thunderous echo reverberated through her ears, a companion streak of lightning radiated from her shoulder.

She saw red and then black.

Then nothing.

"Ma'am?" Someone touched her hand. "Ma'am, you all right?"

I'm not a ma'am. I'm a wolf in sheep's clothing . . . er, a girl in boy's clothing, Darys thought. She opened her mouth to correct Nick, but all she could manage was an ear-shattering screech. The sound shocked her.

Is that me?

The sound must have shocked him as well because he jumped back, as if trying to get out of range of her scream. A moment later, he knelt beside her again, this time without touching her.

"I'm so sorry, ma'am. I didn't know you were a girl." He stared at her, his gaze dropping to the button which had been ripped open when she landed in the middle of the dirt road. Only the smallest glimpse of cleavage had been revealed, but evidently a little was enough. "Uh . . . I mean, a woman. I would have never asked you to . . ." He blushed. "I'm really sorry, ma'am."

She found that if she tried to whisper, the words came out in something less caustic than a shriek. "Say 'ma'am' one more time and I'll scream."

Nick blanched. "Yes ma'—" he paused "—yessum." He reached over and picked up her cap which had fallen to the ground. He offered it to her as if it was a peace offering. "Are you all right?"

"No," she gritted between clenched teeth. A tear trickled down her face and disappeared in the dirt. "I think my arm's broken."

"Gee willikers, I hope not." He helped her to her feet, paying careful attention as to where to place his hands to help. She wondered if he was being solicitous of injuries or her womanly attributes. She remembered her brother at this same age; awkward, gawky, unsure where to touch, where not to touch, and secretly eager to learn the difference.

"My Uncle Ford warned me something like this could happen. He calls it a 'design flaw.'"

She shot him a dirty look. "How reassuring to know I'm nothing more than another statistic of failed automotive design. Don't forget to thank your uncle for me, for his belated insight." She waited a few moments until the shooting pains in her shoulder stopped firing. "What kind of design flaw?"

The boy swallowed hard. "When this model backfires, the engine crank reverses direction really fast."

"Tell me about it," she grumbled, having firsthand . . . er . . . shoulder knowledge of exactly how fast it reversed.

Nick took her literally. "My uncle said it would be relatively easy to correct it. If you could install some sort of ratchet—"

She used her good arm to gesture dismissal. "Never mind the car. Let's talk about repairing me."

"Uh yeah . . ." He pulled his hand back from her uninjured arm and blushed, again. "Uh . . . my mother's a doctor. If your arm's broken, she can set it for you. If it's only a dislocated shoulder, she'll be able to put it back in place for you, ma—"

Darys drew a shaky breath and watched spots of black start to fill her vision. They danced along with the pounding conga line of pain radiating from her shoulder. "Just as long as she has some neural path blocking agents."

Nick stared openly at her. "Some what?"

"Painkillers," she said between gritted teeth, trying to remember what name they went under in the past. "Drugs."

Nick thumbed toward the car, which was idling merrily. "The sooner we get there, the sooner she can do something about stopping the pain. At least the lizzie's running now."

Darys grimaced at the car which broke the peace periodically by belching smoke every once in a while. "Sure, it's running. But at what sacrifice?" She shook her head. "Lead on. Just keep it under a hundred on the curves."

"A hundred," he repeated with a laugh. "That's a good one."

Although the trip to the house seemed as if it took forever, Nick assured her it was only three miles. He tried valiantly to stay out of the ruts and away from the bigger holes, but the vehicle seemed to have a mind of its own. By the time they arrived at the infirmary, Darys had stopped groaning; it took too much energy. She sagged in her seat, almost falling on top of him and not really caring.

"We're here." Nick blew the horn mounted to the side of the car then gingerly righted Darys. Instead of screaming, she allowed the little black dots to swell, hoping that as they blotted out her vision, they would blot out the pain as well.

"Ma'am?" a distant voice spoke.

She didn't respond.

"Ma'am?"

She opened one eye. "Am I dead yet?"

"No ma'am."

"Then kill me."

"C'mon. My mom will take care of you." He turned toward the building. "Mom. Mom?" He drew a deep breath. "Mom!"

Ford Nolan heard the "ah-oo-ga" of the Model T above the din of the machinery. He shook his head. Nick had taken entirely too much time for a simple trip into town to pick up a package. The boy had probably lollygagged over some dime novel or magazine at the store. Or perhaps Nick had gotten caught up in his admiration of the storekeeper's youngest daughter.

Ford couldn't help but smile. When he was fourteen, he'd tended to lose track of time, too, especially when there were pretty girls to usurp his attention.

The squawk of his nephew's voice rose above the sound of the drill press.

"Mom? Dad? Uncle Ford?" Nick's voice cracked with the uncertainty of youth. "Anybody!"

Ford hit the lever which lifted the rotating bit from the wood, causing the noise level to drop significantly.

"Somebody . . . help!"

Ford hit the workshop door at a dead run, knocking it out of the way as he exited into the bright sunlight. Nick stood by the Model T, his knees almost buckling under the weight of his companion.

"She passed out. I can't move."

Ford grasped the woman around the waist, which allowed Nick to regain his balance.

"Careful. Her shoulder's hurt."

Ford shifted her gingerly and she reacted in pain even in her semi-conscious state. "What happened?"

"The lizzie stalled out again and I couldn't get her going. The lady walked up, gave me a hand—"

"With the car?"

Nick blushed to the roots of his blond hair. "I thought she was . . . a he."

"A what?" Ford looked at the woman settled uncomfortably against his chest. Sure, she had on men's clothing, but only an inexperienced boy could mistake her for a man. He heaved a sigh which made the woman grimace in pain.

"Go get your mother. Pronto."

A moment later, Emma scurried out of the infirmary door. "Nick says we have another car crank injury."

Ford nodded. "I thought it would be best not to move her any more until you got a look at her."

Emma performed a cursory examination with the woman still draped in Ford's arms. "I don't think it's broken, but merely dislocated."

The patient opened one eye and squinted at Emma. "I'm covered for this."

Ford looked at the woman then his sister. "What?"

The injured woman drew a shaky breath. "Health insurance. I have the standard government health maintenance policy with a remote location-emergency coverage rider."

Huh?" Ford watched his sister stiffen as she gave the woman a detailed once-over. "It—it must be the pain," he offered in explanation, "making her spout such nonsense."

Emma ignored him. "Tell me . . . do you like . . . television?"

The woman opened the other eye, now staring in perplexed pain at Emma. "Television? What in the world does television have to do with my health coverage?" She straightened, wincing in pain as she gave her surroundings a quick scan. "This better not be one of those reality medicine shows. I'm not signing any waivers. You're not putting this on the air—" A wave of pain choked off the rest of her ravings and she sagged in Ford's arms.

He shifted her dead weight. "She's delirious, I tell you."

Emma planted her fists on her hips. "No, she's not. I'm afraid I know exactly what she's talking about." She turned toward the house and cupped her hand to her mouth. "Barrett! Come quick."

Ford's brother-in-law, John Barrett Callaghan, peered from around the barn door and spotted the threesome. He trotted toward them, wiping his hands on a rag. "What's wrong?"

She nodded toward the woman and released a sigh. "We've got another one."

CHAPTER 3

*A*lthough they were both adults, Emma still possessed an older sister's ability to make Ford feel inept, awkward, and terminally young. He almost plowed into her when she paused in the examination room door. She stood there, arms crossed, and pale determination filling her face. It was a look he knew all too well. And one he still feared.

"John Barrett will take it from here. You wait outside."

"But—"

"But nothing, Ford. Just wait outside." She placed her palm against his chest and pushed him back.

She was a still a slight woman. He'd passed her in height when he was thirteen, and now stood nearly a foot taller than her. But she could still hold him at bay with a steely gray stare and the merest of gestures.

He sighed. "Yes, Emma." As the door closed in his face, Ford tried to sort through his thoughts. Certainly, propriety had something to do with his sister's reaction, but Ford sensed a different undercurrent to the proceedings. There was something that Emma didn't want him to see, and it had nothing to do with the more delicate side of rendering medical attention. Whatever the woman was prattling about, Emma seemed to infer some sort of important meaning from it, some meaning that he wasn't supposed to hear. Or understand.

Ford sighed. His sister and her secrets . . .

How many times had he walked in on her and John Barrett in mid-conversation, only to realize the topic had changed to something innocuous the moment he stepped into the room? Surely two newlyweds didn't care to discuss some topics around a twelve-year-old boy, but ten years later?

Twenty years later?

Hadn't he loved and lost? Married and mourned? Found a way to lose himself in the rigors of research rather than be mired in memory? He hung his head and released a small laugh. His Mary, the schoolteacher, would have not appreciated his extended alliterations.

"Stop it," she would have said. "You're not supposed to sound like a book. You read entirely too much Arthur Conan Doyle as a child."

He had. And for that reason, he sat down on the stairs and propped his fists beneath his chin, giving his deductive abilities free rein, anything to distract him from the sudden bout of melancholia.

Perhaps the woman was a foreigner. If so, she spoke English quite well, even if her cadence was a bit unusual. She wasn't from England, he knew that. A traveling band of actors had come through the area several years ago, and from them, Ford gleaned details about London and the adventures of ocean travel, all delivered in crisp British accents that tickled his ears and made him yearn to travel.

Untangling himself from his ruminations, Ford suddenly realized he was no longer alone. Nick had joined him on the step, elbows balanced on his knees and chin propped on his fists. The boy looked for all the world like a petulant child, pouting because he'd been excluded from the grown-up's world. Suddenly, Ford recognized the boy's look and posture; it was a mirror of his own. Ford straightened self-consciously..

He and Nick sat on the stoop in rare silence. Ford marked the seconds, knowing Nick would explode into explanation before he counted to ten.

Nine.

Eight.

Seven—

"Uncle Ford . . . I'm awfully sorry. I know I was late and . . ." Nick's voice as well as his bravado weakened. His face turned a distinct shade of red. "I didn't know he was a . . . er . . . that he was a she." He swallowed hard. "She'd stuffed her hair in her cap and you saw what she was wearing." He shook his head. "Trousers!" he muttered under his breath.

Ford patted his nephew's shoulder. "It's understandable, Nick."

Certainly, only an inexperienced young man like Nick would fail to see the undeniably feminine curves only partially hidden by the woman's masculine shirt and vest. After all, the boy was barely fourteen. Of course, those shapely dungarees should have been the dead giveaway.

Ford savored the memory of her unusual appearance for only a moment before changing the subject, fearing that he, too, would turn beet red and betray thoughts an upstanding citizen shouldn't readily have. "So why was she manning . . . er . . . handling the crank on the lizzie?"

"I'll show you." Nick stood up, brushed the dirt from the seat of his pants and stalked over to the automobile. Ford followed, and together, they folded back the vehicle's hood.

Everyone in their family had a role to play. Emma was a masterful doctor of human physiology, who diagnosed and treated her patients with respect and care. John Barrett had an uncanny ability to see into the hearts of people and divine their true criminal tendencies or lack thereof. Nick was a schemer and a doer, always trying to execute a plan to bring them all great power and wealth. His older brother, Tim, was a dreamer, enjoying his final summer of freedom before heading to college. Although he spent much of his time with his head in the clouds, what airy thoughts he conjured always had a note of practicality to them. John Junior, at age eleven, possessed a combination of his brothers' worst tendencies. He was a doer with no practical sense, meaning he, alone, got into more trouble of a highly inventive nature than any other child in Margin. Many times, John Barrett had to look no further for his culprit than their own dinner table.

But it was because of Nick's urges, Tim's sense of vision, Emma and John Barrett's support and faith, and John Junior's disinterest in the entire proceedings—and therefore his lack of involvement—which led Ford to patent a few of his own ideas.

"It must be something about the name, Ford," Nick said, his body half hidden in the belly of the automotive beast. "Henry Ford and Ford Nolan, two great men of vision."

Ford reached for a wrench. "You have it all wrong. He builds cars. I merely repair them."

"He's no smarter than you, Ford. You'll do it someday. You'll invent something so marvelous that America will knock down your door to get to it."

Ford straightened up and wiped his greasy hands on a rag. "Then maybe I ought to invent a better deadbolt for the front door."

"No, seriously, Uncle Ford. You can do it. Maybe the invention in the barn is your ticket to fame and fortune. You *are* going to file the patent papers on it, aren't you?"

Ford straightened "Just what do you know about my invention? I thought I told you my workshop was off-limits."

Nick held up his dirty hands in surrender. "All I did was take a peek. I didn't touch anything."

Ford stared at his nephew then sighed. Nick's definition of "not touching anything" usually resulted in three hours of intense repair work to return something to working condition. "Nicholas Nolan Callaghan, if you so much as turned a single screw, I'll . . ." He allowed the threat to trail off; the advantage of dealing with an imaginative youth was that the punishment he conjured was usually far worse than the one Ford would have devised.

"I'm sorry, I'm sorry . . . there was a loose wire and I thought—"

Ford ducked back into the engine compartment. "A loose wire like this loose wire?" He pulled out and held up the offending piece that he knew hadn't vibrated itself loose but was likely another victim of Nick's enthusiastic but unskilled tune-up attempts. "Do me a favor, Nick, don't touch anything. Okay?" He couldn't help but sigh. "Just leave the Model T and the things in my workshop alone. Understand?"

"Sure, Uncle Ford." The boy wiped his hands on the seat of his pants and strolled away. When Nick spotted his brothers coming up the road, he ran toward them.

Ford couldn't help but smile. How could three boys who looked so much alike be so different? Although both Tim and John Junior carried a load of books, Ford knew they were all for Tim. Tim preferred theoretical studies, whereas Nick liked a hands-on method. Frequently they came to the same conclusions but from differing standpoints. Then there was John Junior, who reveled in discovery through chaos.

Nick rescued Junior from his carrying duty and the scamp took off, probably in hopes of getting at least one act of terror completed before dinnertime. Nick and Tim wandered to the house, arms loaded and their heads together, indicating the hatching of a new grand plan.

God help us all. . . .

Ford turned back to the car and the lonesome piece of wire awaiting reattachment. But as he leaned into the car, his thoughts drifted for some unfathomable reason back to Emma's patient.

The first real woman he'd ever held in his arms since Mary passed two years prior.

He closed his eyes and remembered the scent of the woman's hair, tickling his nose when he held her.

Where had she come from?

And why did she smell so good?

BARRETT HAD ACTED as his wife's medical assistant too many times not to understand his role to distract the patient. Dislocated shoulders were a damnable nuisance, because you had to create nearly the same amount of pain to put the shoulder back in place as it took to pop it out the first time. Even worse, the patient tended to tense up in anticipation or even worse, flinch, which made the job that much harder.

But this time, the woman needed no distraction. She ignored Emma and turned her abject attention to the room, slowly scanning it, evidently trying to soak in every little detail. Her gaze settled on the far wall and her eyes widened. Barrett followed her line of sight, realizing she'd fixed her attention on the calendar.

July 1912, it boldly pronounced.

Barrett reddened slightly; they'd forgotten to tear off July to reveal August. But since it was only the second day of the month, certainly that wasn't sufficient to warrant her expression of shock.

He shot her a smile. "You know what they say—*Tempus Fugit*. That's Latin for—"

"Time flies," she supplied. She shuddered visibly. "You have no idea how appropriate that is."

"Well, I do know we haven't been properly introduced. I'm John Barrett Callaghan and this is my wife . . ." He stared at Emma, suddenly losing track of his thoughts. She had that effect on him, as if every time he looked at her, he fell in love with her all over again. Time had indeed flown, twenty years of it. His love was stronger, deeper, sweeter . .
.

Emma cleared her throat and he straightened, trying to regain the threads of introduction. ". . . and this is my wife, Dr. Emma Callaghan. May I ask your name, ma'am?"

"Darys Ki—" Her attempt to speak trailed off in a yelp of pain. She turned to Emma. "Can't you give me some sort of anesthesia?" she pleaded. She glanced ruefully at the calendar and added, "You *know* what anesthesia is, don't you?"

Emma sat up straighter, her face reflecting a mixture of excitement and trepidation which Barrett recognized all too well. But why now?

"I know what it means. I even know how to spell it. But I don't think we'll need any because—" Emma made a sudden movement which made the woman screech in pain and then go pale "—because your shoulder's back in place."

It took a while for the woman to regain enough control and composure to speak. She leaned her head back and closed her eyes. "You're good," she admitted between clenched teeth. "The last time this happened to me, it took a doctor three attempts to get it back in place." She grimaced. "That crank sure packs a wallop."

"One of Mr. Ford's unexpected legacies, I suppose." Emma reached into her supply cabinet and withdrew a small jar and a neat bundle of clean rags. She paused and gave the woman a penetrating stare. "You do know who Mr. Ford is, don't you?"

Barrett watched as the two women communicated on a level beyond him. Whatever secret the woman possessed, Emma knew. And the woman knew Emma knew.

Woman stuff—more complications than Barrett was willing to stand at the moment. "If you don't need me anymore, I better head into town. It's time to make my rounds." He kissed the air in the direction of his wife and made a beeline to the door.

"Barrett."

He was stopped by the serious undercurrents in Emma's voice.

"Barrett . . . she's from the future."

His heart froze in his chest. *The future. . . .* He couldn't move, couldn't turn around.

The enigma of how he'd gone back in time was surpassed only by the concern that he might one day have to return to a world with which he was now unfamiliar. Certainly, he still had his journals in which he'd initially chronicled everything he remembered about his life in the future. But as the memories faded, so had the logic in the words he wrote and the explanations he'd given himself. His words came out in a croak. "How far in the future?"

He provided his own answer. It could be tomorrow, the next day, next month, next year. It could be—

"Twenty-one-forty-two."

The young woman rattled off the numbers so easily. *Twenty-one-forty-two.*

2-1-4-2.

Not 2015. Barrett allowed himself to relax a little. He pivoted, trying to find a proper smile. "So what brings you to the twentieth century?"

She gaped at them. "You're so calm!"

Barrett shrugged, slightly pleased that he could hide an earth-shattering revelation from her. Of course, Emma knew. Emma knew exactly what was going through his head right now, the leaps his stomach was performing, why there was sweat trickling down his back.

"I don't understand," the young woman continued. "How could you even conceive of the idea of time travel?" She turned toward Emma. "Anybody else would simply assume I was delirious. Or crazy. How in the world do you know anything about time travel?"

Barrett looked at his wife, seeking confirmation in her hooded glance. She gave him a barely perceptible nod.

His smile faltered as the words tumbled out. "I came here twenty years ago . . . from 2015."

"2015?" She stared at him, her brows knitted first in perplexity, and then in obvious doubt. "Something's wrong here. People didn't know anything about traveling through time back in the late twenty-first century. In fact . . . people didn't start traveling through time until thirty years ago. They legalized the process in 2112. December 8th, to be exact." She allowed herself one harsh bark of laughter. "It's a hard date to forget. It was the day I was born."

Barrett tried to speak, but found himself unable to explain his curious adventures through time. How could he explain what he didn't actively remember?

"He didn't do it by himself," Emma supplied. "He had some help from a traveler from the future. Someone helped Barrett to come back in time from 2015 to 1892." Emma shot him a look which made his toes curl. "And Barrett decided to stay," she added in a whisper.

Emma—full of delicate strength. She'd been able to understand and accept a man who really didn't belong anywhere. She was the one who made it so easy for him to forsake a prosperous life in the future for true love in the past.

The injured woman's confused stare turned into a dubious glare. "Someone from the future *helped*?" She suddenly paled. "Someone *helped* by picking up a hitchhiker from one time period and taking him to another? Someone like . . ." Her voice trailed off. After a frozen moment, she sagged, wincing as she put undue stress on strained muscles. She tried to speak, faltered, then tried again with more success. "This person's name wouldn't have been Harvey Kirk, would it?"

The sweat running down Barrett's back turned ice-cold. "You know Harvey?"

The young woman met his false bravado with a troubled gaze. "I'm his daughter, Darys." She drew in a deep breath. "He's missing and I came here, looking for him. Tell me you've seen him . . . please."

Barrett shook his head. "Sorry. Not lately."

A small flare of hope flickered in her eyes. "'Not lately? As in not yesterday or the day before that?"

Even before he got the words out, he could see the hope extinguish in eyes. "*Not lately* as in not in twenty years or so."

DARYS GRIPPED the cot with both hands, ignoring the pain that radiated from her tender shoulder. "Twenty years?" she whispered. "I missed him . . . by twenty years one way and a hundred and five the other? Oh no . . ."

As she tried to stand, the woman intervened. "You're not ready for that. You've had a shock. Sit."

Darys complied, wondering why the cot was rising to meet her so quickly and why the room suddenly spun to the left. Lacking much in the way of physical balance, she attempted to steady herself mentally, taking stock of her situation.

It was the right place, but the wrong time.

What was her next step?

She had a sinking feeling if she went back to the vacation center, Bellanger wouldn't be able to schedule a return trip for her. Her only recourse was to return to the time portal and try to navigate forward to 2017 from the controls located there.

"—and rest and I'll be back to check on you later."

Darys roused sometime later to discover she was no longer sitting on the cot in the infirmary, but tucked in a bed in a cheery sunlit room. Here she'd believed she was deeply mired in thought and instead, she'd evidently passed out. What a strange world she'd fallen into. . . .

Like Alice falling down the rabbit hole.

Or has that book been written yet?

Darys settled back into the plump pillow. If not, she could always write Alice's adventures, make a zillion bucks, and buy her own vacation center so she'd always know exactly when and where her father was on his jaunts back in time.

Oh, Dad . . .

She shifted away from the place where her tears formed a wet spot on the pillowcase. Her shoulder hurt, her head ached and her stomach had shriveled up into a hard knot in her belly.

Wrong time. Wrong place. Wrong everything.

FORD STARED AT HIS INVENTION. Whatever Nick had done had shorted out the entire system. Sure, it would be easy to haul the boy in and make him indicate the area of his "repair," but Ford knew that getting Nick into the workshop was the easy part; getting him to leave was another matter entirely.

He opened the housing which hid the mechanics of the machine. Everything looked normal. It would have been far too convenient to see a dangling wire or gear out of place. Nick's addition would be small, seemingly insignificant.

And enough to make the whole thing grind to a halt.

Ford pulled a stool up to his workbench, donned his watchmaker's glasses, collected his tiny screwdrivers, and went to work. Quickly caught up in the challenge of repair, he lost all track of time. It wasn't until the light began to fade that he realized morning had passed to midday and was speeding toward evening. He heard the scrape of the opening door behind him and, beneath the corner of his magnifying eyeglasses, he caught a blur of motion, approximately the size of a penitent nephew.

"Tell Emma I'll be there in a moment."

A feminine voice responded. "She said you'd say that."

Ford stiffened. He ripped off his glasses and pivoted to stare at the woman, no longer dressed in the costume of a boy. The flowered dress clung to a different set of curves than her trousers had. Ford found himself mesmerized by the differences.

She politely ignored his stare. "Dr. Callaghan also said that you'd probably wander in an hour later, gobble down a cold dinner, and come right back out here again."

He offered a weak smile in the face of such damning but accurate truth. "I'm a creature of habit." He examined her fine features, trying to make himself view them with a critical eye rather than admire the rather pleasant aesthetics of her face. He sensed lingering pain in the depths of her clear brown eyes. "Should you be out of bed, Miss . . . Miss . . . ?"

"Kirk," she supplied. "Darys Kirk." She managed a shrug with her uninjured shoulder. "Dr. Nolan said the sooner I get up and use it, the faster it'll heal. If it were up to me, I'd still be in bed. Of course, doctors always hate it when I ignore their advice. But I'm not generally fond of them, either."

"Including my sister?"

"She seems more understanding than most. Her advice is a lot more practical than the other doctors I've seen. And this salve she put on my shoulder . . ." Darys slowly flexed her arm. "It's really working. My shoulder's starting to feel better." She peered past him toward the workbench. "What are you working on?"

He usually heard that phrase articulated a little differently. People in Margin who, throughout the years, had suffered through some of his less successful inventions usually said, *"What are you working on, now?"* with just the slightest tinge of exasperation. It was refreshing to find someone new to inform, to instruct . . . to bore.

He stepped aside, allowing her a closer look. "It's what I hope will be accepted as a new alternative to the existing geoscientific theory on how to measure seismographic activity. It was working fine until Nick walked by and decided to do a little rewiring. Now, what I'm trying to figure out what he did to it and how I undo his 'repair.'"

Darys stared at the machine, her eyebrows knitted in deep thought.That was no surprise; most people didn't understand the thrill of scientific analysis and the excitement that occurred when theory and application met. Nevertheless, his initial reaction when introducing visitors to his project was to plunge into a spirited discussion of the mechanics of the machine, his technological triumph, and the annoying problem he was having with the central magnet assembly.

He drew a deep breath. "Do you recall six years ago when the San Francisco earthquake hit?"

She cocked her head to one side, still staring at his invention. "Vaguely."

Her answer caught him off guard. *Vaguely?* How could she have forgotten one of the most devastating events in modern history? He cleared his throat. "Um . . . this machine is used to measure the vibrations in the ground caused by shifting tectonic plates which helps indicate the intensity and location of an earthqua—"

"Wait." Her face lit up. "I recognize this!"

Sure you do. . . .

"It's the Nolan variation on the Wiechert inverted pendulum."

He stared at her, unable to say anything.

"A seismograph." Darys paused then colored quickly. "Uh . . . at least . . . that's what I think they call it."

But this time, his usual enthusiasm veered in a new direction. His mind raced ahead, trying to find a logical reason for her singular perceptibility. She recognized not only the similarities between his machine and Wiechert's but the changes . . . er . . . improvements he'd made. How could this woman know anything about such a specialized field as seismology?

Then the obvious answer hit him like a wet snowball in the face.

CHAPTER 4

*I*t was a joke.

A practical joke.

One of his nephews had set this up. Set *him* up. How like them to find great amusement in making their uncle think he'd found a kindred soul, a colleague familiar with, perhaps even appreciative of, the world of scientific instrumentation, where mechanics and science met in rousing success.

How could he be so foolish as to fall for what had to be a practical joke?

There was only one way to save face: play along. He released a short bark of laughter. "The *Nolan* variation." Hopefully, his smile wasn't as strained as it felt. "That's a good one. Who put you up to this? Nick or Tim?" He watched her swallow hard, clasp her hands behind her back, and dig her slippered toe into the dirt floor.

"I . . . uh . . . wouldn't want to get anyone in trouble." She looked up with guilt painted across her face in a fine blush. "No names. Okay?"

He shrugged. *Have it your way.* "So do you actually know

anything about the science of seismology?" *Or are you merely a quick study when it comes to getting someone's goat?*

She looked at the machine for a long moment with a critical gaze then turned away, seeming even more uncomfortable than before. "Uh . . . I know enough about earthquakes to not want to live in California." After a brief moment of very obvious thought, she opened her eyes wide and shot him a patently simpering smile. "I'd ask you to explain it all of this to me, but I'm afraid it's time to eat."

There, for one shining moment in time, Ford had thought she might actually listen to his explanation and maybe even understand it. But her blank smile and near vacuous expression revealed a mind evidently capable of parroting words without understanding them. He bet the young designer of this particular joke was doubled over in laughter at his uncle's expense.

"Why don't we—"

His seismograph began to chatter and paper tape started spilling out of it. He reacted immediately, reaching for the strip and stretching it out between his hands.

Darys stepped closer to the machine and stared at it. "Does that mean it's detected an earthquake?"

"Probably not." Ford examined the readout, interpreting the lines and spikes that signified what looked to be a small amount tremor activity. "I suspect someone's blasting underground again."

"Blasting?" She shot him a perplexed look.

"You're in mining country. There are mines running all under these hills, mostly dating back from the days of silver. But some of the mines have copper veins that are still being actively pursued."

"And, of course, an early generation machine like this can't determine the difference between an earthquake and an underground explosion."

It didn't escape Ford's attention that she had spoken as if this was a declaration of fact rather than a question. She may have been sent to play a practical joke, but her statement betrayed some semblance of logical thinking beyond the scope of a simple razz. He suddenly found it very satisfying to learn her vapid smile was merely a gimmick to camouflage her obvious interest.

"A tremor is a tremor. The only way anyone can identify what it truly signifies is by sending the data to the people who are collecting similar seismic information from all parts of the country."

Darys pointed to the largest of the spikes drawn on the paper. "Of course, you could check to see if anybody in the local area blasted at around the same time frame." She winced. That was twice. When would she ever learn to shut up? She'd learned the three "I's" of time traveling when she was just a child:

Don't intervene.

Don't inform.

Don't invent.

. . . which all boiled down to: watch the past, but don't be a part of it.

And she'd just gotten through making two observations, neither of which was too terribly astute, but they did suggest there might be more to her knowledge of mechanical devices than met the eye.

Like a degree in mechtech engineering and a minor in cyber systems.

But he wasn't trying to meet her eye. His gaze was stuck somewhere in the vicinity of her feet. For a brief moment, she was afraid the holosuit had failed in some way. But she still wore the dress she'd copied from Emma's closet.

His gaze rose slowly. Darys knew the type of appraising glance men in olden times usually gave women, calculating their worth either in terms of beauty or ability to perform hard labor.

But as his glance inched upward, he paused at the waist of her flowered dress then skipped quickly past the bodice where she figured his interest might have lingered. For some reason, his gaze stalled at her chin.

She supposed chins were safe places to rest a glance. They were neither titillating nor likely to incur a hostile retort such as "Please, sir! You're staring at my chin!"

As far as chins went, Ford had a well-formed one and a strong jaw, too, with a hint of a dark beard that added more character to his classic good looks. Darys was content to let her attention remain in the safety zone of his chin, but he spoiled everything by smiling. His bottom lip grabbed her attention as it curved into an enticing smile, complete with a single roguish dimple.

She was a goner.

And it was definitely the dimple's fault.

There was something about it that forced her to work her way up higher, so as to get the full effect. She had to know if there was a sparkle in his eyes—whether he possessed a sparkle of intelligence, of parroting ignorance, or of mocking humor. When he finally made eye contact, the expression she found was made up of equal parts of intelligence, gentle humor, and a surprising sense of shyness.

A blush slowly stained his cheeks and suddenly she realized she was staring. "We'd better go eat," she managed to croak, looking away.

He swallowed. "Sounds like a good idea to me . . . Miss . . . Miss . . ."

"Kirk," she managed in a voice which sounded distinctly strangled. She shook herself, regaining more control. "Darys Kirk."

He arched one eyebrow. "Kirk? You wouldn't by any chance be kin to a man named . . . Harvey Kirk, would you?"

She nodded. "He's my father." A rush of memories assaulted her, making her eyes water. "And he's missing." She stopped and clutched Ford's muscular arm. "Tell me you've seen him."

Ford shook his head. "Not since I was . . . eleven or twelve years old. I think he left town right after the wedding—Emma and Barrett's wedding. I haven't seen Harvey since."

THE GOOD DOCTOR looked conspicuously uncomfortable during the meal. Darys tried not to saying anything to Ford and the three boys that would reveal her origins in the distant future, and that was hard, because it was clear that they were curious about her.

Ford, particularly so. When he mentioned her seismic gaffe about the "Nolan variation," Emma shot Darys a look that could have sterilized a knife at twenty paces. Then the woman pointedly changed the subject. After their meal was finished, the three boys were ordered to clean up and Emma marched Darys into the dispensary for a follow-up examination. John Barrett vanished into another room, and Ford presumably returned to his workshop.

Darys lifted herself gingerly to the examining table and unbuttoned her dress to allow Emma to rub in a fresh batch of salve into the injured shoulder. The woman's hands might be warm, but a frozen sheet of silence hung between them like a brick wall.

After several uncomfortable moments, Darys gathered the nerve to speak. "I've tried to be careful like you asked."

"Your shoulder will heal just fine," Emma snapped.

"No, I mean about talking. About the future. I gather it's not a popular subject around the supper table."

More uncomfortable silence reigned as Emma paid an inordinate amount of time to the detail of wiping her hands on a towel. Finally, she pivoted, her face a blank mask. "They don't know."

Darys stared at her. "What?"

"The boys . . ." She faltered for a moment. "The boys don't know their father is from the future because it's not important for them to know."

"Not important? Of course it is."

"Why?" Emotion flashed across Emma's face. "It doesn't affect his role as a father, as my husband, even as the sheriff of the town. He doesn't yearn for the comforts of technologies that haven't been invented yet because he has no memory of his life in the future. It's faded away, just like your father predicted it would."

The mention of her father made Darys's heart skip a beat. What if the same thing had happened to him? What if he had become stranded in time and lost all memory of his life in the future? What if he forgot he had a family?

What if he forgot her?

"Anyway, they're children. They wouldn't understand. No one knows but Barrett and me." Emma had continued, unaware of Darys's momentary lapse of attention.

"But what about Ford? He's no boy—he's a man, a smart man at that. You mean to tell me that in the past twenty years, he's never realized that his brother-in-law was a time traveler from the future?"

"No. And you're not going to tell him. Not about Barrett and not about you. As far as he should know, the future is unwritten. Especially his."

THE FUTURE?

Ford sagged against the side of the house, abandoning his listening post. He clutched at reason, at logic, at anything that would help him make sense of what he'd just overheard his sister say. Harvey Kirk and Barrett Callaghan—time travelers? And this woman, too? He drew in a deep breath. *Only a fool would believe . . .*

But there were no fools involved in this situation. Emma was one of the sanest, most logical people he knew. Progressive, yes, but in a practical sense. And Barrett? As sheriff, he acted with a sense of unerring justice tempered with compassion. As a father, he was a loving and responsible parent to three rambunctious but good boys. As a brother-in-law, Barrett started as Ford's father figure and, later on, became the brother Ford never had.

Then when Mary died, Barrett became more than just his brother-in-law; Barrett became his best friend, providing a shoulder when he needed support, distraction when he needed escape, assignments when he needed to lose himself in work. All this time, Ford had thought of his brother-in-law as an intuitive yet uncomplicated man. But according to Emma, locked somewhere in Barrett's mind were technological concepts that probably made Ford's inventions look like a caveman rubbing two sticks together. Essentially, Barrett had forgotten more than Ford would ever learn or have a chance to learn.

The overwhelming need to know surfaced again in Ford. He pushed to his feet, intending to reclaim his listening post.

If only I could have a glimpse at the—

A hand closed down on Ford's shoulder and a quiet voice whispered in his ear. "I don't think Emma would like it if she knew you were eavesdropping on her."

Ford looked into the eyes of his brother-in-law. Concern tinged the sad smile Barrett wore.

"It's true?" Ford's voice threatened to break. "You're from the future?"

"Not that I remember much about it." Barrett shrugged.

"But w-when? How?"

Barrett motioned for them to move, evidently so the eavesdroppers wouldn't be eavesdropped on. Once they stepped around the corner, Ford started to speak, but Barrett shook his head.

"Not here. Little pitchers have big ears. . . ." He nodded toward the boys' bedroom. "Let's go someplace where we can't be overheard."

They walked in silence all the way to Ford's workshop. After the door closed safely behind them, Ford turned, ready to explode in a barrage of questions. But before he could say anything, Barrett raised his hand to stop him.

"Just be quiet and let me talk. Then you can ask questions. I came here twenty years ago from the year 2015. Johnny Callaghan was my great-great-grandfather and we exchanged places in time. From what I've been told, my name was Barrett Callan and I was some sort of businessman who lived in Denver, and who owned a mining company here in Margin—but in 2015. I didn't meet Harvey until I got here. He helped me . . . acclimate myself to the area, to fool everybody into thinking I was Johnny. No one ever caught on, except for Emma."

Ford released a sigh. "And here I'm supposed to be the observant one, and I never had any suspicions."

Barrett smiled. "You know your sister, Ford. Nobody can't pull much over on her. That's just one of the million reasons I fell in love with her." He stared off into the distance, his face relaxing for a moment until he evidently became self-conscious of his expression. He cleared his throat. "I had the opportunity to come back and I guess you can say I took it. And stayed. I've never regretted it ever since."

"Two-thousand and fifteen. . . ." The words, the concept sounded almost exotically foreign to him. "That's the twenty-first century! I can just imagine what it's like—the advances in science, in medicine. Are the people different? Are there any wars?" The questions poured out of him like a tidal wave, picking up momentum as it rolled along.

"Whoa!" Barrett raised one hand, gesturing for Ford to stop. "You heard what Emma said. I don't remember anything about my life in the future. Harvey is the one who helped me stay here and he told me my memories of how things were . . . are in the future would fade away, and they did."

Ford tried to imagine how he would act, react in a similar situation. "But didn't you leave yourself notes? Information? Instructions?"

Barrett nodded. "I did write down as much as I could, but lots of it doesn't make sense, now. I talked about men walking on the moon, movie boxes that sit in your living room, powerful lights that can cut a hole through metal. It's like reading fiction, science fiction. A lot of ideas, of concepts, but no explanations of how they work, or why. And you, of all people, know—" he quickly scanned the room which brimmed with inventions in all stages of development "—inspiration without perspiration isn't worth much in this world."

Ford sat, locking his hands around his knee. The future. Rocket ships to the moon. Time machines. An absurd tale told by credible people. Better that than the reverse.

"It takes your breath away, doesn't it? Thinking about the future?" Barrett sat on an empty apple crate, picked up a twig from the dirt floor, and pulled out his pocket knife. A silver dollar fell out, hitting the dirt floor with a soft plop. He picked it up, brushed the dirt from it, and handed it to Ford. "Here. For you."

Ford stared at the coin, recognizing it. "But this is your lucky coin."

"Nah . . . it's Johnny's, not mine. Why don't you keep it a while? See if Lady Liberty brings you luck."

Ford shrugged and stuffed the coin in his pocket. "Thanks."

Barrett opened the blade of his knife and peeled off a strip of bark from the stick. "You know . . . it's times like these, when my brain is wrapped around something that's almost too big to think about, that I find I need something to do with my hands. It makes it easier to contemplate the impossible."

Ford fished his knife from his pocket and adopted the same position. "But it's not impossible. You've done it. You've traveled through time."

Barrett paused long enough to look up at him. "Then you believe me? You believe that young woman in there?"

Ford shrugged. "She might have some reason to avoid telling me the truth. But you don't. After all—" he patted his pocket "—Johnny would have never given away his lucky coin."

They both began to whittle.

CHAPTER 5

*B*reakfast was a curious meal.

Emma and Barrett both looked tired, as if they'd stayed up all night talking. As far as that went, Ford felt a little hollow-eyed himself, having his sleep punctuated by dreams of a fantastical and somewhat frightening future. Across the table from him, Darys Kirk looked decidedly uneasy, as if she were ready to bolt from her chair and scramble back to her own time period at the least provocation. She picked at her food, and Ford wondered if it was because she wasn't hungry. Or perhaps people no longer ate such foods in her world of tomorrow.

Only the three boys seemed unaware of the undercurrents at the table. Usually sensitive to the moods of the family, Tim had buried his nose and thus his attention in a book. Nick was distracted by John Junior who was peppering his brother with questions about how to design a catapult.

Lord help them if the boys ever built one.

Darys waited until the boys finished their meal and scattered to their chores before she chose to speak. Even though the boys were well out of range, she kept her voice low, her tone conspiratorial.

"I really appreciate your . . . hospitality, but I must continue searching for my father." She paused for a moment, as if trying to figure out how to continue. "But I do have a slight problem."

John Barrett stood up, his plate in his hand. "What's that?" He crossed to the sink.

Darys stared at her bowl of congealed oatmeal. "I d-don't . . . I don't . . . remember where . . . uh." She lifted a nervous but knowing glance to Emma. "I need to get back to the road where I met Nick." She hesitated. "That *exact* spot."

Emma rose from her seat quickly, as if the speed of her motion would cut off any further discussion of Darys's unusual need. "Why don't we discuss this in my dispensary? I can give your injury one last check before you go on your—"

"Emma." John Barrett placed a hand on her shoulder.

Ford's sister froze in place with her eyes closed in obvious dread.

John Barrett spoke slowly, evenly. "Ford knows."

She drew in a shaky breath which made Ford's chest shudder in sympathy.

"It was time he knew the truth," Barrett explained in a soft voice.

She pivoted slowly. "About—"

"About how I came back in time." They locked gazes. "Why I chose to stay."

There was a moment of silence where several unspoken messages flashed between them. Ford fully expected his sister to explode, demonstrating her noted Nolan temper at having her command of silence broken, but instead of growing red with rage, she paled.

Then she turned to him, wearing an expression which reminded him all too clearly of the time she told him of their father's death. "You were only eleven and such a dreamer." She lifted her hand to his face, but stopped short of caressing his cheek. "I worried that if I presented such an unbelievable feat as time travel to you, then you would have expected other equally impossible things to magically come true. All your wildest dreams come to life." She graced him with the same sort of sad smile she gave John Junior after hearing him confess to one of his many escapades. "You would have spent all of your time dreaming instead of realizing how hard work plays the largest part in making your dreams come true."

Hard work. His stomach turned. *Sure.* Look at all the success he'd derived from hard work. A handful of minor patents that would never make a cent, and a reputation as another "crackpot inventor named Ford." So far, hard work had done precious little to make his dreams come true.

After he lost Mary, Emma had made it plain that he always had a welcome home with her, Barrett, and the boys. Ford saw it only as a stopgap measure in his bid to regain his footing after his grieving, but lately, he'd grown weary of being lumped in as "one of the boys" rather than Emma's adult contemporary. Evidently, she was willing to take care of her little brother forever and that certainly wasn't healthy for either of them.

He cleared his throat. "I don't doubt your motives, Emma, just your sense of timing. What about later? Couldn't you have told me the truth after I was grown?"

She hung her head. "I couldn't bring myself to."

John Barrett stepped forward. "Actually, it was my decision not to tell you anything about my previous life. I'm living my life now, not in some far-flung future that I can't even remember. I don't want a constant reminder that I'm an oddity, that I once held the answers to a thousand questions, the same thousand answers I suspect you're dying to hear."

"But—"

"How could you not ask questions?" John Barrett took a step closer. "Even right now, you want to know everything, don't you? How I came here? What my world was like? What kind of cars we drive in the future? What do we eat? How do we cook? Do we have rocket ships?" His voice picked up strength and he spoke faster. "Have men walked on the moon? Have we broken the speed of sound? When will the next earthquake hit California? When will the stock market crash? When will the Japanese bomb Pearl Harbor? Who shot President Kennedy?"

Barrett stopped suddenly, his building fury transforming instantly into shock. He sagged forward, placing his palms on the table for support. He drew a strangled gasp of breath.

"Barrett!" Emma skidded to his side. For a moment, she was his wife, scared, concerned. A moment later, she transformed to doctor, placing two fingers at his neck to measure his pulse.

"I remembered," he croaked, looking up with a face caught between the throes of ecstasy of memory and the agony of the unknown. "For a moment, it all came back to me. I remember . . . I remember . . ."

"You!" Emma snapped, turning a harsh stare toward at Darys. "It's all *your* fault. He wouldn't be remembering these things, he wouldn't be in pain if it weren't for you. You must leave. Now!"

Darys wrapped her arms around herself, tears forming in her eyes. "I'm sorry. I'm so sorry. I didn't mean . . ." Her gaze narrowed, then she looked down and patted the back of her hand. Suddenly Ford saw a band materialize around her wrist. She stared down at it as if searching it for answers. Her face brightened a little through her tears. "Wait! It must be my temporal stabilizer affecting him." She slipped her fingers beneath a chain around her neck and pulled free a small gold-colored disk, as if it explained her curious terminology.

The disk dangled at the end of the chain, spinning slowly in the air. She turned back to her wristband and fiddled with its buttons. "There. I've minimized the output. As soon as I leave, he'll be out of its range and everything will be all right."

"Then go!" Emma ordered, kneeling at her husband's side, caught somewhere between her role as a concerned doctor and scared wife.

"Emma . . . don't be so hard on the girl." John Barrett lifted his head and tried to smile. "Darys, when you find Harvey—and I'm sure you'll find him—tell him we miss him. Tell him we named the boys after him—Timothy Harvey and Nicholas James." He paused, his breathing eased, his smile growing brighter. "Harvey James Kirk." He managed a snort of laughter. "With that stabilizer thing so close to me, I can remember now why the name was funny. Tell him to—" Barrett's face tightened as if dredging through deep memories "—to live long and prosper."

The chair fell backward as Darys rose awkwardly to her feet. "Y-yes sir. I'll go now." She glanced at Emma. "Thank you," she whispered. She stumbled toward the door, then gave Ford a panicked look. "But I still have to find the time portal."

Ford gestured for her to stay back and turned his attention to his sister. "Emma?"

She looked up, tears cascading down her face.

He knelt beside her. "Emma, I'm going to take Darys to look for her time portal." Suddenly, the transformation was made; he was the adult. She was the child in need. He smoothed her hair. "Are you going to be all right?" he asked softly.

She glanced at John Barrett, who nodded. "Yes," she whispered. She gave him a soggy kiss. "Thank you. I was wrong. You could have handled it. You can handle anything."

Ford lifted a damp tendril of hair off her check. "You

taught me well, Sis. Now you tend to your patient while I play Indian guide."

Barrett reached up and squeezed Ford's arm. "I'll be fine," he said with a small rasp. He turned toward Darys and cocked his head. "It's funny."

She edged toward the door, giving him as much berth as humanly possible. "What, sir?"

"Those questions I was talking about. Right now, I know all the answers to them. And I still don't miss my life in the future." He leaned over and placed a kiss on the top of his wife's head then winced in pain. "My life has always been here."

Ford strode to the doorway and pushed Darys into the morning sunlight. She stopped, blinking against in the harsh light, but Ford grabbed her arm and continued to propel her ahead of him. A cloud of dust rose beneath her stumbling feet.

"Don't stop," he ordered. "We don't stop until we know John Barrett's out of the influence of that . . . thing on your arm. Or you turn it off." He started examining the buttons, wondering which one might switch off the power.

She jerked her arm from his grasp and continued under her own volition. "It only has a fifty foot range and I've narrowed it to ten so he's clear, now. And don't even think about turning it off. If I do, I'm in danger of losing my memories." She stopped in mid-step and smacked her head with the palm of her head. "I bet that's exactly what happened to Dad. Stabilizer malfunction and those idiots at the travel center didn't supply him with a backup."

"This may well be all very interesting to you." Ford gripped her again and continued to pull her away from the house. "But I don't understand a word you're saying. All I know is that the sooner you go back to wherever you belong, the sooner John Barrett Callaghan returns to normal."

"And the sooner I find my father." She started walking faster as if to prove her dedication to the task at hand.

Ford lengthened his stride in order to keep up with her. "Nick told me where the lizzie broke down. Do you think you can find your . . . portal from there?"

"I should be able to. The temporal stabilizer will help me locate the door and make it visible."

"It's not visible right now?"

She nodded. "I couldn't have a . . . native stumble across it. It would be awfully confusing for them."

"A native." Ford contemplated the word and all its more rustic meanings. An image filled his mind's eye—a picture of the citizens of Margin dressed in loincloths and clutching spears in their hands. Right out of *The National Geographic Magazine.*

"Is that how we appear to you? As savage natives, blithely unaware of your world, unable to understand the complexities of your technologies?"

She paused in mid-step. "No. I mean *native* as someone who lives in this area." She picked up her pace again. "I suspect that given enough—pardon the pun—*time*, you could understand the scientific theories behind temporal travel."

"And while I'm at it, given an infinite amount of time, a backward savage like me could even understand the way the big ball of fire travels across the sky and becomes a silvery disk at night."

Darys stopped in the middle of the road, balancing her fists on her hips, a gesture he'd seen his sister performed a thousand times. It just served to prove that no matter what century, some things never changed. "My goodness," she said with a sneer, "we aren't a little bit overly sensitive about all this, are we?"

Ford couldn't help but bristle. "Overly sensitive? How

would you like it if someone impugned your ability to reason and think?"

"Cut me some slack, okay? I know it's been a shock to discover your brother-in-law isn't quite who or what you think he is, but you don't have to take it out on me."

Ford took several steps, leaving her behind. Then he stopped, shoved his hands in his pockets, and closed his eyes. She was right, damn it. He *was* angry. Angry at Emma, at John Barrett, at the whole world in the past, present, and future. Who were they to censor his world? Who were they to determine what he could and couldn't know?

Ford sighed.

And who was he to heap some of the blame on Darys Kirk? She was as much of a victim of circumstances as he. When he opened his eyes, he realized she'd caught up with him.

"I know what you're feeling," she said in a soft voice. "My mother got sick when I was young and the doctors convinced my father that it would be best if I didn't know. So instead of understanding why she couldn't do the same things as other mothers, I spent most of my time resenting her for not *wanting* to participate in my world. It wasn't until I was an adult that I realized the truth. That's when I got really angry." She placed a hand on his shoulder. "Don't make the same mistake I did, and blame them for trying to shield you."

They fell into step together.

"But this situation is different." Ford rattled the change in his pocket nervously. "Harvey was shielding you from pain concerning your mother and, even if it was a misguided reaction, the intent was noble. But Emma wasn't protecting me from anything bad. On the contrary—" he released a large sigh "—she was keeping a magnificent truth away from me."

A magnificent truth? Visions danced through Darys's head, images of problems that continued to plague her world: aggression, intolerance, inequities based on favoritism. How could an otherwise reasonable, even intelligent man still believe in a Utopian society?

"You think the future will be magnificent?" she prompted.

He shrugged. "Isn't it? You have machines that propel you through time. Certainly you've invented ones that propel you through space, too."

She shrugged. "Among other things. But you have to realize that with increased technology, there are unforeseen complications."

"Such as . . . ?"

She started to speak, but closed her mouth suddenly. He wasn't going to trap her into saying something she shouldn't. How many lectures had she endured about avoiding that possibility? How many fictional horror stories had she read about unsuspecting time travelers destroying their own future with a slip of the lip?

"You can't stop now," Ford complained. "Complications like what?"

Darys quickened her pace. The sooner she got to the portal, the sooner this would be over. "Like someone going back in time and shooting off their mouth and tearing a big hole in the fabric of time."

"A hole in the 'fabric of time.'" Ford scowled as he kicked a rock. It sailed into the underbrush beside the road, causing several birds take flight from their hiding place. "That sort of explanation ranks right up there with explaining the nighttime as the Pacific Ocean extinguishing the flames of the sun." He straightened his shoulders. "I'm not an ignorant savage, you know. There is no 'fabric' of time."

She ignored his sarcastic sneer. "Suppose for a moment that you went back in time and prevented the assassination of Abraham Lincoln. What sort of ripple effect might that have caused?"

"Ripple effect?"

"Like a stone tossed in the middle of a lake and the concentric circles it causes in the surface of the water."

Ford drew a deep breath. "If Lincoln had lived, the aftermath of War Between the States might have been handled differently. Johnson could have never won the election on his own, so either Lincoln might have run for a third term or Grant might have been elected sooner."

"And certainly Lincoln's plans of reconstruction would have fared better than Johnson's?"

Ford lifted one shoulder. "His plans would certainly have been less harsh than Johnson's."

Darys pushed a little further. "And therefore, there might have less division between the North and South. Maybe no division at all by now. See how one simple change can have an increasing larger snowball effect?"

Ford nodded with reluctance. "But that's an extreme example, right? Lincoln's survival would affect the course of action for an entire nation. But I'm no one. What big difference will it make if I know a few things ahead of time?"

The obvious retort popped out before she could stop herself. "How do you know you're no one?"

He stopped in mid step and stared at her. "Pardon?"

She refused to stop. "Maybe you're going to be someone famous, someone influential, maybe not. I'm not going to take any chances. Telling you about the future might have no ripple effect at all. Or it might cause a major temporal rift."

A moment later he caught up with her. "Imagine . . . ," he muttered under his breath. "Being a possible historical linchpin. Me—William Crawford Nolan."

To her credit, Darys didn't stop. She continued on as if her heart hadn't skipped a beat. *Nolan? William Crawford*

Nolan? The *William C. Nolan? The founder of the first serious twentieth-century American study on seismography?* Darys swallowed hard.

Up to now, this nice young man was just that—a nice young man. Attractive in a sort of studious, professorial way. She certainly hadn't thought of him as a famous historical figure, as someone having any technological significance that could have parlayed into her world.

Good Lord, she'd even done a high school paper on Dr. Nolan, discussing how the strides he made in the early twentieth century in the field of seismology shaped the future of accurate earthquake prediction in the twenty-first century. But the only pictures she'd seen of him were as a gray-haired man.

Distinguished.

Unsmiling.

Old.

Certainly not the very vibrant, young man walking next to her, simply named Ford.

Had she said anything dangerous? Anything leading? Anything that could be construed as an unauthorized transfer of information to a person or persons in the past? Temporal police were always on the lookout for the shock waves that rode in advance of temporal distortions.

She stopped, wondering if officials would materialize at any second and defuse the situation, by wiping out Ford's memory of her and by hauling her off to jail. She searched her mind, wincing when she remembered her flippant remark: *"It's the Nolan variation of the Wiechert inverted pendulum."* Certainly the Powers That Be couldn't blame her for that innocent slip. After all, she merely thought he owned this particular version of the seismograph, not that he was actually the inventor of it.

But another thought hit her.

Up to now, she'd been worried about telling him something he shouldn't know. But what if she was keeping him from making his next discovery? What if he was supposed to be in his laboratory right now, making his next great leap in seismographic logic, rather than being with her?

The best course seemed to be to break contact with him as soon as possible, before she could cause any more possible temporal damage. She glanced around, thankful that the landscape seemed familiar and that no police intervention patrol had landed. She punched the "seek" button on her holosuit control cuff which would unmask the portal as soon as she got into range.

"I know where I am, now, and where the portal is." She stumbled on the loose rocks as she hurried up the grassy slope toward the spot where she'd last seen the portal, trying to put as much distance between them as possible. "Uh . . . you don't have to stay with me anymore."

"And give up a chance to get a glimpse of the future? Not on your life!" He caught up, reached out, and placed strong hands on her waist, steadied her as she slipped on a loose stone. His innocent gesture suddenly felt almost provocative, which served only to further confuse Darys.

Ford Nolan was history. Literally.

Someone from a distant past who, in just a few moments, would be left behind as she continued her search for her father. Where she was going, even in the early twenty-first century, Ford Nolan was nothing more than a dusty memory, not a living, breathing, strong, muscular . . .

She shook herself mentally.

The portal shimmered into existence, activated remotely by her holosuit.

"Great balls of fire!" Despite his reaction of awe, Ford moved closer to the silvery portal, placing himself between it and Darys as if protecting her.

"It's all right. It's the time door."

After a moment or two, he reached tentatively toward the sparkling door frame. "It's beautiful."

Darys shifted so that she stood between Ford and the portal. Every once in a while, the shimmering door would focus, giving whoever was in range a clear view of the future. A man as smart as Ford Nolan might be able to interpret what he saw, to make good use of a quick glimpse into the future. She couldn't afford to let things get any more complicated. "I think you'd better leave now."

Several emotions and thoughts passed visibly across his face. As a scientist, he had to be intrigued by the technology. As a logician, he evidently understood the dangers of knowledge out of time. But as a man, how could he not be curious, much too curious to simply walk away?

He drew a deep breath. "I . . . understand." He reached down and held her hand for a moment.

She felt a sudden rush of warmth, understanding, and protection with her hand enclosed in his.

"You'll find your father. I know you will."

She nodded, unable to speak.

"And when you do, tell him we're doing . . . we did fine." He dropped her hand, gave the portal a lingering, almost hungry glance and then turned around. He took several steps away, stopped, and faced her again as if wanting one last look at the future.

"Tell your sister, thank you. And the sheriff, too."

He nodded.

Darys entered the time portal and synchronized her control band to the base unit. The portal pulsed on a normal sine wave, as both units began matching speed. Light pulses filled the area, making it difficult to see Ford as he gaped at the silvery spectacle of a time portal approaching critical jumping mass.

She raised her hand to wave good-bye. Suddenly, the portal lurched drunkenly to one side, causing Darys to lose her balance. She slammed hard against the portal wall and dropped to her knees. Something was going terribly wrong.

FORD STARED in shock as a harsh rumble filled the air, snatching away her screams. He took an instinctive step forward to help, but the earth trembled beneath his feet, causing him to stumble. Was it an earthquake or the effects of Darys's time traveling machine? A boulder broke loose from above them and rolled toward the time door. Ford shouted a warning, but Darys evidently couldn't hear him. The rock struck the side of the door and it buckled inward. She was rising from her knees one moment and thrown through to the door a second later.

Ford scrambled back up the slope, gaining slow purchase over the crumbling soil beneath him. This was no normal earthquake. He knew the area too well, knew where the stresses were, where the minor fault lines locations were. The underlying structure here was solid. Whatever reason there was for an earthquake, it was coming from the time machine.

When Darys didn't jump immediately to her feet, Ford felt his heart wedge itself in his throat. When she screamed again in terror, he reacted automatically, not even flinching when he perforated the thinning silver screen which separated them. He got an arm beneath her shoulders and hauled her to her feet.

"Let's get out of here!" he shouted, hoping to be heard over the rising winds that sucked through the hole he'd made. He pulled her toward the hole, but the winds pushed them back.

"I have to stop it!" Dazed, Darys pulled away from him and started pounding a series of buttons on the buckled wall of the time portal. Flashes of light and electricity sparked from the console.

"Too late," she mouthed. She started pounding on the faint scar left by the hole which had magically mended itself. Ford joined her. Together, they managed to tear a small hole in the screen and, working on opposite sides, they started widening the rent.

The sound and fury of the wind rose to an unbearable shriek, compelling them to stop and to cover their ears. Ford pulled her into the relative safety of his arms, trying to shield her from the noise while protecting himself, too. They sank to their knees, cowering together. He wondered how much more they could take before their eardrums would burst and their hearts explode from sheer terror.

The world around them turned into jagged bits of broken time and metallic noise. It defied any other description. As Ford drew what he was certain would be his last breath, felt his heart struggle to complete its last beat, the world shattered into a shower of silver shards.

ho knows when . . .
    Ford felt something sticky and cold clinging to his face. He lifted his head high enough to brush away the flakes of snow.

Snow?

But it's summertime.

He opened his eyes. Sunlight blinded him for a moment, reflected by the clean expanse of snow that surrounded them. His eyes grew accustomed to the bright glare and he slowly became aware of his surroundings. They were on the same slope, at the same location as before, but now it was winter. As he struggled to move, he discovered Darys wrapped around him. A strange feeling twisted in his gut as he realized that she had wrapped her legs around one of his in what he could only describe as a very provocative position.

She chose that moment to rouse, giving him a sleepy smile which faltered as she realized their predicament. She hastily unwrapped herself from him. When she opened her mouth to speak, nothing came out. At least he didn't hear anything.

Ford tried to respond, but based on Darys' expression, she couldn't hear him, either Something had obviously affected both of their hearing.

Where are we? he mouthed.

Darys looked around and shrugged as her answer.

His gut twisted again. Maybe "Where are we?" wasn't quite as important as "When are we?" If it was now winter-time, then more than a couple of months had passed by. Emma and Barrett would be worried to death if he'd been missing for that entire length of time.

Ford helped Darys to stand. Although she was initially a little wobbly, after a few moments, she was able to remain upright on her own. He squatted down and used his finger to trace the word, *Margin*, in block letters in the pristine snow. After a thought, he added a rather large question mark.

She lifted her shoulders. "I don't know," she mouthed.

"*When?*" he wrote on the next line.

She gave him another blank look. Then an idea seemed to fill her eyes with a ray of hope. She punched a few buttons on the control band that circled her wrist and a few seconds later, her outfit started changing. Emma's nicely conservative flowered dress turned into a garish one-piece suit. The material clung to her figure, leaving practically no curves to the imagination. Ford felt the blood pool in his cheeks at the rather libidinous nature of the clothing and the rather scandalous nature of the thoughts they inspired.

Finding great need to distract himself, Ford forced himself to notice the less libertine details of her outfit. The new suit she wore was deep purple with the brightest, ugliest glowing pink stripes he'd ever seen running down her sleeves and pants legs. A set of protective goggles formed across her eyes and thin brightly painted planks appeared at her feet, strapped somehow to odd-looking boots. Two thin poles wavered into shape, hanging from leather straps that circled each of her wrists. In response to his perplexed, almost rude stare, she used the metal tip of one pole to trace the letters "*S-K*" into the snow. Her hand wavered when making the last letter.

"Sky?" he thought. He looked up at the clear blue sky above him, noting nothing of concern at first. Squinting, he began to make out an odd, thin strip of white clouds, feathery at first, but narrowing until it led to a small silver . . . object flying through the sky.

Ford stared at the object, finally making out a silver tube with . . . wings. Then he realized it wasn't standing still in the air. He shaded his eyes against the sun and focused on the sleek silver metallic bird, streaking through the air.

This wasn't his sky.

Not *his* sky. Not *his* Margin.

He took an involuntary step forward and felt his foot slide awkwardly in the snow. As logic went, so went balance. As he fell, he focused for a split second on the word "ski" before he started sliding uncontrollably down the snow-covered hill. As he tumbled head over foot, his mind latched onto the correction. Not "sky."

Ski . . .

"FORD? ARE YOU ALL RIGHT?" a familiar voice croaked in his ear. Darys. At least he wasn't alone in this debacle. This was Darys's world. She would know what to do.

Another voice intruded. "Ma'am, if you'll step back, we can take a look at him."

Hands poked and prodded Ford. He faded in and out of caring.

"Where's his coat?" someone asked.

"He doesn't have one," Darys answered.

"You mean he went skiing without one? Sheesh!"

Another voice spoke, "Look . . . no ski boots. Whatever he was doing out there, it wasn't skiing."

"Oh great . . . another crackpot."

"He's not a crackpot," Darys argued. "He was—" she paused and Ford wondered if she would blurt out his identity "—lured out there."

Lured?

"That's right. Lured out. And robbed," she added dramatically. "Check his pockets for identification."

Ford felt someone checking the contents of his pants pockets. Darys? The thought made him smile.

The male voice spoke again. "She's right. There's no wallet. No ID. Maybe someone rolled him for his cash, then finished the job by rolling him down the slopes."

Someone released a short bark of laughter. "A thematic crook. What'll they think of next?"

A new voice intruded, this one full of spit and vinegar. "I think it's criminal that your security is no better than this. A poor soul can get mugged in the middle of a ski slope."

"He's coming around. Sir, can you tell us where it hurts?"

Mugged? Is that some sort of new-fangled word for falling?

A chorus of voices suddenly joined in, all echoing the same concerns, all protesting lax security measures. Ford noted that Darys's voice wasn't part of the brigade of concerned citizens. He cracked open one eye and saw her concern being manifested in another way. She sat in the snow, cradling his head in her lap. An incredibly soft lap, he decided.

Ford slowly focused on the new face that wavered in front of him. Not one, but two faces. Was he seeing double? A pair of heads bobbed in his vision, both dressed in identical bright orange hoods and both wearing silvery goggles that offered Ford's distorted reflection in their curved lens.

Ford stared harder, realizing that one of the creatures was pulling back his orange skin and reveal odd equipment strapped to his head. It . . . he pulled a piece of it toward his mouth.

"Chopper One, this is Rescue One. Let's hold off on the pickup. Patient is conscious, his vitals are steady, and he seems to have no broken bones. Over."

A disembodied female voice answered, "Rescue One, this is Chopper One, we copy. Returning to base. Out."

The hooded man unstrapped something from Ford's arm which had wires attached to it. Ford looked at his skin, expecting to see a set of holes left from their equipment. There were no holes. But somewhere in the back of Ford's fuzzed mind, he remembered reading a story about aliens who came to Earth to conquer it. They wore communication devices strapped to their heads and stuck wires into people. And they wore glasses with darkly colored lens across their eyes so you couldn't see that they had red eyes.

Red-eyed aliens from the red planet of . . .

Mars!

Ford gaped at the spectacle, finding his voice at long last. "Take me to your leader. . . ."

DARYS REFUSED TO LEAVE FORD, even when he grew adamant about seeing the "leader." The rescue workers consulted some higher-up on their radios and soon, they were both standing in a dry, warm anteroom, ready to meet and receive an official apology from the resort owner. While they waited, someone produced a sweater and coat for Ford who was still shivering. Whether it was due to the weather or fright, Darys wasn't quite sure. He hadn't said much since they arrived, and she wasn't sure she blamed him for staying silent.

Someone else shoved two steaming cups of coffee into their hands and that seemed to perk Ford up a great deal. As he sipped his cup cautiously, he started to pay attention to their surroundings.

It wasn't until Darys tasted the rich coffee that she pointedly realized that this wasn't her world. Up to now, she'd thought she was in one of the popular retro-resorts, one that had been restored to its earlier splendor for clients who preferred communing with expensive reproductions and antiques.

But what she was drinking was coffee. Real coffee. Not a cheaper synthetic substitute. This was real—rich, strong, freshly ground from honest-to-God beans coffee. She closed her eyes for a moment and savored the taste.

"More?" the young woman asked, holding out a steaming pot.

Darys looked down and realized she'd drained her cup. Two cups of real coffee? In one day? One month? One year? *Zounds!*

Nodding blankly, Darys held the cup out and the woman refilled it without a moment's hesitation.

"The boss will be through with his meeting in just a moment," the secretary said, glancing at a closed door. "And he's quite anxious to make sure that the gentleman and you are all right. We will, of course, be comping your room tonight," she added with a concerned smile.

"Comping?" *Different world, different language,* Darys thought.

The young woman smiled indulgently. "Giving you a night's lodging for free. It's only fair after having something like this happen to you."

Darys sighed. So this was a hotel . . . ski resort. Good.

She'd need some sort of home base to work from as she searched for her father. As far as things went, Ford looked as if he'd need some sleep before she could march him up the slope in the dead of night and pack him back to his rightful time period. She watched him dart a hooded but inquisitive gaze around the room. The sooner she limited his exposure to the technology of the future, the better.

Darys cleared her throat. "I'm afraid we haven't . . . checked in, yet."

The woman's smile broadened. "Then please allow us to put you up for the night in our very best suite, compliments of Margin Mountain Resorts."

Something buzzed on the desk and Ford jumped in response. Coffee sloshed everywhere. The young woman responded immediately to the instrument on the desk then to Ford, helping to wipe the spill.

She dabbed at a puddle on the low table beside them. "That was the boss . . . J.B. He's ready to see you. Shall I bring in another cup of coffee for you, sir?"

Ford shook his head. "No thanks, ma'am." He managed a weak smile. Once he turned his back to the attentive woman, he leaned over to Darys. "If that weak stuff is what they call coffee in the future, I'm glad I live in the past."

Darys grabbed his hand and pulled him toward the office door. "Don't volunteer any information," she said between gritted teeth. "Especially not comments like that. Just play along with what I say, okay?" She watched him as he gazed with open curiosity at a cumbersome computer on the secretary's desk. "And whatever you do, don't stare!"

He swallowed hard. "Yes ma'am."

As they stepped into the office, the first thing Darys noticed was the giant stained glass peacock that hung over a large polished oak desk. The framed glass had been back-lit to show off the bright bits of colored glass that formed the bird, with plumage unfurled in glorious display.

It was an impressive, stunning piece of work, but certainly not stunning enough to warrant Ford's look of gaping amazement.

Not amazement, but sheer unadulterated awe.

"Don't stand there with your mouth hanging open," Darys prompted. She turned a nervous glance to the desk where she could see the back of a large leather executive chair. She could see only a partial side view of the man sitting there. He spoke into a communication instrument, only half aware of their entrance.

She took advantage of her last chance to instruct Ford. "Now remember, don't say any—"

"The Crystal Plume!" Ford said in an oddly strangled voice.

She stared at him. "The what?"

"That sign." He pointed to the stained glass peacock. "It hangs . . . er . . . used to hang over the entrance to the biggest bar in Margin. How did it get here?"

Darys motioned for him to lower his voice. "I don't know what year this is, but evidently, it survived from your time period until now. That, or it's been replicated from old pictures from the past. Nostalgia runs in cycles like that where people have unusual interest in history and—"

"Sorry, folks." A voice spoke from the desk. "The phone never stops ringing around here. But I've instructed my secretary to hold all calls so we won't be interrupted again." The man stood and held out his hand. "I'm J.B. Callaghan, owner and operator of Callaghan Resorts and Margin Mountain. I'd like to apologize for any—

"John Barrett?"

Ford's quiet interruption stopped the man's introduction cold.

Darys turned and watched the color drain from Ford's face. He wore a look of utter shock.

"Sheriff?" he repeated.

She looked closer at the man behind the desk, suddenly seeing the similarity between this J.B. Callaghan and the much older sheriff. Johnny's name had been Callaghan, too, hadn't it?

J.B. Callaghan scratched his chin as he stared back. Slow perplexity filled his eyes. "Most people called me—" he hesitated for a moment "—Johnny." He stared openly for a moment longer then obvious recognition blossomed. "Ford?" he croaked. "Ford Nolan?"

Ford nodded.

Darys was lost. How could someone from—she strained at the man's desk, reading his calendar upside down—2017 know a man from 1912?

J.B. Callaghan stood up, obviously amazed. "Good God . . . it's you. It's really you! Look at you, Ford, all grown up." Both men met halfway, grasping each other in what Darys's dad always called "manly hugs" with lots of good-natured back-slapping and such.

Ford seemed pleased yet confused at the same time. "I don't understand. You came here when Barrett came to my time period?"

J.B. "Johnny" Callaghan nodded. "It was an exchange program of sorts." He held out both palms as if they were the pans of an imaginary scale. "It balanced out both worlds."

Ford still gaped. "But you're so . . . young. You look . . . my age! John Barrett's in his fifties."

"What year is it where you came from?" Johnny asked, as if this was an off-hand questions he posed twice a day.

"N-nineteen hundred and twelve."

Johnny nodded wisely. "Then Barrett's been in the past

for right at twenty years." He shoved his hands in his pockets. "I've only been here for two years."

"Two? I don't understand. According to Emma, you changed places with Barrett at least twenty years ago. Why haven't you been here for that same length of time?"

Johnny shot them an enigmatic smile. "Whose clock do we use to measure time with? Yours or mine?"

Ford's expression switched from amazed to confused and Darys knew she needed to step in with some sort of simple explanation he could comprehend. "Allow me," she told Johnny. She turned to Ford. "When you travel through time, you can land anywhere, any time. Time isn't linear. I'll return to my world exactly one week later than when I left, no matter if I spend days, weeks, months or years in the past. In my case, it's the safest time for me to appear back at the vacation center. But normally—" she ignored Ford's expression when she said the word *normally* "—the only requirement you have when it comes to scheduling your return is to make sure you arrive back home *after* your departure time. If you return before you've actually left, then you can rip a whole in the fabric of time."

Johnny turned his sudden attention to her. "By that rather concise explanation, I take it you're not from 1912. Or even 2017, for that matter."

She tried not to blush. "No, I'm from 2142, and I'm afraid Ford's an unintentional hitchhiker."

Johnny Callaghan smiled at Ford. "You mean to tell me that you *didn't* jump through the portal in order to seek your fame and fortune? I'm surprised. You certainly were impulsive enough as a child to do something like that."

Ford seemed too stunned to answer so Darys did it for him. "He jumped into the portal to save my life. Something went wrong. I'm not sure what."

Johnny's smile broadened. "Aha! Saving a damsel in

distress would have been my second guess." He slapped Ford on the back, proving the gesture was ageless. "As God is my witness, I honestly never expected to see anyone from my past again. The last time traveler I knew was afraid he was going to face some stiff penalties for encouraging Barrett and me to change places." Johnny perched on the corner of his desk and crossed his arms. "Hell . . . he did more than encourage us; if it weren't for him, Barrett would have remained in the present and I would have stayed in the past —both of us as miserable as two men could possibly be. I owe a lot to that traveler." Johnny narrowed his gaze and aimed it at her with less goodwill than before. "No matter what anybody says, he's a helluva guy."

It was the first encouraging word she'd heard about her father since this whole time swap debacle had begun. According to the Court of Temporal Appeal, what Harvey had done was nearly criminal and nothing good had come of the switch. The two Callaghan men were lucky they'd been allowed to remain in their chosen eras and not forced to return. Only her father's most persuasive arguments had prevented the exchange.

Now, it was sweet justice to hear her father praised for an act over which others had damned him. "You don't know how glad I am to hear you say that about him. Harvey Kirk is my father."

Johnny's cautious glint brightened into a grin. "You're Harvey's daughter? That's marvelous." He stepped over and pumped her hand furiously. "I'm sorry. I suddenly thought you might be one of those time cops he was afraid of."

She extracted her hand from his exuberant grip. "No, I'm no cop, but if I don't find him, he's going to be in very big trouble again with the authorities. He's missing . . . in time."

"In time?"

She nodded. "His last known coordinates place him here,

in this area in 2017. I overshot the location to begin with and landed in 1912."

Johnny seemed to understand. "Where, I guess, you picked up this lug as a traveling companion." He ruffled Ford's hair as if he was still a child then reddened. "Sorry. I still think of you as a youngster, fresh-faced, smart as a whip, and very protective of your sister." He gave Ford a critical once-over. "You're not a child anymore. Hell, we're practically the same age now, right?"

Ford nodded blankly.

"And exhausted, too, right?"

Ford shrugged. "Time travel is more . . . taxing than I expected."

Darys stared at Ford, suddenly seeing the signs of strain in his eyes, the toll of all this excitement.

Johnny continued, "And there's so much of this new world you want to see, to try out, to investigate, right?"

Ford started to speak, but Darys stepped in. "But let's not forget that temporal pollution is our number one thing to avoid if possible."

"Pollution?" Both men spoke with one voice.

"He can't stay here for long." She turned to Ford. "You're going home just as soon as I find the time portal. The less you know about the future, the better."

Ford's expression darkened. "But—"

Johnny cut him off with a dismissive wave. "She's right, Ford. You've already seen enough to jump-start that clever mind of yours. I bet you'll go home and invent a thousand new things."

Ford's gaze had already settled on the Johnny's desk where several pieces of equipment seemed to have captured his attention. "I can't help being curious. After all . . . wait . . ." Suddenly, he jerked his gaze back to Johnny. "You know I'm an inventor?"

It was Johnny's turn to blush. "Well, I . . . got curious one day about you and looked you up in some history books."

"You found something about me in a book?" Ford asked in honest awe.

Darys gave Johnny a disapproving glance. Surely the man understood what a conundrum he could cause by revealing Ford Nolan's accomplishments before he'd even had a chance to accomplish them.

Johnny seemed to understand her censure. "Uh . . . let's not worry about that. The important thing is that you're somewhere safe. I can offer you the best room in the house for as long as you need it." He turned to Darys. "And that goes double for you. If there's anything I can do to help you find your father, I'll do it. Harvey played a very pivotal role in my life and I owe him a great deal."

She dug her toe into the carpet. "Well there are some ways you can help."

He grinned. "I suspected so. Where shall we start?" He moved gracefully around his desk, dropped in his chair, and indicated that they should all sit.

Ford moved leadenly to his chair, exhaustion masking his features.

"Not you, Ford. Quite frankly, you look tired. Why don't I have my secretary take you to your suite where you can get some sleep while Miss Kirk and I start on the search for her father?"

Ford nodded. "I *am* awfully sleepy."

Johnny punched a button, talked into an instrument, and a moment later, the young woman who'd served them coffee bounced into the room.

"Yes sir, Mr. Callaghan?"

"Please see Mr. Nolan to the Presidential Suite. He doesn't have any luggage, so we'll provide him with every- thing he needs for a comfortable night's stay at Margin. Get whatever you need and put it on my personal account. Miss Kirk and I have some things to discuss."

The woman gave Ford an appraising glance and her dimples deepened. For a fleeting moment, Darys felt her hackles rise. The woman's glance was much too predatory, much too proprietary for Darys's likes.

"Why I'd be delighted," coffee woman purred.

To Darys's relief, Ford stumbled behind the woman, seemingly unaware of her come-hither glances. Just the thought of it made Darys's stomach turn. As Ford left the room, her stomach flopped again.

It must be the coffee.

She'd only had real coffee maybe two, three times in her life. And it didn't taste nearly as good as what—

Her stomach surged again, this time, her sense of balance was equally upset.

Johnny noticed her discomfort. "Are you all right?" He leaned forward, concern shining in his eyes. "Perhaps you've had a more difficult trip than you expected."

"I have thirty-six hundred hours under my belt. I didn't even get time sick when I was a child." Her bravado weakened as her stomach lurched one more time. "Then again . . ."

They heard a commotion outside in the hallway. The coffee woman burst in the door, looking much less composed than before. She spoke in a torrent. "Mr. Nolan has passed out. He started complaining of not feeling well and suddenly he almost fell right on top of me. I've called the EMTs and they're on their way." She rushed out.

Darys stumbled to her feet, despite the waves of upheaval that crashed through her body. Right now, passing out sounded like a delightful suggestion, and she intended to do so just that as soon as she knew Ford was being taken care of. She staggered toward the door, her strength coming back somewhat slowly as she made her way across the room.

But as she reached the doorway, her knees buckled. She grabbed it for support, thankful for the strong arm Johnny placed around her waist. They looked up together, both spotting Ford who had landed in an awkward heap on the carpet. The secretary hovered over him, administering first aid.

A surge of jealousy pushed away the worst of Darys's sickness. With Johnny's support, she stumbled into the anteroom. When she saw Ford rouse and sit up, relief helped her to regain more control. The closer she got to him, the quicker the queasiness faded. She pulled away from Johnny's supportive arm and had no trouble maintaining her balance. Ford seemed to go through a remarkable recovery as well.

A flash of heat erupted across her chest.

Relief?

No . . . her temporal stabilizer—it was overloading.

She jerked it out of its hiding place, but dared not take it off. Rule Number Twenty-Nine of the Time Travelers Code: Never remove your temporal stabilizer.

The disk began to generate so much heat that it started to discolor the fabric of her holosuit. Any hotter and it would leave a serious burn. She held the stabilizer away from her skin by its chain and cautiously examined it.

Evidently overloaded, the disk had fused shut. Try as she might, she couldn't pry open the tiny repair access door. What if the stabilizer stopped working? What if their sickness was merely the first stage of destabilization? She took a hasty glance at her control cuff which monitored her relative stability in time. The readout pulsed steadily, indicating that although fused closed, the stabilizer was still functioning properly.

But as she switched screens, something odd popped up. The stabilizer indicated it was handling a double load.

A double load?

She glanced at Ford, who seemed to have recovered as quickly as she had.

Recovered only when the distance between them had been decreased to only a few feet.

Two people on one stabilizer.

It all made sense to her now. Logical, frightening sense . . .

argin Mountain Resort, February 2017

"LET ME GET THIS STRAIGHT." Ford propped his elbow on the chair and tried to ignore the black spots that threatened to fill his vision. "We're stuck here? Together?"

Darys sat in another chair beside him, lacing and unlacing her fingers. "No . . . yes . . ." Her head bobbed in indecision. "Let me start over again. Something happened when we went through the time door together. The door malfunctioned because of the tremors."

"Tremors?" He thought back to moment when he'd seen Darys slammed against the silvery door frame. "Impossible. I know earthquakes and I promise you, that was no earthquake."

She pursed her lips then sighed. "It was something called a temporal shock wave—a type of time-loop feedback problem. It happens when a location has hosted too many different time doors. The whole area gets unstable, including the ground."

The room spun to the left, and Ford's stomach lurched along with it. "Too many time doors?"

Darys glanced around the room and her gaze finally settled on the stained glass peacock hanging over Johnny's desk. It was an uncanny reminder to Ford that these two worlds, the past and the future, were inexplicably connected.

"Margin's been a popular place for time travelers," she said, turning away. "My father visited here in 1892, 2015, and 2017, too I hope. And then I came in 1912 and now again, 2017. One location simply can't handle that much temporal traffic. When I activated the time door again, the area must have reached temporal saturation and that caused the residual shock waves we felt."

Ford stared at the peacock. In his time, it still hung in over the bar at the "Crystal Plume." But the 'Plume was no longer a bar and house of ill repute, having made the change to a hotel when Earl, the bartender, retired and his oldest son took over. Ford took a closer look at the office, seeing other pieces of memorabilia from the Margin that he had known so well. A framed section of the *Margin Gazette* hung on the wall. *"Sheriff Re-Elected to Fourth Term."*

Ford remembered that election, remembered that issue of the paper. He recalled watching Barrett recoil from the photographer's flash. Or was it Johnny?

It was a Margin that no longer existed outside of aged newspaper clippings.

A Margin that no longer existed for him.

Ford turned his attention back to Darys who looked almost as bad as he felt. He reached up and caught her hand in his. "Darys, I didn't know what to do when I saw you fall." Ford felt a flush start somewhere in the vicinity of his collar.

"I was afraid you'd been knocked unconscious or something like that."

She graced him with a smile that didn't quite erase the fatigue in her eyes. "So you charged in like a knight in shining armor to rescue me." Her expression faded. "But unfortunately, you got caught in the temporal undertow and came along for an unexpected ride." All evidence of her smile disappeared from her face. "But that's not all." She dropped her head into her hands and released a soft sigh.

"What?" His stomach lurched again.

She didn't answer.

"Darys, I have a right to know. . . ."

She sighed again. "Traveling through time places several unnatural stresses on your body. You have to overcome the normal tendency of matter to stay in its natural place in time. We use temporal stabilizers to help boost our personal stability when we travel. Without a stabilizer, the molecules of your body attempt to return to your natural place in the time stream."

It sounded like hokum to him, but he could tell by her expression that she was being serious. He made a stab at comprehension. "So you're saying I could return to my own world at any time?"

She winced. "Not exactly. The molecules break down at different rates. Your body would tear apart and go back, one molecule at a time."

Ford closed his eyes. What she was describing agreed unerringly with what he'd felt . . . as if his body was breaking down on an elemental level.

She continued in a leaden voice. "When you got dragged through time, the portal tried to process you just like it does me. Only . . . there was only one stabilizer in use at the time. The portal had no other option than to treat us as one person."

"Can it last long like that?"

Her strained smile contained only the slightest amount of reassurance. "Yes. It's not going to quit on us any time soon. But there are some limitations."

"Like what?"

She explained everything with an air of clinical detachment. Essentially, if Ford stepped beyond the equipment's range, he'd suffer something she described as "time sickness"—a headache, a queasy stomach, a fever. Then his body would slowly disintegrate as his molecules return to the early twentieth century. The only problem was, they wouldn't necessarily reassemble on the other end.

Ford would cease to exist.

Her voice cracked. "And so will I." She cleared her throat and made an obvious attempt to hide her growing emotion. "Whereas your molecules will try to return to the past, mine will attempt to return to the future."

"So we're stuck with each other." It was a statement rather than a question.

She nodded. "Until I find my father." A tear trickled down her cheek. If Ford knew anything about strong women, it was that he could recognize the signs of an emotional dam under too much strain.

"If we find my D-Dad, then I can switch to his stabilizer and we can send you back home with mine. But if we can't find him . . . or his stabilizer has malfunctioned . . ." Her voice broke. "We'll be stuck . . ." Emotion choked off the rest of the explanation.

Ford sat up and shifted so that their knees were touching. He rested his arms on her shoulders and pulled her forward until her damp cheek rested on his chest.

"Don't worry," he muttered into her ear. "We'll find him."

"But he could be any place. Any time!" she said with a sniff, regaining some control.

"We have to start somewhere. And Johnny—Johnny will help us. He's a sheriff. He knows how to find missing people."

There was a rap at the door and as if on cue, Johnny stepped into the room.

"Everything okay?"

Darys wiped away her tears on the back of her hand and straightened. "I was just explaining the situation to Ford. About what's happened to us."

Ford pulled her hand into his and gave it a squeeze. "And I was telling her that you're a sheriff. You know how to find people, right?"

Johnny ambled over to his desk and sat down. "I *was* a sheriff. But that was well over a hundred years ago, by the world's calendar. Now I'm a business executive."

Ford stared at him. Certainly, the surroundings were different. Instead of a scarred desk with a broken drawer, Johnny could see himself in the perfectly polished surface of his workplace. There was no upturned nail for messages, no wanted posters tacked on the walls.

But what about Johnny?

Had he changed as well?

"Then you won't help?" Darys adopted an aggressive stance at the corner of his desk.

Johnny shot her a lazy smile. "Now did I say that? I've had two years to learn a lot about this modern world I live in now. The most important lesson I learned was that you have to be careful about everything. Do background checks on all the employees, check the credit rating of guests before the bill gets unmanageable, and of course, always make sure to go after unpaid bills." His grin broadened, becoming almost conspiratorial. "I have a man on my payroll who is a cracker-jack private investigator. He can find anybody. Including Harvey—"

A knock interrupted him.

"This could be him. I asked him to drop everything and report to me." He faced the door. "Come in."

The door opened and a woman leaned into the room. "Johnny, I—" She noticed Ford and Darys and blushed prettily. "I'm sorry. I didn't realize you had guests."

Johnny's smile turned into something which Ford could only describe as "sappy." The man sprang from his chair. "Angela, I want you to meet some old friends."

As the blonde stepped into the room, Ford lumbered to his feet, finding the task more draining than it ought to be. When he finally looked up, he realized that, even in this century, clothing couldn't camouflage a woman's delicate condition. Judging by her size, Ford figured the woman would be lucky to reach the chair before the birthing pains started.

She shot Johnny a raised-eyebrow look as she waddled toward the desk. "*Old* friends?"

Johnny gave her a quick nod then ushered her to his chair where she settled herself gingerly. "Angela, I'd like you to meet Darys Kirk and Ford Nolan. Darys, Ford, this is my wife, Angela Callaghan." He reached down and gave her protruding stomach a gentle pat. "And our very first little Callaghan who is scheduled to arrive two weeks from today."

Ford could do nothing but stare at the woman. Johnny's wife? His child? It hadn't occurred to Ford that the sheriff might have made quite a comfortable life for himself in this century. But Johnny had; he had obvious wealth, the power that money can generate, and, like his counterpart, Barrett, Johnny had a devoted and expanding family.

The woman smiled and covered Johnny's hand with her own. "Nolan—as in Nolan-Callaghan Memorial Hospital? Same family?"

Ford glanced at Johnny, hoping the man might supply the answer. The last thing a woman in her condition needed was the shock of learning about their unbelievable trip through time. But apparently, Johnny didn't share the same concerns.

"Ford is Emma Nolan Callaghan's brother. And Darys is the daughter of Harvey Kirk. Remember me talking about him?"

Ford didn't know what to expect. Hysteria, fear, shock, surprise, maybe even labor pains. But instead of any of these dangerous emotions, a serene look crossed her face.

"Time travelers? How nice. I hope your trip here was uneventful. Are you here on vacation?"

Uneventful? Ford gaped openly at her. How in the world could someone even hope to describe what they'd gone through as uneventful? Traveling through time was an event. A big, unbelievable, stretch-your-imagination-beyond-all-limits event. How in the world could he even find words to express his utter shock at landing somewhere else in time?

To Ford's relief, Johnny supplied the answer. "I'm afraid they're here on business, sweetheart. Harvey's missing."

"Missing?" Her brow furrowed. "How terrible. What can we do to help?"

Johnny picked up her hand and laced her fingers in his. "I've offered them a place to live while we start a search for Harvey. After all, we have one of the best bloodhounds in the business working here. If anybody can find Harvey, Tucker James can." He turned to Darys. "Angela and I owe Harvey a big debt; if it weren't for him, I wouldn't be here. We wouldn't be together at all." He paused to shoot his wife an indulgent smile which faltered only when he looked back up again. "I know Harvey caught hell for helping Barrett and me to exchange places in time."

Darys ducked her head. "He was banned from time travel for two years. No time-share vacations at all. It almost killed him."

"And you think he headed back here as soon as his suspension was lifted?"

Uncertainty filled her eyes. "That's the problem. I'm not so sure his suspension was officially lifted. It appears he may be traveling illegally and might have used equipment which might have been in less-than-perfect working condition."

"And if he's not supposed to be here, he might try to hide from the authorities and be inadvertently hiding from you as well."

"That's exactly the reason why I need to go look for him all by myself. He won't trust anybody but me."

"But you won't be by yourself," Johnny offered.

Ford cleared his throat. "Don't forget me."

She pivoted around as if to argue, then realization took the wind out of her sails. She sagged against the desk. "That's right. We're stuck together. Unless Dad recognizes you, he'll probably think you're some time cop using me as bait to flush him out in the open." She leaned more heavily on the desk. "Oh no . . ." She dropped suddenly to her knees.

Ford rushed to her side, adrenaline supplying the energy he'd lacked before. "Darys, don't worry. It's okay. We'll find a way to get to your father. I promise."

"It's n-not that," she said between raspy sobs.

He knelt beside her, stroking her hair and trying to murmur encouraging things, but she pushed away his attempts to comfort her. She nudged her hair out of her eyes, straightened and shrugged off Ford's attempt to help her.

She stood, pale and erect. "If you'll excuse me, I need to go someplace where I can be violently ill. When I was little, I'd have delayed reactions to time travel and this time it's going to be a doozy."

It was an effective end to their conversation. Moments later, they were safely ensconced in a private suite with a large accommodating bathroom in which Darys locked herself. Ford didn't need to inquire about her sickness. He learned quickly that there were other levels on which they were connected. He lunged for the trash can.

AFTER FIFTEEN RATHER UNPLEASANT MINUTES, Darys emerged from the bathroom. She spotted Ford, draped bonelessly across the bed. A nearby garbage can confirmed her worst suspicions.

"You too?"

"Like clockwork," he muttered, making no effort to nod. "Every time you . . . had the urge, a similar urge hit me about a minute later." He grimaced. "And rest assured, they weren't sympathy pains. Whatever technology holds us together seems to want us to share all the same symptoms as well."

"Sorry."

He managed a weak smile. "Just assure me you hold no unordinary fondness for spicy foods."

She grimaced at the thought. "Please. Not now." She dragged herself over to the bed and sat on the floor beside it, leaning her head against the edge of the mattress. "I don't want to think of food. All I want to do is sleep. I can't effectively look for my father if my head won't function." She massaged her temples. "It hurts to think."

"Sleep." Ford flexed his long body. "Sleep sounds almost decadent, especially in a room like this."

Darys took a double handhold of bedspread, tugged herself up to her knees and then into a sitting position on the edge of the mattress. She glanced around at the room, finding it ordinary by her standards. Perhaps even a little antiquated.

She'd already discovered in the bathroom that the lights had to be turned off manually rather than with voice controls. Water temperature had to be mixed by combining scalding and frigid water together in an almost random fashion. Turn the controls too far one way and you were burned. Turn it too far the other and you thought you were washing in the run-off from Mount Everest.

And she thought Ford lived in an antediluvian world. . . .

Darys slid to a reclining position, confident she could sleep quite well across the foot of the bed. "Hand me a pillow, okay?"

Ford sat bolt upright in the bed, his ailments evidently forgotten. "What are you doing?"

She tucked her aching body into a more comfortable position. "It's called sleep. I thought we covered this topic a moment ago."

He struggled to his feet. "Get up."

A sleepy buzz had begun to form in her ears. "Why?"

"Because I need the coverlet."

She yawned. "Why?"

"Because if I'm going to sleep on the sofa, I need some sort of cover." He pulled at the material beneath her.

As she grew even sleepier, the word became more of a mantra for her than a question. "Why?"

"Because, if you haven't noticed, it's damnably cold in here." He tugged at the bedspread. "Roll over, okay? You're too heavy."

She ignored his insult. "Computer access."

Instead of a computer responding to her voice request, she heard only Ford's dubious, "Pardon?" At least he'd stopped pulling at the material beneath her.

"Computer, access environmental controls," she commanded.

Silence filled the room.

"Voice responder must have—" a huge yawn interrupted her, creating black spots in her vision "—malfunctioned. Live with it." She surrendered to the fatigue that washed over her like a heavy blanket of molten lava. Somewhere in the back of her sleep-addled mind, she realized Ford had successfully pulled the bedspread from beneath her and dragged the material as well as himself into the next room. She inched into the warm spot he left behind and closed off her mind to everything, including dreams.

In what seemed like a split second later, a shrill ring pierced her brain, bursting her bubble of sleep. She pulled the pillow over her head, not caring if the noise was an alarm, a warning, or a communication device.

It blasted the room a second time, and she heard a muffled shout and the sound of a body hitting something hard. Cracking open one eye, she focused through the doorway into the next room where she spotted Ford. He sprang up from his awkward position on the floor beside the couch. He looked like a wild man—hair sticking out at odd angles, eyes bugging out, bare-chested . . .

She smiled. *Nice pecs.* The bedspread was tangled around his waist and legs, making it appear as if he had no clothes on.

That fact alone finished waking up Darys.

"That n-noise!" he stuttered. He ran one hand through his disheveled hair while maintaining a death grip on his bedspread.

"A vidphone," she answered. At his puzzled look, she added, "A communication device. A telephonic instrument." She sighed in exasperation and searched for an antiquated reference he might understand. "A cell. A telephone."

"But where?"

It was a stupid question. Or was it? In her day, you wore your comm. In this century? She dredged up a memory of a history text showing large units in various places throughout a room. Darys looked around. Where was the silly thing? She scanned the room, looking for a likely piece of equipment. A small black keypad sat next to the lamp on the bedside table. She picked up the keypad, punched the button marked "Power" and held it to her ear.

"Hello?"

A man's voice answered. "It's delicious. I would have never guessed it wasn't ground roast coffee. So full-bodied."

"What in blue blazes?" Ford demanded as he stumbled into the room and toward the bed, almost tripping over the trailing bedclothes.

Darys waved him away. "Room service, I think. Something about coffee." She turned her attention back to the instrument. "We didn't order coffee. We're sleeping. Leave us alone."

Another shrill ring split the air.

A dozen booming voices filled the room. "—two-three hundred, Empire! Get your carpet today!"

Darys focused on the screen which had jumped to life in the corner of the room. A man's face stared at her. Darys jerked the covers up out of age-old instincts. "Computer. Cut the video access." She pushed another button.

Yet another man appeared on the screen, one wearing a too-big-to-be-genuine smile. "Case and Starborn has revolutionized the freeze-drying process so you can enjoy the same rich cup of coffee, today, tomorrow, and every day!"

Darys stared dumbfounded at the screen. What sort of crazy world had she been dropped into?

At the next beep, Ford halted, cocked an ear then pounced on a piece of equipment on the desk near the screen console. He found a hand-set which he tentatively shoved to his ear. "H-hello?"

Darys almost laughed. Whatever that bulky thing he held was, it was no vidphone. She glanced at the keypad she held, trying to find the proper controls that would kill the video portion of the call.

Relief flooded Ford's voice. "Johnny, it's you."

Don't tell me he *found the vidphone.* She punched another button on the keypad she held and the screen flickered, suddenly replacing the man's face with a picture of a ship flying through space.

A distinguished voice spoke. "Captain's Log, Stardate 43989.1."

Not a tele*phone*. A tele*vision*. Now she remembered. She searched on the keypad for the power button and hit it. The television screen went black.

"Yes. No . . . yes . . . that would be fine. Now, I guess. Thanks." Ford moved numbly, dropping the instrument to the desk.

She pointed to the empty cradle. "If you don't put it back in there, the call won't disconnect," she said, demonstrating her total knowledge of antiquated telephone systems. Lord help her if he asked her anything else about telephones.

Ford fumbled with the receiver and managed to return it to its proper place. "According to Johnny, we've been asleep for twelve hours."

She glanced at her control cuff and read the time. "T-Twelve hours? It seemed more like twelve seconds."

Ford nodded. "To me, too." He glanced at the telephone. "Johnny wanted to know if we wanted breakfast now. I didn't know what to tell him so I said yes. I think I'm hungry." He reached up and splayed a hand across his stomach. When he realized he wore no shirt, he blushed and jerked his covers up.

Unfortunately, all that succeeded in doing was to expose his bare legs. In full flush, he reached down to get his jeans which had been thrown to the floor in a wadded heap. As he bent over, his covers parted and Darys got a full rear view of early twentieth-century underwear.

And she liked what she saw in them.

"Excuse me," he said with a gulp. He disappeared into the bathroom, his trailing bedclothes getting caught in the closing door. He opened the door again, grimaced, and pulled the bedspread free. A moment later, the door opened wide enough and long enough for him to toss the offending material back into the main room.

"And next time—I get the bed," he shouted through the closed door.

CHAPTER 8

*D*arys and Ford ate in silence, almost matching bite per bite. They yawned at the same time, they reached for the butter at the same time, they even said "excuse me" at the same time.

If they had been lovers, it would have been encouraging, perhaps even cute to see herself in such sync with a man.

But they weren't lovers.

Artificial means had connected them, causing them to fall into a synchronous rhythm that, quite frankly, unnerved Darys. They were two separate people, not two halves of a whole. When their hands brushed as they reached simultaneously for the cream, Darys exploded.

"Stop, damn it!"

Ford withdrew his hand. "Sorry. You first."

"That's not the point. I don't use cream in my coffee."

He smiled. "Good. Means more for me."

"But don't you see why I reached for it?"

He took a bite of toast and shook his head.

"Because you wanted it."

He quirked an eyebrow at her. "Really? Isn't that a bit childish?"

She threw her napkin down and pushed away from the table. "Come on—you're more observant that that."

"Right now, I'm hungry. I'll be observant later." He continued to eat, evidently oblivious to the strange connections between them.

"Think of a number."

He looked up, his mouth full. "Hmm?"

"Think of a number between one and ten."

He shrugged *okay.*

"Two," she declared.

A small smile of surprise touched his lips and he nodded.

"Another number," she continued. "This time between one and twenty-five."

He wiped his mouth. "Okay."

"Eighteen."

His eyes narrowed. "Right, again."

"Between one and a hundred."

He pushed back in his chair, balancing it on its rear legs in a too-casual manner. "Got it. Guess."

She squinted in concentration, as if it might help her to "see" his mind more clearly. But she realized she wasn't reading his thoughts—merely expressing her own. "Seventy-one."

The chair almost lost its precarious balance. "Aha!" A grin of triumph creased his face. "The number was seventy-two. You missed." His expression faded into confusion. "By one. You missed it by only . . . one." He turned away from her, spending an inordinate length of time recovering his balance. "I suppose you want me to believe you're a mind reader as well a time traveler?"

He still didn't understand. "I'm not reading your mind,

Ford. I'm just telling you the numbers I would choose if someone asked *me* to guess."

"So it's merely coincidental that we would choose the same number or close to it?" He stood a bit too quickly. "I could believe that with a ten number range, but not in a range of a hundred numbers. It's statistically . . . improbable."

"But not impossible." Darys crossed her arms. "Okay, let's go for broke. Pick a number between one and one thousand."

He began to pace, his head bobbing with every step and concentration forming neat wrinkles in his forehead. Finally, he stopped and nodded. "Go."

She closed her eyes, letting a conga line of numbers dance through her brain. During the other times, the answer came to her as if it was her own creation, not a matter of divining his. But this time, nothing. Darys opened one eye and simply guessed. "Eight-hundred and thirty-nine?"

He released his pent-up breath in a whoosh. "Nope. Six."

"I ask you to choose a number between one and one thousand and you choose *six*? No one chooses six when they're guessing a number between one and a thousand."

He shrugged. "That's exactly why I chose it. But the question is: why didn't you guess it? You think it has to do with the range? The larger the range of answers, the less likely we choose the same number?"

She nodded. "That makes sense. In a field of twenty-five or less, we coincide exactly. In a field of a hundred, our guesses were damned near close. In a field of thousand, they were nowhere near each other—just two random choices."

"But are you reading my mind?"

A chill went up Darys's spine. "Or are you forcing your thoughts on me?"

He took an involuntary step back. "I'd never do something like that."

"Not knowingly. But what if you can't help it?"

He pointed to the breakfast table. "Sit. We need to test this hypothesis. Is our ability to make free choices being influenced by someone else?"

Darys took her seat again. "So how do we test it?"

"I'll ask you a question and then count to three. We'll say our answers simultaneously. Okay?"

She nodded.

"Pick a number between one and twenty. One, two, three—"

They answered in unison. "Nineteen."

"Okay, what is your favorite color? One, two, three—Red."

"Blue." Darys smiled. "Okay that's one for individualism. Let me ask the next one. If you're given a choice between an apple, an orange, and a peach, which do you choose? One, two, three—"

"Apple." Their voices blended together.

"Okay, I want to try something. Go stand by that window."

Ford scratched his head, but complied. With his long legs, he reached the window in only a couple of strides. Darys moved to the opposite side of the room, putting the greatest distance between them that the room would allow.

"Pick a number between one and twenty. One, two, three —twelve."

"Thirteen. Hey, you may be onto something here. Maybe we can assume that distance has something to do with this—this connection between us." Ford took a step toward her.

"No, go back. I'm not through. What is your favorite—"

Favorite what? Song? Holoprogram? I can't ask him twenty-second-century questions.

"Favorite month?" Ford supplied.

She nodded in relief. "Okay, favorite month—one, two, three—December."

"May."

"One last question: if given a choice, which would you choose? An apple, a banana, or an orange? One, two, three —apple."

"Banana."

His answer caught her off guard. "Why the change?"

Amusement flared in his eyes. "I've never had a banana, before. Heard of 'em, but never eaten one." His gaze narrowed, extinguishing his brief bout of humor. "But all this doesn't necessarily prove that proximity is the only factor here. It certainly seems to have an influence on those answers that can be influenced."

Darys returned to the table and took a sip of her coffee, finding fortification in its foreign richness. "I agree. When we're coming up with what is essentially a random answer or action, we do it in synch, depending on the distance between us. Like the numbers. The closer we are, the more likely we'll guess the same."

"But when it comes to reporting a preference, something which we've probably had for years, there's no outside influence. I say red because I've always liked red."

"And I say December because that's my birth month. It doesn't matter how near or far we are from each other."

The both settled in their chairs, across from each other. Their gazes locked and an uncomfortable silence filled the room.

"So now what?" Ford picked up his coffee, took a healthy swig and made a face. "Take the show on the road as a mentalist act for vaudeville?"

Darys's mind went blank. "Who's Vaudeville?"

He lifted his shoulders in a small shrug. "Not who, *what*. It's a type of . . . roving entertainment show. We don't get much of it in Margin, but it's big business down in Denver if you're willing to make the trip. They have singers, dancers, comedians, and mentalist acts—that's where someone on stage reads the minds of people in the audience." He shot her a devastating grin. "We could make a Denver Mint of money with an act like that."

Darys sighed. Lord save her from inventors with oddball senses of humor. "Be serious. This is merely another side effect of the temporal stabilizer. Speaking of which . . ." She pulled the stabilizer from beneath her blouse and held it by its thin golden chain. "I think I can maximize our range to about thirty-five feet. If we stay within that area, we're fine. If we go beyond it, we'll both start to get timesick." She paused for effect. "And worse."

"Will the range be decreased by structures such as walls?" He looked around the room as if searching for something. "You know . . . like with a wireless radiotelegraphic signal?"

She shook her head. "No. Walls, furniture, trees—nothing will decrease the range. But at thirty-five feet, one inch, we'll start to feel sick. At thirty-six feet, we'll start to lose consciousness and at thirty-seven feet, the reversal process begins."

Ford winced, indicating that she'd evidently impressed him with the seriousness of the situation. Good. What she didn't need was an absentminded scientist apt to meander off at the least provocation and forget about their limited range. Or, for as far as that went, a partner who would hamper her search for her father.

Ford stood, interrupting her thoughts. "If you don't mind, I think I'll wash up." He padded off to the bathroom, but before entering, turned and graced her with one more smile. "I guess I don't have to tell you not to wander off."

The door closed behind him.

She sighed. Lord save her from twentieth-century comedians.

Darys turned back around and stared at the remains of

their breakfast. Guilt settled in her stomach, turning her meal into lead. She rose from the table. How could she have even thought about food at a time like this? Her dad was lost. Possibly hurt. It would be up to her to find him.

She scanned the room for a netlink. She knew computers had become popular in the late twentieth century, so it should be hard to get on the netlink and find Harvey by searching for his stabilizer frequency code. She picked up the keypad from the side table, pointed it at the most likely candidate for a netlink, the television, and pushed the "power" button. The screen jumped to life, displaying a man dressed in white and stirring something in a pan.

"—three egg whites, finely beaten and just a pinch of salt. This is a great recipe for those of you who have cholesterol and sodium problems. Now we—"

Darys pushed another button marked, "Up."

". . . Olivia, you know I've supported you against the President in the past, but I can't this time."

A dark-haired woman appeared on the screen, evidently upset. "Can't or won't? You've fallen in rank with the rest of those bureaucrats," she spat. "It's critical that I be able to trust you and now I worry that—"

Up.

"—deadbeat dad who can't find the money to pay his back child support but comes up with the bucks to throw at some insane inventor with an unbelievable product." A woman sat in a chair with her arms crossed and an ugly sneer on her face.

The scene cut to a man with his arms crossed as well. "The guy's not crazy. Weather forecasting is the wave of the future. Anyway, you gotta spend money to make money, right? Well I'm gonna invest in my future, in the kids' future, by investing in—"

Up.

Darys checked every channel, finding nothing that resembled a netlink. What other equipment in a hotel room might be used to access the net? She scanned the area, her gaze settling on the telephone. Upon examination, she found a small rectangular-shaped hole on the back of the instrument, marked "DATA PORT" in raised letters. Curiosity overtook her and in just a few short moments, she'd used a blunt knife from their breakfast table to unscrew the casing and reveal a collection of colored wires and old-fashioned silicone waferboards.

She winced. *Hopeless.*

"Fantastic . . ."

She turned and saw Ford standing beside her, peering at the exposed guts of the telephone. He seemed totally entranced by the sight, but she found herself more captivated by the sight of him.

Ford was undeniably handsome, in a sort of old-fashioned way. And he was different from the men of her world. Certainly, he viewed things from a unique perspective due to his level of technological expertise, or lack thereof. But it was more than that that interested her. More than his unhesitating heroics. More than his almost child-like fascination with the new world unfolding at his feet. More than—

"What does that do?" He pointed to a round black disk, shattering her thoughts.

She tried to drag her mind back from its musings. The word "wander*lust*" had just gained a whole new meaning. "Maybe it's the ringer. I don't know much about these old . . . er . . . these systems."

Ford ignored her gaffe and snagged a pen from the desk. "What about this?" He used the tapered end to point to a waferboard. At that moment, the phone emitted a shrill beep. They jumped back, flashing each other guilty grins.

"Did I do that?" he asked sheepishly.

The phone beeped again.

Darys realized she'd been holding her breath. "Guess not." Ford joined her in nervous laughter. "We better reassemble this thing so it'll work."

Beep.

"I spotted another one in the bathroom." Ford pushed back his chair.

"There's one beside the bedroom in the other room . . ." Darys stopped. Ford had already disappeared into the bathroom.

From there, she heard a muffled, "Uh . . . yes?" She moved to the bathroom door, not willing to step in and share a rather personal space with him. After a moment's thought, she laughed silently. Until she either found her father or discovered a way to send Ford back, practically all they would have would be considered personal space.

"It's Johnny," Ford called out. "Yes? Yes. Ten minutes?" He gave Darys a questioning look and she nodded. "No problem." He paused then smiled. "Yes . . . it's been pretty eye-opening. Almost more than I can comprehend." Another pause. "In your office. All right." He punched a button on the telephone, giving it an appreciative look. "Miraculous."

Darys raised a critical brow. "Depends on your perspective I guess. Compared to what I'm used to, it's an antique. And look, it's even tied into the wall. Do they have that much problem with theft around here?"

Ford adopted a grin of superiority. "You're kidding, right? Everyone knows you can't have a telephone system without telephone wires." His grin faded. "But the parts that stump me are these buttons." He pointed to the keypad on the receiver. "I wonder what these numbers are for."

Darys balanced her fists on her hips and mimicked him. "Everyone knows that each telephone has a special identifying code and you punch that number in to reach that specific telephone."

His sheepish grin returned. "With our telephone system, a central operator connects you to your party."

They stared at each other for a long moment. Somewhere down the line, he'd lost his serious, studious look. Maybe it was the hair. He'd worn it sort of flat, almost slicked down. It was probably the height of fashion in his time. But she preferred how he looked now—tousled, comfortable, almost sexy . . .

A fine red flush suddenly crawled up Ford's face.

A shock of recognition flowed through her. At this very close proximity, could he read her thoughts?

He swallowed hard. "Uh . . . by the way, Johnny called to tell us that his private investigator has arrived."

Darys straightened, thankful for the distraction. "Good. Now maybe we can start looking for Dad." She pivoted and retreated into the bedroom.

Ford remained behind and the prickles that had risen on the back of his neck finally relaxed once she disappeared from sight. Darys was definitely the cause of his rather schoolboy reaction. She was exotic, with an intoxicating beauty and an intelligence that far out-distanced his own. But he had no problem dealing with smart women. His Mary had been smart—book smart as well as practical and wise. Emma had introduced them, saying they were well-matched, and she'd been so right.

How tiring it must have been for this twenty what? . . . twenty-second century woman to deal with what amounted to his stone-aged world.

But what about Johnny's world? Ford thought about a small hand-held machine that blasted a hot stream of air, a shower that pulsed seven different patterns of heated water, and a toilet without an overhead tank. What he viewed as a technological advance, she considered backward and antiquated.

He sighed. If Johnny's world was backward, then what sort of magnificent future did she come from?

Ford sighed again. The only way to know for sure was to ask. He stepped out of the bathroom. "You know, Johnny said he's been here only two ye—" He stopped.

Darys stood in front of him, her clothes metamorphosing.

He spun around quickly, fairly sure that a gentleman shouldn't watch a lady change clothes, even if the clothes were merely changing on their own.

"It's okay, Ford. There's nothing to see."

For a brief moment, he wondered if she was disdainfully discussing her attributes rather than the glimpse of flesh he might get as she changed. "You sure?"

"Turn around, silly."

Ford drew a deep breath and pivoted. She stood by the desk chair, dressed in a tight gray suit-skin which clung to her every curve, giving the imagination a definite blueprint to follow. He'd only seen something like it once before, when a traveling circus came to Margin. The lady who flew the trapeze wore something similar. Ford had been sixteen and he and his friends had been full of curiosity. His interest had been in the trapeze riggings and theory behind their gravity-defying art. His friends had been more enticed by the allure of her costume and the curves it held. Back then, women were a complete enigma to him. But now, at thirty, he under-stood better the constraints and challenges of dealing with life's greatest puzzle.

"It's a holosuit," Darys offered, evidently mistaking his appreciative look as one of curiosity. "It can change to anything."

"I know." He cleared his throat which inexplicably decided to clog. "I saw it change when we . . . landed here."

"That time, the controls were set to adapt automatically. I'll be in control of it from now on, especially since we'll be dealing directly with . . . natives." She held up a magazine and pointed to an advertisement for a department store. "My father taught me to take my inspiration from what I see others wearing. Fashion changes awfully fast, no matter what time period you're in."

Ford nodded then glanced down at his own clothes. "I suppose I look terribly old-fashioned, don't I?"

She punched some of the buttons of her controls. "You'd be surprised. A pair of jeans and a white shirt are still fashion basics, even in my time." The holosuit transformed into a pair of indecently tight trousers and a bright-colored sweater. Black boots formed on her feet.

"But we might see if Johnny can scare you up some more modern clothes." She flipped to the next page of the magazine. "Something like this."

Ford studied the photograph of the sunken-cheeked, sullen-looking men. They seemed terribly unhappy about something. Probably their clothes. The denim pants were molded so tight to their bodies that couldn't possibly move with any ease. He stared at shirts which, in his world, were considered mere undergarments. "I'm afraid I'd be a little cold wearing something like that."

She glanced out the window at the snow-covered slope. "I suspect you're right. We can leave the fashion sense to Johnny. He'll know what to do."

Ford reached into his pocket to pull out his watch. The hands were both pointing to twelve, but Ford knew it was nowhere near noon. He listened to the watch, hearing no telltale tick. He began to wind it.

"What's that?" Darys leaned closer to look at his timepiece. The color drained from her face, and she looked as if her knees were going to give out from beneath her.

Ford shoved his watch back in his pocket, reached out and steadied her. "Are you all right?"

"That watch . . ." She shook her head as if trying to shake off unsettling memories. "My father had . . . has a watch somewhat similar to that."

Ford closed his eyes and tried to dredge up a twenty-year old memory of the Harvey Kirk that he remembered. A watch . . . did he recall some sort of watch? He'd been a child when he last saw Harvey. And, if Ford wasn't mistaken, the man was drunk at the time. It was at the celebration that turned into an engagement party for his sister. Harvey had slapped an arm around Ford and rambled something about clocks and time and the power of love. And he had rattled his pocket watch once or twice as he offered an incoherent view of the world.

Ford opened his eyes and watched Darys battle with her own memories. The power of love. It was a noble cause that fueled her travel, her search. Due to their unexplainable connection, he could almost feel her concern for her father, emanating in palpable waves. He reached over and patted her hand.

"Don't worry. We'll find him."

She stiffened as if drawing strength from a new reserve. "Damn straight. We'll find Dad, I'll fire a few retros in his direction—" she marched toward the door "—and then I'll haul his rosy-red rear back to the twenty-second century where it belongs."

The slang might differ, but the sentiment survived all translation; Harvey Kirk would be in big trouble when his daughter found him.

CHAPTER 9

*F*ord moved quickly, reaching the door before Darys, and swinging it open for her. She recoiled for a moment, surprised by the gesture. Did he think her incapable of opening the door herself? Then she remembered one of the temporal excursion classes her father had dragged her to as a child. The topic had been decorum and etiquette in centuries past. Unfortunately, she'd been an unenthusiastic student, and couldn't remember exactly who did what, when. All she could think to do here was what she did back in the classroom, years ago—

Fake it.

She stalked down the hallway, leaving Ford to close the door behind them and then catch up with her. When he finally reached her, she'd already found the turbo-lift. She ignored him and faced a control panel beside the lift entrance. "Turbo-lift," she ordered.

Ford released a sigh. "Yes . . . I know—an elevator. I've seen one before."

Elevator. That's what Johnny had called it when they'd

ridden up from his office. She'd been feeling so miserable, she'd paid little attention to how it worked or what he called it. She repeated the command, this time using the proper terminology: "Elevator."

Ford crossed his arms, obviously miffed. Darys couldn't help but share in his impatience. The car was taking an inordinately long time to arrive. She tried again. "Elevator," she called out, this time in a louder voice.

"You don't have to repeat yourself," Ford complained. "I said I knew what an elevator was, how it functions. I'm not a caveman, you know. I've read about elevators—I've even studied their basic mechanics. Heck, I even rode an elevator once in a department store in Denver. For five floors."

Five whole floors. Will wonders ever cease? How would he react to a turbo-lift at her apartment building that had artificial gravity and could negotiate a hundred and forty-five floors and twenty-seven horizontal sectors in twelve seconds or less?

She forced herself to remain civil. "I'm not repeating myself. I'm calling for the elevator. They're usually voice-activated." She looked down, realizing her tapping foot was betraying her impatience. "What's taking so long?" She leaned closer to a communications grill set in the wall next to the door. "Elevator. Now!"

Ford studied the panel for a moment then with an air of superiority reached around her and pushed a button. It lit up, highlighting an embossed arrow pointing down. "I guess you need a twentieth-century man to run a twentieth-first-century elevator."

"I don't need a twentieth-century man to run anything for me, thank you very much." The button light flickered, went out, and the door slid open, revealing polished wooden panels and brass rails.

"What about a twenty-second-century man?"

Darys stalked in and turned around to discover a panel of controls by the door. "My personal life is of no concern of yours." She skimmed the panel quickly and punched a button marked "L" which she assumed stood for "Lobby." After all, she was supposed to be the technologically advanced one, right?

"I guess that answers my question about the future of the women's suffrage movement. I bet Emma wouldn't be surprised at all by that news."

Darys bristled at his dejected sigh. "You're disappointed that women might have won the right to vote?"

"Heck, no." He dismissed the idea with a wave of his hand. "I'm just jealous of Emma—of every scrap of information she might have gleaned about the future." His unfocused stare finally settled on the elevator's control panels. His interest sharpened perceptibly and he ran his finger lightly over a couple of buttons. "I find this place pretty fascinating, but I suppose it's old hat to you."

"Old hat?"

Ford grinned. "Nick likes to use that phrase. It's very . . . popular at the moment. It means being comfortably out of fashion, being in the past. All this—" he pointed to the elevator controls. "You've grown far beyond this, haven't you? Technologically speaking."

"Pretty much." She studied the buttons beside his hand. "Some of the systems, here, are . . . analogous to my world, some aren't." She'd be fine just as long as he didn't ask her to explain what each control meant. She still hadn't figured out the two buttons with the opposing arrows.

"Like the 'voice-activated' thing?" He crossed his arms nonchalantly. "What does 'voice-activated' mean, anyway?"

She allowed herself a mental sigh. Good. A question she

could at least answer. "It's a method by which a computer—hey! Wait a minute . . ." A sudden warning light flashed in her brain; she'd been tricked. And by a master, too. "I'm not going to tell you that."

The elevator dinged and the door slid open to reveal a teeming lobby where people milled about in large clumps. As she negotiated a path between the clusters of bodies and suitcases, Darys spoke between clenched teeth, "You do remember our discussion about President Lincoln and temporal pollution, don't you?"

"Uh huh." Ford dutifully dogged her steps.

"Then don't ask me questions like that."

He sighed. "Fair enough. But there's still one thing I want to know."

Darys stopped and pivoted in order to make eye contact. "Ford . . . ," she warned.

He raised both hands in mock surrender. "I don't think it's a potentially polluting topic. Tell me about—" he nodded toward a knot of particularly brightly-dressed people "—skiing. Do people actually pay money to come to a place like this . . . to put wooden planks on their feet and play in the snow?"

Darys sidestepped a large pile of suitcases and pulled Ford closer. It wouldn't do to have a native overhear such a conversation. "Skiing is a very popular recreational sport," she whispered. "People enjoy the challenge of learning how to maintain their balance, control their speed, and guide themselves as they go down slopes of snow."

"And they pay money to do it?"

She nodded. "Lots of money."

Ford took a surreptitious glance around the room and motioned her closer. "One more question."

She leaned in. "What?"

He gave the room and its people one more furtive scan.

"Then if it costs so much and they enjoy it so much, why aren't they out skiing, right now?"

Darys stiffened as someone jostled her. Good question. People packed the lobby, all talking, laughing. If skiing was indeed such a popular sport, then why was everyone hanging around inside the hotel in large clumps rather than out enjoying their expensive recreation?

The door opened and a gust of cold air swept into the room, bringing with it a blast of snowflakes. Beyond the windows, they both saw a storm in full rage. Snow flew sideways through the gray sky, whipped by strong winds. Benches, tables, everything outside had been turned into anonymous bumps beneath a white blanket of snow.

Ford sighed. "Everybody talks about the weather . . ."

"And if I were home, I still couldn't do much about it . . . ," Darys muttered under her breath. She stopped short, realizing she'd spoken aloud.

A gleam crept into Ford's eye. "If I understand you correctly, then you're saying people can't control the weather in the future?"

"Abraham Lincoln . . . ," she warned, wrapping a hand around his arm and pulling him away from the window. "This isn't the place or the time—"

"But one day in the future, it will be the right time. Correct?"

She ignored him, choosing instead to enter the hallway which led to Johnny's office.

"C'mon, Darys, can't you—"

"No." She spun on her heel and shook her finger in his face. "Don't ask me to tell you anything. Don't try to trick it out of me or coerce it out of me or try to get me drunk or anything. Understand? Your future and mine may depend on it."

Ford merely lifted one eyebrow and followed her into the

outer office. Johnny's secretary acknowledged Darys with a polite nod, but gave Ford a sparkling smile.

"Good morning, sir. You certainly look as if you've recovered nicely from yesterday's accident." She gave him an appreciative glance which could have steamed the clothes right off him. "Quite a storm we're having, isn't it?" She rose from her seat and perched on the corner of her desk, making sure to display a modest amount of cleavage.

Ford nodded, returning her grin with his own goofy one. "Yes indeed. I haven't seen one like this in years."

Darys shoved an elbow into his ribs in warning. "I believe Mr. Callaghan is expecting us," she said to the secretary.

The woman took a deep breath, evidently hoping to capture Ford's attention with one lingering glimpse of décolletage. "He certainly is. This way, please."

They followed her to the door that led to Johnny's office. The woman paused to shoot Ford a blatant come-hither look. "Can I get you anything?" she asked in a breathy voice. "Coffee, tea . . ." Her third option of "me" hung unspoken in the air.

Darys felt her jaw clench automatically. *He's old enough to be your great-grandfather.*

Ford swallowed hard and a flush of red started at his collar. "Uh . . . not for me, thank you, ma'am." He turned to Darys, unable to mask his confusion. "How about you, D-Darys?"

The woman's simpering smile faded into a businesslike expression when she turned in Darys's direction. "Coffee, ma'am?"

And you're old enough to be my great-grandmother.

"Why, aren't you sweet to ask," Darys replied, using the same artificial tone. "Thanks, but no thanks." Grabbing Ford by the arm, Darys dragged him into the inner office where

Johnny stood beside the desk in deep conversation with another man. He broke away when he saw them.

"Ford, Miss Kirk. Good. I've been giving Tuck, here, some of the sketchy details." He nodded toward his companion. "Tuck, this is your client, Darys Kirk, and our mutual friend, Ford Nolan. Darys, Ford, meet Tucker James—the resort's chief investigator."

Ford and James sized each other up for several seconds and Ford wasn't too sure he liked what he saw.

The man held out his hand to Darys first, showing at least a modicum of manners. "Ms. Kirk." James gave her a smile which Ford found a bit too smarmy for his likes. Then the man had the audacity to continue holding her hand as if she was a possession he longed to have.

To make things worse, Darys actually reacted favorably to the lothario's unctuous gaze. It succeeded in making the hackles rise on the back of Ford's neck.

"Pleased to meet you, Mr. James," she responded, in a perfect parody of the secretary with the inviting voice.

"Let's not be so formal. It's Tucker." His smile deepened. "Tuck to my friends." He finally relinquished Darys's hand and turned to Ford. "And ... Mr ... ?"

"Nolan. Ford Nolan."

"Oh? Like the inventor?"

Ford managed a half-smile. Even in this century, he couldn't escape from the shadow of the Great Henry Ford. He tried not to sigh. "Yes, Ford, like Henry Ford."

The man smiled benignly. "No, I meant Nolan. like in ..." He turned to Johnny. "What's that earthquake guy's name? Something Nolan?"

Suddenly, the room grew small, the air, oppressively hot. After an awkward moment of silence, Johnny spoke in a low, almost serene voice. "I believe the name you're looking for is Dr. William C. Nolan."

Ford turned his stare to Darys, who managed only a grimacing smile in return. The blood rushed in Ford's ears, making it almost impossible to hear the conversation. He focused on Johnny's words.

"—suspect our Mr. Nolan hears this all the time. Right?"

Ford nodded numbly.

"Now, onto business."

Ford lost track of what was being said or done. He made no effort to feign interest as his attention was consumed by James's little slip.

Dr. William C. Nolan, the "earthquake" guy. What were the chances that the "C" stood for Crawford? He glanced at Johnny who offered a very slight nod.

Ford pushed back his amazement, letting logic take control. True, he had a great interest in earthquakes and seismic detection, but he hadn't perfected his latest invention.

At least, I haven't done it, yet.

If Johnny's revelation was true, Ford would eventually finish his seismograph and gain some sort of fame for his efforts. But it wasn't the idea of fame or even peer recognition that piqued his interest as much as the other prognostication: a doctoral degree.

Me . . . a doctor. He couldn't keep himself from smiling. He'd thought about going back to school, more than once, but something always got in the way. But according to Johnny, he'd earned . . . would eventually earn a doctorate.

I wonder what field? Engineering? Geology?

"You okay?"

Ford looked up and saw Johnny standing beside him.

Johnny kept his voice low. "I figured *you're* trying to figure out exactly how you went from Ford Nolan, struggling inventor, to Dr. William Crawford Nolan, eminent scientist."

"Em-eminent?" Ford stuttered.

Johnny smiled. "Don't let it go to your head. Knowing what's going to happen doesn't make it any easier. In fact, it'll probably make things harder on you. You'll know what you're going to achieve, but not how to achieve it. You still have to invent the right machinery, study the right books . . ."

"Go back to graduate school?" Ford sighed, then found himself smiling. "The more I think about it, the better it sounds."

"Good." Johnny clapped him on the back. "Now, let's go see what those two have decided to do about finding Harvey."

Ford looked up, surprised to see Darys and James sitting on the couch together. Too close together. Ford drew in a sharp breath and took a step toward the couple, only to be restrained by Johnny.

"Maybe that's not such a good idea, right now, youngster."

Ford stopped in mid-step. "Youngster?" He pivoted and stared at Johnny. "I thought we established the fact that we're basically peers, now."

"Nonetheless, you're acting like a child. A jealous one, at that."

Ford bristled. "Jealous?"

Johnny nodded. "Jealous of Tuck and Darys. You looked like you wanted to punch him the moment he touched Darys's hand." Johnny paused for a moment then crossed his arms. "You two aren't . . . I mean, you haven't . . ." His raised-eyebrow expression left no room for misunderstanding.

"Of course not." Ford tried to disguise his initial reaction as righteous indignation, but buried somewhere in his shock over Johnny's frank question existed a thread of unexpected attraction. "She's a lady."

"A very attractive lady," Johnny responded, as if that were a sufficient reason.

Ford tried not to look at her, but found himself sneaking a peek. "She's pleasant-looking . . . in a sort of futuristic way."

"She's smart. Right?"

Ford nodded. "Very smart."

"And she's sexy."

Sexy? Ford couldn't stop from gaping. "What did you say?"

Johnny wore a conspiratorial grin. "Sexy. The word was coined in the 1920s, but the concept is actually quite timeless. Being openly sexy is a very fashionable thing these days. And believe me, she's quite sexy. Tuck's noticed it. I've noticed it. I just wondered if you'd noticed it too."

Ford stared at Darys. She certainly had some attractive qualities he couldn't readily define, but proper gentlemen weren't supposed to categorize them in such a . . . blatantly physical manner.

At least not in polite company.

"You really think she's—" he stumbled over the word "—sexy?"

Johnny nodded. "Definitely."

"And being sexy is a good thing?"

Johnny's grin grew wider. "Definitely."

"But you're—" Ford stopped to scan the room. He lowered his voice "—married."

Johnny matched his hushed tones. "Married, but not dead. In this century, it's perfectly acceptable for a married man to openly appreciate the female form, even to admire another woman, just as long as he refrains from doing anything else of a more personal nature." He clapped an arm around Ford's shoulders. "The twenty-first century is quite different from when and where we're from. I've learned how to accept the differences between the two societies and while you're here, you might learn a thing or two."

"It's okay to . . . appreciate?"

Johnny nodded. "Look, but don't touch." He glanced up and a new light danced in his eyes. "And here's the woman I love to look at *and* touch. Angela?"

Angela Callaghan stood in the doorway and responded to her husband's gesture to enter. She held a piece of paper in her hand which she seemed reluctant to show Ford. Johnny excused himself and moved to another spot to talk with her.

Ford turned his attention to Darys and James. The man had somehow gotten hold of her hands again, and that fact rankled Ford. He stalked over to them, in time to hear a snippet of their conversation.

"—everything I can do, but all this secrecy is really going to hamstring the operation."

A puzzled look crossed her face. "Hamstring?"

"You know . . ." James fluttered his hand as he searched for a definition of the term.

"It's a method of hobbling an animal," Ford supplied. He made a slicing motion at the back of his calf. "You cut their hamstrings to keep them from wandering far away."

A brief flare lit James's eyes then he turned a spurious smile in Ford's direction. "Oh. A farm boy, I see."

Normally, Ford would have risen to the unspoken challenge, but James had a distinct advantage: the truth. Ford was, in essence, a farm boy, albeit an educated one. How could he hope to compare to James's sophistication and appeal?

"Tuck?" Johnny motioned to the man. "Could you come here for a moment?"

James excused himself and slithered over to Johnny and Angela. Ford dropped into the man's empty seat and waited until he was out of range before speaking. "So, does this guy think he can find Harvey?"

Darys hung her head. "He doesn't hold out much hope. If Dad has lost his memory, he may be using a different name. Apparently, the government uses a numerical system to track their citizens, but, of course, Dad doesn't have one of their 'socially secure' numbers."

"Socially secure?"

"Tuck mentioned it. Sounds like nonsense to me. The point is, without any sort of identification papers, all I can do is describe what Dad looks like and hope he can be located that way. Tuck calls that . . . a pin in a haystuck?" Confusion and devastation drained the last bit of life from her eyes.

"A needle in a haystack. It translates into long odds, but not impossible ones."

"Impossible enough."

"We'll find Harvey," he said, hoping he sounded resolute. "I'll help you."

"How? I don't even have a photograph of—"

The quiet conversation on the other side of the room suddenly erupted, filling the air. "It's a confidence game, I tell you!" Johnny bellowed.

Angela patted her husband's arm. "It's not a con, sweetheart. It's a chance to get in on the bottom floor of a new technology."

"If it actually exists." At her disappointed expression, he heaved a sigh. "Okay, suppose this thing is true." Johnny stabbed at the piece of paper James was examining. "If so, then essentially, this man is asking for extortion money."

Angela pouted. "But I've—"

"But nothing, honey. It's nothing but some gimcrack tomfoolery to separate Junior here—" he patted her protruding stomach "—from his inheritance." He turned to the detective. "Listen, Tuck, after you find Harvey, I want you to look into this."

Angela crossed her arms, balancing them as best as possible along the top of her stomach. "But what if you're wrong? What if it's really true? Think of the possibilities."

Johnny glanced nervously at Ford and Darys. "Can we talk about it later, sweetheart?"

"But Johnny . . ." Tears welled up in her eyes.

James shook his head. "No problem, J.B. I can scare up enough manpower to handle both cases at the same time." The man graced Darys with a reassuring smile. "We'll find Harvey J. Kirk and return him to his loving family." He turned to Johnny. "And we'll also find this—" he consulted the paper in his hand "—E. Marsh of Reykjavik—that's in Iceland, right?—and prove his 'foolproof weather forecasting' machine is nothing more than a bunch of crap."

"His what?" Darys stood up.

James laughed. "Some guy is trying to peddle a machine that can supposedly give a one hundred percent accurate forecast of the weather."

Ford found himself entranced by the possibility. After all, he'd already witnessed and believed six impossible things before breakfast. What was one more like accurate weather predictions? "I can imagine that could be useful in a place like this," he said in hopes of cheering Angela who seemed crushed by the general air of disbelief.

"That's what I thought. Very useful," she said with a sniff.

Darys nodded. "Oh it is . . . definitely. Er . . . it could be." She flushed and took a sudden interest in her shoes. "That is . . . if you believed such an invention could exist in the first place."

James nodded, unaware of her unique foresight. "Yeah. If we'd known a freak storm was going to hit, I would have stayed in town. As it is, I'm probably stuck here until it lets up."

"No problem, Tuck. You can take over your brother's office during the duration and turn it into your missing persons operations center." Johnny turned to Darys and Ford. "Tuck's brother is my assistant who's off on his honeymoon." Johnny shoved his hands in his pockets. "Damned inconvenient of him to decide to get married during the peak season."

Angela looked taken aback by her husband's slip. "Johnny!"

He offered an apologetic smile. "Sorry, sweetheart. Can you see that Tuck gets everything he needs? A computer, a printer . . . whatever else?"

"Well . . . of course, dear." She shot James a dubious smile. "Is that all right with you, Tuck?"

James's reaction dripped with perplexity and suspicion, but his words remained noncommittal. "Looks like our only option. For now."

"Good. Tuck, you go with Angela then, and give her a list of what you need. We'll catch up with you in a little while."

Everyone knew what was going on; James and Angela were being railroaded out of the office so that Johnny could talk to Ford and Darys in private. Once James and Angela left and the door to the office closed behind them, Johnny bounded across the room in two steps.

"This machine. Are you telling me it's for real?"

Darys winced. "Well . . . it could be. I know that great strides were made in weather forecasting in the early twenty-first century—better meteorological data sampling and more sophisticated forecasting algorithms."

"So, are we talking foolproof forecasting or what?"

Her forehead furrowed. "I'm not sure."

His drumming fingers betrayed his impatience. "C'mon, Darys. This could be important. This has been a hard season with respect to weather and the resort business. When we thought it was going to be a warm winter, it seemed the right time for my assistant to take off to get married. But one moment we're hitting record highs and the next moment, we're setting records for blizzard activity. If I could get a totally accurate forecast of the weather, that would help." He paused and narrowed his gaze. "Exactly how accurate have they gotten when it comes to forecasting the weather in your century?"

"Well . . . I mean, we . . . um . . ." She faltered several times. "I'm not so sure I should talk about it."

"I'm not asking for details on how to build such a device —only if it's possible. It's important."

Enough was enough, Ford decided. This man might be a dead ringer for the John Barrett Callaghan he called his friend and his brother, but they were two different men. His John Barrett wouldn't need someone to prick his conscience; this man did. Ford took a step forward. "No . . . finding her father is important."

The two men locked gazes. After a long, tense moment, Johnny took a deep breath, taking a step backward. "You're right, Ford." He plowed his hand through his hair. "I'm sorry. I haven't been myself, lately, what with the baby on the way and the recent economic downturns."

He started pacing a well-worn area to the side of the desk. "And the weather. Despite our preparations and our equipment, a good storm can either make us or break us, depending on when it hits. If we could only foresee when . . ." A panicked look flashed across his face. "And what if Angie goes into labor in the middle of a blizzard . . ." His voice trailed off.

After a moment, he dropped into the leather chair and propped his elbows on his desk. "I'm going to be a father for the first time in this or any other century, and quite frankly, it's unsettling. Angela's worried the resort isn't going to be profitable this year, and she wants to make sure we can give our baby a secure future. And I do, too." He shook his head. "This talk about a future . . . a man from the past certainly knows a lot about anticipating the future." He offered Darys an apologetic smile. "I'm sorry. I didn't mean to make it sound as if this was more important than finding Harvey."

She nodded. "I realize that. And if I could remember more specific details about weather forecasting, I'd tell you as much as I could. But I simply don't remember when the big strides were made in weather prediction."

"That's okay." He drew a deep breath. "Now about Harvey. I take it you didn't say anything to Tuck about . . . when Harvey's from."

"How could I?' She shrugged. "He'd think I was crazy. I gave him a description of what Dad looks like, what his basic interests are—translated into twenty-first-century terms, of course."

"Of course. And did he say what the chances are of finding your father?"

A modicum of encouragement filled her eyes. "He said he was hopeful. . . ."

"IT'S HOPELESS." Tuck settled himself in the chair and flipped on the computer. He'd never liked the conference room, and was relieved when Angela offered her own office for his use.

"You know I'll never be able to find this guy." He hooked his foot around the chair next to him and pulled it out for Angela. "Your husband sure does pull odd people out of the woodwork. I'm supposed to find a man who literally doesn't exist—a man with no discernible identity or past. That's damn near impossible."

Angela eased herself into the seat. "You don't know the half of it."

"You finally willing to let your favorite cousin in on some of the gruesome details? Skeletons in the closet? Bodies buried in the snow?"

Angela punched him in the shoulder, just like she used to do when they were children. "You're talking about my husband. Sure, he has his . . . secrets, but they're not earth-shattering. At least—" she made a face "—not too earth-shattering."

"If you say so. I'm just glad he hasn't figured out that I do everything myself—that I don't have a big staff of operatives at my beck and call."

"Johnny wouldn't be upset."

Tuck shook his head. "Maybe not. Still, I have this fancy image to uphold. The more I make people think I run a big operation, the higher-profile cases I'll get. A couple of more referrals from Johnny, and I'll actually be able to afford that big fancy office with a secretary and a couple of operatives to do the grunt work."

She made a face and shifted in her chair. "So if you can't find this Mr. Kirk, what will you do?"

He crossed his arms and smirked. "Oh, I'll honestly look for him. Don't worry about that. But I'll sweeten the bad news by giving Johnny the good news about this Mr. Marsh."

"Good news?" She brightened. "Then you think his machine is real?"

Tuck shrugged. "Who knows? All I have to do is give Johnny the goods on the guy. If it's a scam, then I'll be protecting my favorite client from a con artist. If it's real, then think of the money you can make. I come out smelling like a rose, either way."

Angela wrapped her arms possessively across her stomach. "But it's not going to be easy, is it? Iceland is awfully far away."

Tucker James proudly picked up the letter and waved it under her nose. "He may be from Iceland . . ." He pointed to the envelope which had been paper-clipped to the letter. "But according to the postmark, he mailed this from right here. From Margin."

CHAPTER 10

*D*arys stared forlornly at the television in the lobby. Until Tucker James came back with some sort of investigative report, there was little for them to do. She'd done her duty, following Ford around all day, watching him dart around from one technological wonder to another. He resembled an insatiable bee in a garden of blossoms, unable to decide which flower to pollinate and, instead of selecting just one, trying them all.

She found the whole process boring. Her father was the antique lover, not her. Currently, the television had captured Ford's fascination and it was boring her to tears.

Or was she about to cry because her grand plan to rescue her father had dissolved into a comedy of errors?

"Hold it there—turn it up," someone called out from behind them as Ford fiddled with the channel selector. "Ten o'clock news is on."

Ford's gaze narrowed as he examined the buttons then selected one to punch. Sound suddenly blared from the speakers and he smiled in triumph.

"—freak blizzard hit parts of the Front Range last night

133

and there's no signs of letting up. Here's a report from meteorologist Skip Reitnaur. Skip?"

The picture changed from a somber-suited man to one dressed in a white bunny suit, complete with drawn-on whiskers.

"Right you are, John," the bunny burbled. "The ski areas are all experiencing snow right now, but the town of Margin is getting hit with the brunt of this monster storm. Up to ten inches have fallen already since midnight, and there are no signs of stopping. As you know, John, we were going to do a live broadcast tomorrow from Margin Mountain Resort for their annual "Bunny Slope Days," but the main highway into the town is closed with drifts up to three feet. So I decided to put on the old bunny suit and do my tribute to snow bunnies from right here. We have resort owner, J.T. Callaghan on the phone. You there, J.T.?"

"It's J.B. and I'm here, Skip."

A roar of applause and catcalls filled the room. Darys glanced at Ford who bounced his astonished attention between the television and their uneasy host speaking into a telephone. Johnny motioned for the room to quiet down.

"Is he really talking directly to the man on the screen?" Ford asked in a hushed whisper.

Darys nodded. "Evidently so."

The weatherman wore a smile too big for his face. "Sounds like the natives are restless, J.C."

"Everything's under control. So far, we're measuring twelve inches of new powder out here. We're hoping the storm will stop soon, but there are always other things to do at Margin Mountain Resort."

The man mugged shamelessly. "Like crowning this year's Miss Bunny Slope?"

Johnny winced. "Among other things."

"I hate to think I'm going to miss a chance to be

surrounded by a bevy of beautiful girls, each of them begging me to call out their name as the winner."

A cackle of laughter rose in the lobby. Darys turned to a young woman who was wiping tears of mirth from her face. "What's so funny?"

"He's got the wrong contest. 'Miss Bunny Slope' isn't a beauty pageant; it's a skiing competition for girls, aged ten and under."

The weatherman continued, oblivious of his faux pas. "Make sure to give the next Miss Bunny a big ol' kiss from me, okay?"

Johnny refrained from answering. "What's the forecast for tonight, Skip? Any chance of the snow letting up so we can take to the slopes?"

The man motioned behind him to a map. "Good question, J.G. Let me try to explain what's happening. As you see here, we have a small but concentrated high pressure cell centered over—"

A round of applause drowned out the weather rabbit and someone clicked down the volume.

"Reitnaur does it again!" a young man declared.

Another voice shouted, "He must be the world's worst weatherman."

"Worst dressed, at least."

Another round of laughter filled the room. Ford edged closer to Darys. "Johnny was really talking to that man over a telephone, right?"

She shrugged. "It's not much of a conversation. The man didn't even get his name correct."

"And anyone with a television could hear him?"

She shrugged. "I suppose so."

"Only *suppose*?"

"Remember—" she leaned in closer, lowering her voice "—I'm not from around here, either."

Ford nodded self-consciously. "According to what I heard a woman say earlier, practically everybody in America has a television. If that's true, then why don't you simply talk on television and ask if anyone has seen Harvey?"

Out of the mouths of babes. Darys grabbed Ford by the arm and hauled him across the room.

Johnny smiled as he saw them approach. He held his hand over the phone. "I'm glad this is about over. They're on commercial right now." He mopped his face with a handkerchief. "I hate talking to that idiot. I know more about weather than he does."

Darys shoved Ford toward him. "Tell Johnny what you told me."

Ford cleared his throat. "People all across the entire world are listening to you through the television, right?"

"Not the world." Johnny glanced ruefully at the people gathered around the set. "More like—parts of Colorado. And that's just the folks with their TVs on and tuned to this particular station."

"Why don't you say something about Harvey? Announce to whoever is listening that he's missing."

Johnny scratched his chin. "I suppose it couldn't hurt. Though I'm not sure how I can work it in with a snow—" he held up his hand, forestalling any more conversation "— okay, ten seconds," he said into the telephone. His head bobbed as he mouthed a silent countdown.

Ford turned around just in time to watch a parade of cats dance across the television screen. His mouth dropped open, probably at the sheer absurdity of it all. He nudged Darys with his elbow. "Look."

"Ssh . . . I'm trying to listen to Johnny."

Ford continued to stare at the prancing pussycats. "He's not on yet. How in the world did they train cats to dance like that?"

She glanced at the screen. How in the world could she explain computer-generated images to him? Even rustic, first-generation images like these? "They're not real cats," she admitted, hoping he wouldn't demand a more complete explanation.

Ford took a few steps toward the large screen, still staring intently at the spectacle. Darys cringed as he opened his mouth; she knew what his next question would likely be, but luckily, the screen flickered and then the man in the rabbit suit reappeared.

"Tomorrow's forecast—sunny and cold in Denver, high in the mid twenties, light snow showers for the Western Slopes and scattered storms for the ski area, particularly the area around Margin. And speaking of Margin, let's check in with Margin Mountain Resort owner J.C. Callaghan. You still there, J.C.?"

"Sure am, Skip." It was Johnny's voice.

"Do you have any contingency plans in case the weather clears?"

"Well, we certainly hope it clears. Ticket holders and contestants can call our toll-free number to get a contest update as well as check the current conditions. That's 1-800-555-SNOW."

"Look," Ford whispered. He punched her arm again, marveling as the numbers appeared magically on screen.

"That's great J.D. Now, I'd like to—"

"Skip?" Johnny interrupted. "There's one more thing."

The weatherman seemed taken aback, as if Johnny wasn't following a prescribed pattern.

"Uh, yes, J.D.?"

"I'd like to extend a special invitation to a friend of mine who I haven't seen in a long time. I'm sure he's one of your faithful weather watchers. His name is Harvey Kirk. Harvey, if you're out there, come to Margin. I have a special surprise, waiting just for you."

Skip looked away, as if conferring with someone else then turned back, his bright smile dimming only the slightest. "Uh . . . so if you're out there, H-Harvey Kirk, don't miss a chance to see the prettiest collection of snow bunnies this side of the . . ." he faltered for a moment, ". . . Continental Divide. Our thanks to Margin Mountain Resort owner, J.P. Callaghan."

"Thanks, Flip."

The man reddened visibly. "That's Skip. Back to you, Jeff . . ."

Before the camera cut away, the weatherman's perfect smile disappeared completely. It was painfully easy to read his lips. "What th' hell was that all about?"

Another wave of laughter in the lobby drowned out any replies from the television. Someone turned off the set and the people who'd been watching broke off into small clusters and began to talk.

Johnny motioned for Ford and Darys to follow him to a quieter corner. "That was the best I could think to do on the spur of the moment. Maybe Harvey's out there and he heard me."

"I hope so. Have you heard anything from Tuck?"

Johnny shook his head. "Nothing yet. But it takes a while to get the investigative wheels in motion, especially in weather like this."

Ford took a deep breath, unwilling to look at Darys and watch the light of hope drain from her eyes. He'd run himself ragged all day, trying to keep her mind off her missing father and the storm which kept them hostage. He'd peppered her with questions, demanded explanations, even played dumb a few times to make her work harder to describe how something operated or why people of this century did things the way they did. Sometimes her explanations sounded as if they were based more on fantasy than fact. But to Ford, everything he saw bordered on the fantastical until he could sit down and examine the internal workings carefully.

Of course, he could count on one hand the number of times he had more than three minutes to scrutinize anything. Darys had been too jittery to stay in one place for long, and, due to their unnatural connection, whither she went, he was forced to follow.

Johnny patted Darys on the shoulder. "I trust Tuck. He's a good man and an excellent investigator. He'll find Harvey—simple as that."

Darys stifled a yawn, reacting as if the very act of being sleepy betrayed her dedication to her mission. "God, I hope so. I don't like sitting around here and doing nothing."

Johnny gave her a long, critical look. "You look exhausted. Ford? I think it's time to haul this young lady up to bed."

Given any other time, any other situation, Johnny's words might have sounded a little more provocative. But instead, Ford was hit with a wave of melancholy. He hadn't even looked at another woman after he met Mary. Not while they courted, not after they married and not after she passed away.

"I'm not that sleepy," Darys protested.

Ford glanced at his—for a lack of a better word—roommate, and noticed the dark circles beneath her eyes. She yawned again. He put an arm around her shoulders. "Johnny's right, you know. You'll be more effective tomorrow after a good night's sleep. Come on." They bade Johnny goodnight and Ford guided her through the lobby and to the elevator bank.

He smugly pushed all the right buttons and even remembered how to use the white card to open the door to their suite. While they were gone, someone had magically turned the couch into a bed and even left a small sweet on the pillow. Ford forgot his mission of mercy and turned his attention to the miraculous folding bed in the couch.

When he turned around, his curiosity slaked, he discovered Darys had disappeared into the bedroom. He sighed. He did tend to get overly involved in those objects or concepts that piqued his interest, and he'd forget everything around him. Emma had been yelling at him for years for such antisocial behavior. On the other hand, his professors had openly admired what they called his single-mindedness and attention to detail. Odd how the same behavior elicited such different responses from people.

Perhaps that's what Darys needed—an immediate problem to absorb her attention, to make her forget her troubles if only for an hour. But what?

A mental challenge might not provide enough diversion. She needed something physical. Something which would occupy her entire body, forcing her mind to follow suit. Physical, demanding, mind-consuming, encompassing . . .

But what?

Exercise? Somehow Ford didn't think a healthy dose of calisthenics would sufficiently occupy her mind. He always found his mind wandering off when the body was forced into a regime of exercise.

There had to be something else. Something comprehensive. Something which would distract the mind and body. Something like—

"Sex."

Ford pivoted at the sound of the one word. "P-pardon?" Why couldn't he keep his voice from breaking?

"Sex," she stated as if it was a word she used each and every day. "It occupies the body and the mind. Soul, too, if you're really lucky." She graced him with a tired smile. "But sorry. The last thing either of us need is the complication of a seduction to cross the centuries." She disappeared behind the closing bedroom door.

He dropped to the edge of the bed then shot up, as if the crisp white sheets might entice him to perform an action he wasn't quite prepared to take. It wasn't that she wasn't attractive, even desirable in a futuristic sort of way. Women of the future evidently lacked nothing in that department. But she was treating the idea of intimacy as nothing more than a safety valve. . . .

Wasn't it typically a masculine perception?

Or had things changed drastically in over a hundred years?

Darys stuck her head around the corner. "Not that much has changed."

"You're reading my mind," he complained.

"I can't help it. You're projecting. Go to sleep. Things'll be better in the morning."

TO GET TO THE MORNING, Darys had to survive a night of tossing and turning, and dreams that constantly jolted her awake. When it seemed she'd finally fallen into a deeper, more restful sleep, something loud jangled in the room, startling her so thoroughly that she fell out of the bed. It took a few moments to remember that the noise came from a communication device and a few more to remember where she was. After a few moments of confusion, she finally found the instrument's cord, pulled it down and managed to orient the receiver correctly against her face.

"What?" she growled.

"Darys?"

"Yeah?"

"It's Johnny. Sorry, it just didn't sound like you, there for a moment."

She woke up completely. "Has Mr. James found Dad?"

"I don't know. He's asked me to call a meeting and won't tell me why."

The obvious answer hit her like a two-ton meteor. "Something's wrong with Dad."

Ford's voice echoed from just beyond the door. "Something wrong with Harvey?"

She covered the mouthpiece with her hand. "I don't know. Johnny doesn't know, either. Something's up."

"Can you get down here in fifteen minutes?"

"Absolutely." She hung up the phone and scrambled to her feet. "We're meeting with—"

"—Tuck James in fifteen minutes."

"You heard us talk?"

"More like I felt your answer." He paused. "And no, I don't know how or why. All I can figure is it's that thing of yours, connecting us. I think half of my dreams were yours last night."

She stiffened. That explained why she kept waking up, thinking she had to start the morning . . . what was the word? Chores. Even the word sounded several centuries old. She shook her head, hoping to shake away the intruding thoughts and concentrate on the more important problem.

In less than fifteen minutes, she managed to take a quick shower and adjust her holosuit in order to dress to something she saw in a magazine she'd carried up the night before from the lobby. When she emerged from her room, she saw Ford, already dressed, and folding the bed back into a couch.

"Remarkable," he muttered. The moment he saw her, he blushed. "I know. I know. I'm utterly old-fashioned."

She reached out her hand. "Let's go, Grandpa."

He grinned when he took her hand and followed her into

the hallway. As they waited for the elevator, something buzzed in the back of Darys's mind. Something she'd forgotten. Something she'd seen . . . in that magazine.

The elevator arrived and they stepped in. Suddenly, she remembered what had page had captured her attention—an ad for someone who specialized in locating missing people.

"I forgot something." As the doors began to close, she pulled at Ford, trying to get him to step out of the elevator car along with her. Having caught him by surprise, he didn't move immediately, causing his hand to slip out of hers. Her momentum took her through the opening between the doors a split second before they closed.

"Stop, elevator," she yelled, forgetting that it wasn't a voice-activated unit. She punched the console beside the door. Inside the elevator, she heard Ford yelling something in return.

"Find a stop button," she screamed. If the car dropped more than thirty-five feet down, the chain reaction would begin, ending their life on earth. She heard the smooth hum of machinery and Ford's muffled shout.

She waited in dread, in silence.

An alarm suddenly pierced the air. Or was it the sound of her impending death—the sound of her molecules being torn from each other?

She crouched down out of reflex, as if she could dodge the forces that would end her life. The alarm pounded in her ears, but they didn't drown out sounds coming from the elevator doors and the shaft below. Perhaps her proximity to the stabilizer would shield her for a few moments, allowing her to hear Ford's shrieks as he ceased to exist.

Her heart threatened to explode. She closed her eyes, unwilling to watch her own death, wishing she could close her ears as well and not hear it.

Over the din, she heard a small scratching noise. Then,

she heard the most beautiful words she could imagine to hear, "Darys! Open the damn door."

She threw herself at the elevator door, wedging her hands in the thin crack between the panels. With a grunt of exertion, she managed to shift the doors slightly and give her better purchase. Using the entire weight of her body, she bullied both doors back, revealing the dark shaft and the cables dangling down its middle.

"Are you all right?" she called into the abyss. She squinted down into the shaft and saw him emerge from a trap door in the top of the elevator car. He hoisted himself out and pulled to his feet, his head still a good ten feet below the metal door sill.

"Find a rope or something. Quick."

She glanced around, spotting a window with a handy drapery cord.

"Hurry! If this thing starts to move . . ."

"I know. I know." She sprang toward the window only to be hit with a wave of nausea a few feet short of her goal. She pulled back, realizing the cord sat outside of the range the stabilizer allowed them to have.

"What happened?"

She waited only a few precious seconds for the nausea to subside."There's some cord a couple of feet away, but I can't reach it."

"I can't climb these cables. They're covered in some sort of grease."

The obvious answer made her stomach lurch, this time, not due to the limited range between them. If he couldn't go up then the only solution was for her to go down.

"I'm coming down."

"What?"

"I'll jump."

"But—"

"Do you see any other solution?"

Ford hesitated. "No. Not really. But don't just jump. Try to dangle down as far as you can from the door ledge. Then let yourself drop. Maybe I can catch you."

The whir of machinery started again.

"Darys! The elevator's moving."

She knew she didn't have time to waste. If the elevator descended even one more floor, the chain reaction would start. She dropped down in the open doorway, hung her legs over the side of the ledge and into the abyss. Turning over, she slid down, clinging to the ledge long enough to send up a prayer of mercy to the heavens and a shout of warning down to Ford.

She plunged, feet first, into the black void below, expecting to see her life flash before her eyes. She expected time to either race ahead at breakneck speed—probably breaking her neck in the process—or to slow to a dying crawl. Instead, she fell the grand distance of . . . two feet into Ford's sturdy grasp.

"You can open your eyes."

She did so, watching them pass by the open door and up into darkness.

"I thought . . . when you said the elevator was moving . . . you meant down . . ."

The fading light washed over his wincing grin. "So did I."

She tried to pull in a deep breath, but her body refused to cooperate. His grip tightened. "Are you all right?"

She leaned against his solid warmth, knowing her sense of relief would be communicated to him via the stabilizer. After last night, she'd learned how to rely on the unique properties of the connection between them.

He cleared his throat. "We'd better climb down before someone pushes the button for the top floor." He glanced up ruefully. "Who knows how much head space there is." He helped her drop to her knees beside the open trap door.

"Ladies, first."

She mentally measured the distance from their position to the floor. "No way. You first."

Ford complied, landing in the elevator floor with surprising grace. He stared up at her. "Your turn."

There were no unknown variables. The elevator car was fully lit. She could see exactly how far she would fall and even had someone there, ready to catch her, should, for some strange reason, she not land on her feet. There should have been absolutely no reason for her to be scared.

"C'mon," he coaxed. "You were ready to jump down an elevator shaft. This is nothing in comparison."

"I know." A wave of fear almost paralyzed her. "Maybe it's a delayed reaction."

"It could be. But remember—I would have caught you then, just like I'm ready to catch you now." He stood below her with his arms held up.

Trying to ignore the worst of the lingering effects of fear, she lowered herself down into the elevator car. Ford reached up and grasped her firmly around the knees. Once she released the edge of the opening, she literally slid down Ford's body, thankful for the security he offered. He tightened his grasp the moment her face slid down to meet his. Captive in his arms, she had no other option but to kiss him.

"Thanks," she whispered after they finally broke away. He lowered her to the floor.

"I should thank you. You're the one who was willing to jump blindly down an elevator shaft."

She tried to busy herself with straightening her clothes. "It seemed my only option."

"No matter . . . thanks."

Who was she kidding? Desire coursed through her veins

just like blood, both propelled by the heart in a rhythmic rush. There was no denying what she felt. And with it came guilt—loads and loads of guilt. Was what she felt truly desire or the result of a couple of libidinous thoughts magnified out of proportion by the stabilizer? She stared at the elevator controls and pushed the button marked "L."

"L" for "Love?"

Or for "lust?"

She sighed. Here they were, heading down to hear possibly earth-shattering news about her father and instead of concentrating on that, she was consumed with the idea of pushing the "Stop" button and tearing the clothes off of Ford.

What sort of ungrateful daughter was she?

Ford must have sensed her trepidation because he reached over, pushed the "L" button again and picked up her hand, twining his fingers in hers.

"Harvey'll be okay. I promise."

A thousand prophecies swirled in her mind; the bad outnumbered the good two-to-one. "I hope so. I hope so. . . ."

The elevator started down, and moments later, it opened onto the lobby which teemed with people. As they walked toward Johnny's office, it was very apparent the mood had changed from the day before. People who had accepted the fact they were housebound for one day weren't terribly thrilled at the prospect of being incarcerated for a second day.

"The people are growing somewhat restless," Ford said, after shouldering a path through a loud crowd of would-be skiers who congregated in the hallway leading to the office. The secretary waved them through to the inner office with a smile and an offer of coffee.

When they walked in, Johnny was on the phone. He made a face and gestured that they should sit. Darys paced the floor, unable to face the concept of sitting still in one spot.

Ford perched on the edge of a chair. From all outside appearances, he looked calm—folded hands, placid expression. But Darys knew he was as jumpy as she was; she could literally feel his heartbeat, mimicking hers.

Johnny leaned back in his chair, clutching the receiver in a tight fist. "Honey—I . . . you expect me to—yes, sweetheart, yes . . . yes . . ." He shot them a pleading look. "Darys and Ford are here. I gotta—why don't you just tell me what— okay, just hurry."

He hung up the phone, wearing a slightly glassy-eyed look. "I have absolutely no idea what's going through Angie's head."

Darys paused in mid-step. "What about my father?"

Johnny shook his head. "All I know is that Tucker called and said he was coming out with some important news. He didn't tell me the details. Apparently, he made it back to his office during a lull in the storm and was able to start some inquiries."

"But there's no lull now. How does he expect to get here?"

They all looked toward the window, as if checking to see if, due to some miraculous reason, the storm had stopped.

And it had.

"Will you look at that?" Johnny stood up and strode to the window. When he pushed the curtains farther back, he revealed a sky filled with dark gray clouds which still held the sun captive. However, the blizzard of snow which had been pouring from the clouds had suddenly grown into a meek flurry of flakes. "Finally." He heaved a sigh. "Now maybe I can get these people out of my hair and back on the slopes." He turned to the intercom on his desk. "Suze? Call Boardman and tell him to assemble his crew. If it starts to lighten up, I want them ready to check the slopes. If things look good, we'll start gearing back up."

"Yes sir. Mr. James just arrived. Shall I send him in?"

"Absolutely."

A few moments later, Tucker James walked in, snow still clinging to his hat and the shoulders of his coat. Pulling his hat off, he ran a hand through his mussed hair. "Have you looked outside?"

"It's better . . . for the moment. I just sent word to the ski patrol so they'll be ready to check the conditions of the slope if this holds."

Tucker shot them a toothy smile. "You know what they say about the weather in Colorado. If you don't like it, just hang around. It'll change again in ten minutes. I bet my brother and his bride are sitting on the beach at Maui, having themselves a big laugh at our expense. I heard the weather there is—"

Darys exploded, unable to contain herself any longer. "Forget the weather! What about my father?"

Tucker's face registered a flash of disappointment that made Darys's stomach churn in dread. "According to the United States government, your father doesn't exist. He has no social security records, he's never paid any income taxes, he's never been registered with the selective service, or served any time in the military. I can find no record of him ever having existed." He took a step closer to Darys. "Or you either." He pivoted to face Johnny. "I don't know how you know these people, or what they've told you, but I suspect it has little to do with the truth."

A stunned silence settled around the room like a blanket of suffocating snow. Darys tried to read Johnny's expression; was he going to tell Tucker the truth? Would Tucker actually accept the fact he'd been looking for a man who hadn't been officially born yet?

"Tuck, you're right." Johnny stood up, clasping his hands behind him.

Darys closed her eyes. More time pollution. The last

thing she needed was another overly-informed soul wandering around the past with news of a distant future and some of its secrets.

Johnny walked around the end of the desk and sat on its corner. "You won't be able to find Harvey or Darys in any government record."

Darys felt her throat close. Ford's warm hand slipped into hers, and he gave her a reassuring squeeze.

Johnny folded his arms. "That's because they don't exist."

Tucker gaped at him. Darys and Ford did as well.

"The man we know as Harvey Kirk turned state's evidence on a case again the kingpin of a Colombian drug cartel. Harvey'd been nothing more than an honest accountant who had access to all the wrong data. As a result, he was admitted into the Federal Witness Protection Program. All records of his previous life are gone, eradicated as if he never existed, but his new identity isn't finished, yet. The same is true for Miss Kirk here—" Johnny pointed to her and she tried to return a suitable expression "—in order to protect her from the same forces that want to kill her father. The government may try to stonewall you, but for her sake, for her safety, for that of free America, you must find Harvey Kirk!" Johnny ended his fiction on such a grand note that Darys expected to hear patriotic music in the background.

Tucker seemed to accept the outrageous story without hesitation. He nodded, knowingly. "I should have figured that out, myself. It all makes sense—the missing records, the empty files. Ma'am?" He turned to Darys and took her hands in his. "I'm sorry I doubted you. I'll do the best I possibly can to find your father and not reveal his identity or his location to those people who might want to do him harm."

Darys extracted her hands from his grasp. "Thank you, Mr. James. I appreciate your—" she shot Johnny a look "—discretion."

"Now that the weather's better, you'll be able to step up your investigation, right?"

"The storm?" Tucker stopped then brightened. "The storm! Of course, I almost forgot why I came." He turned his full attention on Johnny, ignoring Darys, her hands which he seemed so anxious to hold all the time, and Ford, who he tended to ignore, anyway. "Remember the letter you received about the weather forecasting machine?"

Johnny shared an exasperated glance with Darys and Ford. "Yes."

"Well I did a little investigation, and, if we act quickly, we can get in on the ground floor of the newest advances in weather forecasting."

Ford watched Darys sag. All her thoughts of anticipation, of hope had been dashed quickly and the conversation summarily changed to something else. He felt her disappointment as if it were own. "Uh excuse me, Johnny? I think Darys probably needs a little air. Why don't I—"

"Ford, Darys, I'm sorry. Just hang there for a minute." Johnny sent him a look that said, *"Let me get rid of this guy and then we'll talk."*

"Yeah, you'll get a real kick out of this," Tucker offered.

Johnny returned to the discussion at hand. "Ground floor? As in an initial outlay-type of financial commitment?"

"Seven hundred thousand twenty-five Gs to start, but that's just for R&D."

Johnny snorted. "You mean the idea hasn't been researched yet? I don't think—"

Tucker waved his hands to interrupt Johnny. "I know it sounds like a scam. I thought so, too, until I got a demonstration that I simply couldn't ignore. The inventor's name is Edvard Marsh and apparently, the folks up in Iceland have made some fantastic strides in accurate weather forecasting."

Johnny looked singularly unimpressed. "How accurate?"

Ford slipped an arm around Darys's shoulder and pulled her back to the couch. If they were going to have to wait, they might as well not do it on their feet. But when she sank down on the couch, he didn't like the blank look she wore. If she'd given up all hope of finding her father, then what would happen next? Would she return to her far-flung future, sadder but wiser? And what about Ford, himself? How could he return to his own world if they were joined at the hip?

Tucker continued, oblivious to the devastation they were going through. "Accurate enough to let me know exactly when this storm would let up enough for me to drive here from my office in relative safety." Tucker dropped into a nearby chair and propped his arms on the desk. "Johnny, it's unbelievable. You saw that storm out there. It has let up, not once, except when Mr. Marsh said it would. Think how much it would benefit the resort to know exactly when the storms would start and stop for the entire season, what temperature it'll be weeks in advance. And if we get involved now, we'll have this technology and Vail and Aspen won't. Our share of the ski market with triple, even quadruple. We can't—"

"Hold it, Tuck. Something tells me that this is a bit too good to be true. If this technology exists, then why is Mr. Marsh so anxious to sell exclusive rights to it to us?"

Tucker pushed back the chair and stood. "I don't know. Why don't you ask him yourself?" Tucker reached over and punched the button on the talking box on Johnny's desk. "Suze, can you bring in Mr. Marsh?"

Johnny crossed his arms. "He's here?"

"Sitting in your outer office, all the way from Reykjavik, Iceland."

The door to the outer office opened and the secretary

stood in the opening. "This way, sir. Mr. Callaghan will see you."

Enough was enough. Ford stood up again, helping the blanked-out Darys up by her arm. "Johnny, we're going back to our room. I don't think—" He stopped, his irritation at Johnny fading away, along with the air in his lungs.

Ford stared in amazement at the barrel-chested man who stood in the door. He was dressed in a bizarre combination of plaids, checks, and stripes, topped off by a garish polka-dot tie. His coat almost dragged the floor as did the striped scarf that had been wound several times around his neck. He wore a floppy black hat that drooped to one side, covering half his face. But Ford saw enough of the face to recognize the perpetually rosy cheeks, the twinkling blue eyes, the sloppy grin.

But Darys was the first one to say anything. She took a stumbling step forward and uttered one word in a strangled voice.

"Dad?"

CHAPTER 11

*H*arvey Kirk looked up, his expression void of all recognition. "Pardon?"

Darys took a faltering step toward him. Her look of fear mixed with hope and concern made something in Ford's chest hurt.

"Dad, is it really you?" she whispered.

Harvey showed no emotion. "I'm afraid I don't know what—"

His words were muffled by Darys who threw herself in his arms. He stood there, wearing a puzzled look and allowing her to sob into his bright-colored coat. "Here's one rainstorm I didn't forecast," he said to no one in particular. After a hesitant moment, he patted her back and adopted a strained smile. "There, there, dear. I'm sure everything will be all right."

Johnny bounded around the desk, his hand outstretched in greeting. "Harvey! Where have you been, old man?"

Harvey's sense of confusion seemed to grow exponentially. He detached himself from Darys and took a step backward. "I'm afraid you two have mistaken me for someone else. Let me introduce myself. My name is Dr. Edvard Marsh. Mr. James has kindly responded to a letter of inquiry I sent your resort concerning a potential business liaison." He reached into his pocket and pulled out a paisley handkerchief which he shoved in Darys's direction. "Here, dear, try to make yourself presentable. Now, Mr. Callaghan—" he navigated around her as if she were a wet splotch on the carpet "—I'll hope you have enough foresight to accept this unique chance to take a flying leap into the latest twenty-first-century technology."

"Twenty-second century," Darys corrected with a sniff.

Harvey paused to give her a critical stare. "Pardon?"

She raised her hand, as if to touch him then withdrew before making contact. "You're from the twenty-*second* century, Dad."

Tucker looked startled, and she made a mental note to explain later . . . or make something up.

"'Dad?' *Dad?*" He turned to James. "Who is this lovely child and why does she insist on thrusting me into such a paternalistic role? Poor delusional thing. Let me show you what I can do." He swept aside the papers on Johnny's desk and plopped a large briefcase in the cleared space.

"I've input all the variables into my computer." He opened the case, revealing a huge sheaf of papers. When he picked up the top sheet of greenish-colored paper, Ford realized all the papers were connected like a giant folded fan. "I've taken into account the time, date, latitude, longitude, elevation, current weather conditions, wind speed, humidity, and a host of other data collected in and around this region for the last twenty years."

"But Harvey—"

"Enough with all this blathering about this Harvey fellow," he shouted, slamming his briefcase shut with his fist. "Please get it into your evidently thick skull that my name is

Edvard Marsh and I come to you from the icy plains of Reykjavik which is the capital of my native home, Iceland. It's a place where we understand snow and ice and have gotten quite adept at forecasting when and where storms will hit. Using a combination of advanced forecasting techniques, combined with a computer simulation program augmented by satellite reconnaissance photographs of the area, I can predict to the second when and where a storm will hit and to the millimeter how much snow will be produced."

"But no one can predict that accurate—"

He puffed up, rising nearly an inch in height. His face turned an unattractive shade of red. "Do you dare impugn my words? Perhaps I've made a mistake in offering you this golden opportunity." He snatched his briefcase from the desk. "Perhaps I should speak first with the owners of Beaver Creek—"

"No!" Johnny stepped forward, placing a restraining hand on Harvey's shoulder. At the man's disdainful look, Johnny retreated. "Forgive me. I didn't mean to be disrespectful." He shot Ford and Darys an imploring look. "And neither did my staff members. Right . . . er . . . team?"

Ford swallowed hard. "Uh . . . right." When Darys didn't respond other than with a slack-jawed stare, Ford nudged her with his elbow. "Right, Dar—dear? We want Mr. Marsh to stay here and take as long as he needs to explain his process, don't we?"

Darys nodded, her mouth still hanging open.

Johnny stepped forward, shifting so that Harvey couldn't see him gesture toward the door. He glared at her, the door, and back to her. His message was painfully obvious. *Get out of here and let me handle this.* "Gee, Doreen, you don't look so well." He made a face, indicating the door again.

"Dear girl looks a bit under the weather." Harvey

chuckled to himself. "Sorry. A little occupational humor, there." He shifted so that he could grace Darys with a patently fake smile. "You be a dear and toddle off. I suspect your big strapping farm boy, here, could be persuaded to bring Mr. Callaghan and me some coffee."

"The name is Ford. Ford Nolan."

"Indeed." Harvey turned away, dismissing him with a sniff.

It was Ford's turn to stare, only to be jerked off his feet by Darys who grabbed his arm and tugged him toward the door. "Get me out of here!" she whispered between clenched teeth.

As they stumbled awkwardly toward escape, Harvey called out, "Oh Edsel, I take my coffee black. It wouldn't do for you to forget."

Once the door closed behind them, Darys exploded as if she'd held her breath since the moment Harvey had stormed into the room. "My father," she said between pants, "doesn't . . . recognize me. I've never . . . seen him . . . like that." She pivoted, her face suddenly tight with anger. "Why did you stop when you were about to use my name? Dad might have recognized me if he'd heard someone use my name."

"I panicked. I didn't know what to do. I was afraid the shock might make him panic, and he might leave if you kept pushing him." Ford steered her to the nearest chair. "What I can't believe is that he looks just like he did the last time I saw him—twenty years ago. He hasn't aged at all!"

She gestured toward the closed door. "Twenty of your years. Two of his. But that's not the problem. It's those clothes. That name." She paused and made a face. "That *attitude!* He's not acting like my father. Not like him at all!"

There must be a reasonable explanation, Ford told himself. He stopped for a moment. "Reason" ceased to exist the moment he fell into the time portal to save Darys. He swallowed hard. "Could it be someone else? Someone who merely looks like your father? After all, Johnny and Barrett were dead ringers for each other."

"But Johnny and Barrett are relatives. Any similarities between them are a result of an unusually dominant genetic code sequence." She shook her head. "I made sure to check the family tree before I came to see which relatives lived where. It wouldn't be wise to run into them and risk changing your entire history because of an innocent remark or unintended influence. In 2015, I had four great-grandfathers alive, seven great-great-grandfathers and thirteen great-great-great-grandfathers. It can't be that much different in 2017. I know that none of them lived in this area and for sure, none of them were named Marsh or lived anywhere near Iceland."

The secretary who had been sitting silently at her desk cleared her throat, calling their attention to her presence for the first time.

Ford and Darys looked at each other and then at her; she couldn't have missed any of their conversation. For a moment, Ford contemplated several explanations, each one more foolish than the one before it. Even the truth sounded like a fanciful tale from a dime novel. Rather than spin a yarn, he simply thumbed over his shoulder to the inner office. "They're asking for coffee. The big guy wants his black." He grabbed Darys by the arm and began to drag her out of the office.

She dug in, standing her ground. "No! I want to go back in there."

"And do what? Try to convince a man who is clearly out of his mind that he's your father?"

She jerked her arm out of his grasp and wiped away a stray tear with the back of her hand. "It might work."

"And it might drive him away. Then where would we be?"

"We? He's my father!"

"Yes, but without your father, I don't have a way home. You said we needed two stabilizers in order to return to our own time periods. If you scare off Harvey, we lose our only chance at finding that second stabilizer."

A fresh stream of tears spilled down her face. "Is that all this means to you?" she shouted. "A trip home? What about the future? My future? Our fut—"

The door to the inner office opened and Johnny stepped out. He moved quickly toward them, grabbed their forearms, and propelled them to the door leading to the hallway. "Go away."

Darys fought to pull out of his grasp. "No, I want to stay—"

Johnny ignored Darys's protest and continued toward the door. "I'm trying to have a nice conversation with Dr. Marsh and your argument is disturbing us. You don't want to disturb us, now do you, dear? Go away."

"But—"

In the relative safety of the hall, Johnny relaxed his grip. He spoke in a low voice. "Darys, believe me—I'm doing everything I can to keep him here so we won't lose him again."

"But the weather forecasting—"

"—is a cockamamie invention." Johnny dismissed the notion with a wave of his hand. "But I'll pretend to believe it works and do whatever I must to keep him happy. But I can't do that if I can't hear myself think because you two are arguing loud enough to be heard all the way to China. Now go!" He pushed them out the door. "I'll call you later." The door slammed shut behind them with a decisive bang.

Darys balanced her fists on her hips, her face one muscle shy of developing a full pout. "See what you've done?"

Ford sighed. By provoking an argument with her, he'd hoped he could help her escape the debilitating effects of fear, and translate that emotion into constructive anger. He didn't anticipate getting thrown out. But . . . despite their unexpected change in venue, his plan was working. She was no longer caught in the grip of panic and dread.

Now she was just plain mad. His next best tactic was misdirection.

"What are the chances that Harvey's machine in there really works?"

"It doesn't matter." She headed for the lobby, her footfalls echoing like gunshots down the hallway. "What I have to do is figure out how to jump-start my father's memories."

Ford caught up with her, falling in step. "Think, Darys! You cited all sorts of warnings about temporal pollution and conundrums when I wanted to know something about the future. Is your father polluting this past? Is there potential . . . temporal damage he can create with this so-called weather-forecasting machine?"

She edged away from him. "As far as I remember, there was no meteorological breakthrough of this magnitude in the early twenty-first century. This technology that Dad is talking about doesn't really even exist in our world, today . . . er . . . tomorrow."

"Then why in the world did you make it sound like he was exposing the world to premature technology? If it doesn't exist, then why worry?"

Darys rolled her eyes. "It's just as damaging to tell you that something categorically doesn't exist as to tell you that it does. What if you're supposed to be working on some other idea and instead, you switch to weather forecasting because I said it's possible. Or conversely, forecasting is the initial goal but your experiments lead you somewhere else. If I tell you it can't be done, would you abandon a line of valuable research that might lead to other discoveries?"

Ford shrugged. "I see your point."

"Good, then let's get back to the real problem. Whatever has happened to him that has robbed him of his memory has evidently affected other parts of his mind."

"He's crazy?"

"No. Just . . . mixed up. And it might not even be a physical or psychological ailment."

"What's left?"

She chewed her thumbnail. "It could be equipment malfunction. His stabilizer could be misaligned and shielding only part of his memories and brain function. I have no idea why he'd think he's somebody else."

"So what do we do about it?" Ford prodded.

She faltered.

"What do we do, Darys?" he repeated, not wanting her to give her fear the latitude to resurface.

She waved his away. "Give me a minute."

"C'mon, Darys, think. If Harvey doesn't recognize you, then how are you going to get close enough to get a look at his stabilizer?"

"I'm not sure."

"If you can see it, will you be able to figure out what's wrong with it?"

"I should be able to." She turned so that she wasn't facing him anymore.

"Should? That's not good enough. Not only do you have to diagnosis it, but you'll need to be able to fix it."

"I know that."

"Then let's make a list of what you'd need to fix something like that."

"A list!" She turned around, the harried light of challenge in her eyes. "Let's make a list."

She grabbed him by the hand and hauled him toward the elevator. As soon as they got there, a *ding* indicated an arriving car and the doors slid open to greet them.

They both hesitated before stepping into the elevator. Darys looked at Ford and he looked back at her. Neither of them needed a stabilizer in order to read each other's minds. A second later, they were trooping up the staircase which continued up sixteen floors to their room.

"F-fourteen," Ford read in a breathless voice as they passed the sign indicating that floor. "Who would have thought . . . ?"

"What?" Darys called down from the landing above him.

He paused to catch his breath, holding onto the railing. "I didn't realize how exhaustingly tall an eighteen-story building could be."

Darys started to say something, but stopped herself.

He continued, calculatingly oblivious of her silence. "Oh, I realize this isn't all that tall, even for my day. Back home, they say a building in New York City is supposed to be completed soon that'll be fifty-five stories tall. Can you imagine that? Fifty-five stories, looming into the sky."

Darys nodded without saying anything.

Ford made a face as realization hit him one statement too late. "Oh course you can imagine that. I bet buildings in your day and time rise well over one hundred stories high. Probably even higher."

She shrugged as she started plodding up the stairs again.

"I'd sure hate to try to walk up a building that tall," he called up to her.

"Uh huh."

Ford took the next flight two steps at a time until he could reach out, touch her shoulder, and make her stop. "Listen, Darys . . . back there . . . I'm sorry I got you mad. But that seemed the best way to help you."

"Help me?" She shifted so that she stood two steps above him, making her slightly taller than him.

He nodded. "To regain control. It's okay to be scared, but

it's not okay to let your fear shut down your mind and your ability to think through things logically."

He moved up one step, putting their faces on the same level, placing her within tempting reach. He reached around her, locking his arms around her waist. "The hardest part is over. We know exactly where your father is."

She ducked her head, very evidently fighting the emotions that demanded control over her. "You're right. We have him now, safe and sound . . ." Darys paused and made a face. "Okay, safe and only relatively sound."

He grinned. "How about safe and 'madder than a March hare?'"

She managed a small smile in return. "Or safe and 'madder than a kayaker on the Niagara.'"

Ford stared at her. "Huh?"

"It's a punch line to an old joke . . . er . . . a new joke." Her sad smile grew. "One of Dad's favorites."

"Sounds like Harvey. And he'll sound like Harvey again." Ford tightened his hug. "We can do it, Darys."

"We?"

"Until we get that second stabilizer, I'm stuck with you, remember?"

They stood on the stairs for an inordinate length of time, finding solace in each others' arms. Darys finally pulled back far enough to brush an errant lock of hair from Ford's forehead.

"Do you miss your home?"

He nodded, making the curl fall back into place. "It feels as if we've been here . . . forever. If I didn't come from a family of time travelers, I'd worry that they'd be concerned."

Darys leaned closer and planted a kiss on his cheek. Tucking her hand in his, she led their way up the stairs at a more sedate rhythm. "That's another side effect of time lag. Your normal sense of timing is . . . jostled, temporarily knocked out of alignment. Things that you think took forever, only took a few minutes. Things that take only a short period of time, seem like they last forever."

Ford didn't respond, at least not verbally. Judging by the reddening around his collar, he must have been thinking about their love-making session. *How did he categorize it?* she wondered. Too quick or too long?

He stopped on the sixteenth floor landing, his hand resting on the doorknob. "What about us, Darys? What about our future?"

She deliberately chose her own definition of the word, *our*. "Don't worry, you'll have a future. I'll get you back to your wonderful world where you can complete your wonderful inventions and fulfill your wonderful destiny." The word, "wonderful" rang through the hallway little more sarcastically than she meant it too.

"I 'wonder,'" he countered as he opened the door for her, "if I should be allowed to see my future with quite so much clarity."

Evidently, he hadn't been talking about "our future" as in their future together.

Ford stuffed his hands in the pockets and started walking toward their suite. The fire door closed behind them with a metallic *ka-chunk*. "Darys, how in the world am I going to be able to go back home and forget all this? I'll be afraid to work on any inventions for fear that I'm profiting from knowledge that I picked up here."

She fell in step beside him. "What do you mean?" She knew exactly what he meant. The mind's ear heard her father, a lover of people, books, and songs from the ancient past, singing in the shower. Every time he returned from one of his temporal jaunts, he'd constantly be serenading her with his favorite centuries-old song about *How Ya Gonna Keep 'em Down on the Farm, After They've Seen Paree.*

Ford led the way toward their suite. "I might be stealing an invention and its patent from its rightful owner, merely because he hasn't invented it yet. Can't you see what sort of havoc that could play with the threads of history?"

The unsavory results of such an act filled her imagination. Nolan Investments—"Profits 'R Us."

He paused, glancing down to the floor at a discarded room service tray. A wrinkled newspaper screamed its headlines at them. "Dow Jones Hits Record High." To Darys's relief, he reached past the paper, and retrieved a gaily-painted can someone had left behind as well. "See this? They're everywhere. *Diet Coke.*" he read aloud.

"You never heard of Coca Cola?"

He rolled his eyes. "Of course I have. That's not the point. It's this can." He picked it up, weighing it in his hand, rotating it for a better look. "Look at it. Seamless construction. I wonder what metal? Aluminum? Probably. It's been extruded, somehow. The lid. See? It's a separate piece, crimped to the open end of the sleeve. And this drinking hole in the top. It's simple, effective. It requires no tools, no can opener." He held the can out to her. "Do you know what I could do with this can in 1912?"

"Drink it?" she asked weakly.

He released an exasperated sigh. "I could copy its construction. It might take a while, but I'd have an advantage over the original inventors of these processes; unlike them, I have a finished example to copy. Frequently, the most difficult part of inventing something is coordinating its component pieces with people who don't share your same sense of vision. They simply don't understand what you're trying to accomplish because they don't 'see' what you see in your mind. Drawings, schematics help some, but with a sample, I could essentially give them the same vision I have of the intended result."

He cradled the can in his two hands as if it were a precious stone. "I could make a bushel basket of money from something relatively simple like this, and it would upset the whole balance of history." He made a face as if something twisted in his gut.

"Darys," he whispered in a hoarse voice, "you have to get me home before I learn too much."

She calmly plucked the can from his hand and tossed it into a nearby garbage can. "Now you understand why I have to get my father home. You're starting to understand how much damage you might create; he has no idea. He could do anything—bring any of our technologies to the past. And if they got into the wrong hands . . ."

"Now, Mr. Marsh—"

"Doctor," Harvey corrected.

Johnny gritted his teeth. It had taken every ounce of ingenuity to get Tucker out of the room. The last thing he needed was Harvey playing stupid word games with him. "*Doctor* Marsh, you're making some very . . . bold claims. What sort of data do you have to back up your claims?"

Harvey sniffed derisively. "Certainly you realize that empirical data is only as effective as the person interpreting that data. Are you a trained meteorologist?"

"No."

Harvey beamed. "Which means I could show you a list of numbers and you'd have no idea whether they backed my claims or not." He leaned forward. "Mr. Callaghan, you strike me as a practical man."

Johnny crossed his arms and shifted in his chair. "I'm not into needless frills, if that's what you mean."

"Indeed. And as a practical man, you certainly believe in what you can see and what you can hear. Am I correct?"

Johnny shrugged. "Not exclusively, but certainly seeing is believing in most cases."

"Well . . . what if I told you at precisely—" he tapped his paperwork with his forefinger and then pushed back his sleeve to expose an expensive gold watch "—eleven-fifty-eight, the storm will end and the sun will come out?"

Johnny glanced outside where the gray clouds had renewed their winning battle in the sky. Snow flew sideways, blurring the landscape with its mind-numbing whiteness. "You think the storm will be over in—" he consulted his pocket watch, one of the few remainders of his earlier life and made a quick calculation. "—fourteen minutes? I don't think so."

Harvey pulled off his wristwatch and placed it in the middle of the desk. "Are you a betting man, Mr. Callaghan?"

Johnny shrugged. "I've made a wager or two in my day." The chair squeaked as he leaned forward to examine the watch.

Real gold.

A Rolex.

Whatever Harvey had been doing during his vacation, it must have been highly profitable. "My father once told me that the only bet a man ought to take is whether the sun would set or not. Do I understand it correctly that you want to bet . . . on the weather?"

Harvey nodded. "My watch against . . . yours, that the storm will end at eleven-fifty-eight. Not fifty-seven, not fifty-nine. Exactly eleven-fifty-eight."

Johnny turned his pocket watch over in his hands. Perhaps he was being silly to cling to this last reminder of his life in the nineteenth century. Unhooking the fob from his belt loop, he dropped it gently within the circle formed by the Rolex.

He met the man's gaze with his own unwavering one. "You're on."

Johnny pushed back in his chair and laced his fingers over his stomach, still maintaining eye contact with Harvey. If Johnny won, he'd wear the Rolex. If he lost, he'd buy himself a new watch. Maybe even buy a Rolex. After all, any man who could accurately predict the weather could run a helluva efficient, not to mention, lucrative ski resort.

Together, they watched the sky. Clouds continued to dump snow for twelve of the thirteen remaining minutes. Harvey reclaimed his watch merely to act as a time keeper.

"Sixty seconds."

The snow slowed to a thin, lacy curtain.

"Forty-five seconds."

The snow stopped completely.

"Thirty seconds."

The clouds began to break up, a couple patches of blue peeking out.

"Fifteen seconds."

The small splotches of blue began to combine, forming one larger expanse of clear sky.

"Five, four, three, two . . ."

Sunlight spilled through the window, reflected into brilliance by the vast expanse of glittering snow. As bright as it was, it failed to compare to Harvey's gleaming smile. He reached over to the desk and picked up Johnny's watch by its chain.

"You know? I had a pocket watch once, but it broke. I've always wanted another one. . . ."

CHAPTER 12

*A*ngela waited until the oddly dressed man disappeared with Suze, Johnny's secretary, before bursting into her husband's office. "How'd it go?" She expected to see him, furiously scribbling at his desk, excited at the prospect of this new venture. But instead, he stood at the window, staring out at the sunshine.

He sighed.

"Well?" she prompted.

He shoved his hands in his pockets and pivoted, giving her a sad smile. "That's not Edvard Marsh of Reykjavik, Iceland."

An uncomfortable pain flashed across her stomach, and the baby kicked in response to it. "He's not? Then the forecasting . . . it's all a lie?"

He tilted his head. "Who knows? He gave me one demonstration which was pretty hard to ignore. But that's not important. The important thing is—"

"Not important?" she interrupted. It irked her how his old-fashioned attitudes simply burst out of nowhere and it would be up to her to explain the modern ramifications. "Of course it's important. You know as well as I do that exclusivity boosts business. When we offer something no other resort does, people beat a path to our door. Think of what we can do with one-hundred-percent accurate weather forecasts! With Dr. Marsh's help, we can—"

Johnny raised both hands in a quieting gesture. "Sweetheart, calm down. It isn't good for the baby. His name's not Marsh. It's Kirk. Harvey Kirk, and he's Darys's father."

She stared at her husband. "The man you've been looking for?"

He nodded. "A man from the future who seems to have lost his way as well as his memories in the past."

"From the future?" Angela's thoughts skidded back to the moment two years ago when she'd kissed the man she loved, discovering he wasn't the same Johnny with whom she'd fallen in love. For a few horrible moments, she'd wondered if she'd lost Johnny—*her* John Barrett Callaghan, forever. But, to her relief, he'd returned, crediting his mysterious reappearance to a "man from the future."

Bells started ringing in her head. "Wait . . . is he the one who helped you change places with the other John Barrett?"

"The one and the same." Johnny dropped into his chair and leaned back. "Harvey James Kirk. Only, he doesn't remember that's his name. And since he is definitely from the future, I can't help but figure his forecasting technology might possibly be legitimate."

"If it is, then we can—"

"Then again," he interrupted, "it may simply be a matter of Harvey knowing, in a historical sense, when certain storms are going to start and stop." A lazy grin flitted across her husband's face, signifying an oncoming homily.

Johnny was full of homilies.

"It's like the old joke about the Baptist preacher who walked across the lake. The Methodist and the Presbyterian preachers are astonished until he explains that it's easy when you know where the stepping stones are." He laughed at his own brand of dated humor.

It didn't make sense to Angela. She crossed her arms as best as she could. "Why would he remember something as historically mundane as when a certain snowstorm started and stopped in the past? I can't even tell you when it started, and that was only a day or two ago."

"When it comes to Harvey, who knows why he remembers what he does? The important thing is for us to do whatever we must to keep him here until Darys figures out how to get him back home."

Angela saw a ray of hope amid the clouds of doom. "So . . . at least while he's here, we can try to investigate his claims, can't we?"

Johnny stared at her. "Is it that important to you?"

"Not just to me, silly, but to you, too." She ran a hand across her stomach, feeling the child within shift. "Not to mention the baby. When it comes to my baby, I'll do whatever I must to provide him a stable, prosperous home."

"Or her?" Johnny pulled her gently into his lap and leaned forward, planting a kiss in the middle of the sweater stretched tightly across her stomach. "Ol' Thumper here could be a girl."

Some of the worry lines disappeared from his face. "My daughter," he declared proudly. "You just might be carrying the first female born on my side of the family in the last century . . . er . . . two centuries." His eyes widen. "Three!"

Angela couldn't help but smile at the width of his paternal streak. He'd been reluctant at first when she mentioned having a family, but he came around quickly enough. Once he started staring at the guests' children with more awe than dread, she knew he was ready.

She splayed a possessive hand across her belly. "I told you the sonogram technician said it was boy."

"Sonogram, smonogram." He dismissed the notion with a curt wave. "I'll gladly put my faith in new-fangled equipment, but it's the people running that machinery I don't quite trust."

"What if your son turns out to be a technological type of child?" She grinned at him. "You know . . . computers, the Internet, VR goggles . . ."

"Then I'll have to learn all about computers, the Internet, Game Girls . . ." His face lit up with sudden revelation. "We haven't even picked out a girl's name, yet." He shot her an almost evil grin, a sign that he was about to start what he always called "tomfoolery."

"What about . . . Johnetta? Johnita? How about Juanita?"

The baby started a rhythmic kick and Angela grabbed Johnny's hand, placing it for maximum kick reception. "See? Even the baby doesn't like that idea."

"Angela Jr.? Angelina? Angeletta?" he offered. Another kick. "Guess not."

The next kick hit her squarely in the bladder and she couldn't help but wince in pain.

Johnny's face softened in response. "We only have two more weeks, sweetheart. That is, if Junior here can tell time."

She deliberately masked her response to the next twinge that slid across her belly. "I feel fine. And the doctor says it's more like three weeks."

He shook his head. "Forecasting the weather is fine, but I'd sure have appreciated it more if Harvey had the means to predict the exact moment you go into labor and when Junior will make his or her grand appearance."

"Where did Dr. Mar—Mr. Kirk go?"

"Upstairs. I've invited him to stay, free of charge, so we can keep a close eye on him. I want to give Darys a chance simply to talk to him, first. Maybe she can shake loose some of his blocked memories. Barring that, we may have to tackle him and restrain him to let Darys figure out how to force him back to his own time where the doctors there can treat his amnesia."

"What about the doctors, here? Nolan General has an excellent neurology department. Couldn't they—

"—be asked to treat a man who doesn't remember he's actually from the future?" he supplied. He made a face. "I don't think so. They'd probably try to commit me for observation merely for suggesting the possibility. And if I slipped and started telling them about my true past, it would be a one-way ticket to the nearest asylum for me."

She patted him on the arm. "We don't have asylums any more, sweetheart."

"Good thing." He leaned over and kissed her on the cheek. "I wouldn't want Junior to think her Daddy was a couple of bricks shy of a load."

She nodded knowingly. "That your elevator doesn't rise to the top floor."

"That I'm one taco shy of a combination platter." He laughed and threw his arms around her as best as he could. "Have I told you lately that I love you, Angela Callaghan?"

She kissed his nose. "Not since this morning. I missed the ten o'clock declaration of undying love." She pretended to pout, which always drove him crazy.

"Then let me make it up to—" The phone rang insistently on the desk. Johnny shifted to reach for it, but Angela pulled him back.

"Let Suze get it." She tried her hardest to distract him with another kiss.

He shook his head, making her miss his mouth and rake her lips across his cheek. "Sorry, hon. She's charming Harvey, a.k.a. Mr. Marsh, into his room. I have to get this." He managed to free one hand and picked up the phone. "Hello? Yes? No . . . absolutely not. What? I'll be right there." He hung up the phone and began to untangle himself from Angela's arms.

"Sorry, sweetheart. It's Harvey. It seems that he's not happy with his accommodations. I guess he's forgotten that the last time I offered him lodgings, it was a cell in my jail back in my Margin."

"Let Suze—"

He shook his head. "Evidently, even the lovely but persuasive Suze can't charm him into accepting our hospitality, such as it is. He's starting to make noise about taking his offer to Keystone or Breckenridge. I have to go stop him."

Johnny gave her a quick peck on the cheek and headed for the door. Angela followed him as far as the outer office and watched him move swiftly down the hallway toward the lobby elevators. He dodged Tuck at the corner, forestalling any discussions with a curt "Not now."

As Johnny disappeared, Tucker headed down the hall, approaching her with his arms tightly crossed and a smile draped too casually on his face. He wanted something—like usual.

"What's his problem?" He jerked his head in Johnny's direction.

"A disgruntled guest."

He leaned in closer, a conspiratorial smile firmly in place. "So, what's the scoop on Dr. Marsh? Is J.B. excited by the prospect of knowing everything there is to know about weather prognostication?"

Angela opened her mouth to explain then shut it again. Johnny's previous life in the past was their secret. Tucker might be family, but he didn't need to know anything about it. Two of the reasons why he was such a good investigator were his nosiness and his opportunistic streak. Together, they could make for a lethal combination to upset the comfortable life she and Johnny were creating for their family. She suddenly wished Crawford was back from his honeymoon. He could always be counted on to keep Tucker's feet on the ground and his head out of the clouds.

Clouds. How appropriate. . . .

"Uh . . . Johnny's not so sure the claims this man is making are true."

"Not sure?" Tucker's mouth dropped open. "Has your husband even looked outside lately? When Marsh says the snow will stop at a certain, time, it stops. That's what I call an accurate weather forecast."

"Still . . . it pays to be careful."

Tucker shrugged as he shoved his hands in his pockets. "If you say so . . . I just hope J.B. doesn't let a golden opportunity slip though his fingers."

"He won't." Angela's stomach flip-flopped and the baby followed suit. "He won't."

"HARV . . . Dr. Marsh, I don't understand. This is one of our best rooms. If you'll tell me what's wr—"

Harvey stomped across the room, waving his arms madly. He pointed to the original Vianté hanging on the wall. "Everything. The decor! How pedestrian. Your so-called luxury appointments remind me of something I'd see at a cheap roadside motel."

Johnny clenched his teeth. "This is one of our best suites." *Not to mention next door to Ford and Darys so they can keep an eye on you.* Johnny searched for some sort of compromise short of handcuffing the man to the bed. "Perhaps I can make things a bit nicer by having our room service bring up a selection of complimentary hors d'oeuvres and a selection of fine wines."

"And flowers," Harvey added with a flourishing gesture. "I require plenty of fresh flowers to help generate oxygen. It's bad enough that ski resorts must be located at such ungodly altitudes where the air is pitifully thin, but to add insult to veritable injury by housing me in the . . . attic of the hotel. It's almost criminal." He scowled at the surroundings.

Johnny adopted his best *I'll smile because I have to* innkeeper's face. "There are still two more levels above you, but our best rooms are located on this floor because of the spectacular view." He stalked over to the window and pulled back the curtains to review a magnificent view of the mountains. "But of course, I'll be glad to make sure there are plenty of fresh flowers in the room."

"Good." Harvey sniffed. He waved toward the window. "While you're at it, make sure the wine is very French and very old. Absolutely no domestic swill. And inform your chef, I cannot tolerate preservatives in my food. And before you leave, do close those curtains. The glare aggravates my sinuses, you know . . ."

Johnny responded by jerking the drapes back across the window. He was lucky he didn't end up pulling the material from the rod. Biting his tongue, he told himself Harvey must be suffering some sort of brain damage that altered his personality from personable and pleasant to dour and demanding. All he had to do was play along for a while.

A short while.

Harvey's grating voice called out once more before the door closed. "Oh . . . before I forget, you must see to it that—"

A very short while.

DARYS STOOD AT THE WINDOW, watching the slopes come to life. It hadn't taken long for the resort personnel to make their safety checks and for business to resume again. She leaned her cheek against the cold glass. "It stopped snowing. . . ." She stared vacantly at the exposed patches of blue sky.

"Uh huh." Sprawled in a chair, Ford pointed the remote at the television set and kept flashing through the channels at an irritating speed.

"—next on Dr. Phil—"

"—welcome today's contestants, an accountant from Jacksonville—"

"—with Ellen's guests—"

"—and the case of the 'Damaged Dog Run' with Judge—"

"Would you stop it, please?"

Ford looked up, surprised. "What's wrong?"

"I can't concentrate with you doing that. Can't you simply leave it on one channel?" Men and their remote controls—it had to be some inherent weakness in the male genetic structure. Ford had only been introduced to television less than forty-eight hours earlier, yet he switched entertainment channels with the same irritating frequency her brother Darrell used.

Ford switched the television off. "Sorry." The silence sounded strangely empty after the constant barrage of broken sound bytes. He cleared his throat as if trying to recapture his conversational skills. "People sure like to talk a lot on the television, don't they?"

"I guess."

"And what they talk about . . . well . . ."

Darys heard him sigh. With her back to him, she couldn't tell if he was blushing or not. He certainly sounded as if he was.

"The topics seem . . . a little personal. I can't imagine discussing with anybody some of the things they talk about.

Especially not in front of that large crowd people in the audience."

"Or a couple million of your closest friends watching the program."

"M-million?" he stuttered.

She turned away from the window. "This is a very big world you've stumbled into, Ford Nolan. Big enough to get lost in." She paused, trying to fight the pounding headache that threatened to beat a hole in her temples. "What's taking Johnny so long? I thought he said he'd be right up."

Ford stretched his arms over his head and groaned. "Maybe he doesn't like elevators, either."

"That's not funny. I want to know what my father said. We need to figure out how to bring him back to his right mind."

"You ready to talk about it?"

She flopped on the couch, her stomach tightening into an ungainly knot. "He has amnesia."

"Actually it's worse than that. He has a new identity."

She glared at him. "Remind me to never send you to talk in a jumper."

Ford looked puzzled. "Huh?"

"Never mind. Dr. Edvard Marsh of . . . Where did he say he came from?"

"'My name is Edvard Marsh, and I come to you from the icy plains of Reykjavik which is the capital of my native home, Iceland' Ford repeated in a fair approximation of her father's voice.

She shivered in spite of herself. "Why Reykjavik? We're from Chicago."

"Maybe he visited there once."

"Not that I know of. Iceland isn't what you'd call your number one vacation spot in the world."

Ford clasped his hands around his knees. "I remember

reading a *National Geographic* article about Iceland. If I'm not mistaken, Reykjavik isn't on any 'icy plain.' It's a port city."

"E. Marsh, Reykjavik." Darys muttered the phrase twice then her gaze narrowed. "Is there paper and pen around here?"

Ford pointed to the desk. Darys shot up, rifled through the desk drawer and produced a sheet of stationary and a writing instrument. "E. Marsh, R-E-Y-K . . ." she pronounced slowly as she scribbled.

Ford moved closer so he could see better.

She stared to reorder the letters, and a moment later, wrote down, *Harvey James Kirk.*

She threw down her pen in disgust. "It's an anagram. His addled brain must have taken the letters from his name and jumbled them into another name."

Ford pulled the paper closer to him, to verify her findings. "Are you sure?"

"See for yourself."

Ford ticked off the letters, realizing that, indeed, *E Marsh Reykjavik* unscrambled to become her father's full name. He sat back and scratched his head. "Scrambled name, scrambled brain. Stands to reason, doesn't it?"

She balled her hands into fists. "Just wait until I get my hands on Ferrin Bellanger's scrawny little neck. I bet he had something to do with this."

"Who?"

Her face tightened in anger. "The slimeball who sent Dad out with obviously defective equipment. I ought to—"

Ford covered her fist with his hand. "Does it matter? The important thing is to play in to your father's . . . fantasy. If we want to keep him here, he must feel as if we believe what he's saying."

A voice came from the door. "You can believe it, all right."

They both turned in surprise to see Johnny standing in the room.

He held up a keycard. "Sorry. I let myself in with the passkey. You weren't responding to my knock." He stalked over, dropped in a chair and plowed his hand through his hair. "You looked outside lately?"

They nodded.

He released a deep sigh. "Your father predicted exactly when the sun would come out. Exactly." He grimaced. "And he's not the Harvey Kirk we all know and love."

"He's an amnesiac," Darys offered.

"Among other things, he's an extortionist."

"A what?" Darys gasped then realized that Ford had blurted the words simultaneously. She nodded gratefully at him. No matter if it was the influence of the stabilizer or a shared sentiment, she was simply glad not to be alone in her faith.

"Mr. Callaghan, I'll have you know my father is one of the kindest, most gentle people you'll ever meet. He'd give you the shirt off his back, his last dollar, his—"

"He took one look at the operations and doubled his prices for 'exclusive rights to his forecasting information.'" Johnny ground one fist into the opposing palm. "It would serve him right if I created a consortium of all the resorts and offered him only half of the original price."

Ford looked shocked. "Johnny!"

He shook his head, sighed, and leaned against the back of a large arm chair. "I know, I know. No one is getting anything from Harvey. No matter how tempting, his technology doesn't belong here. Neither does he." Johnny crossed his arms and stared at Darys. "So what's next? We've found him. How do we send him back?"

"I need to get a look at his stabilizer." Darys fingered her own stabilizer nervously. "Maybe I can recalibrate it and bring him back to his senses." She allowed herself a deep sigh. "It's on his person or in his room, somewhere. But how do we get to it without Dad knowing?"

Johnny smiled and pulled out his passkey card. "Leave that to me."

≈

HER FATHER REMAINED in his hotel room for the rest of the day and night. According to Johnny, the insistent, badgering calls to room service and the front desk petered out around midnight. They waited an extra hour, hoping that would give him enough time to either fall asleep or into a drunken stupor.

Johnny handled the break-in, using his passkey to open the door a few inches until it stopped, indicating Harvey utilized the inside security measures. Johnny pulled out two pushpins, a small length of elastic cord and in seconds, he defeated the restraining mechanism.

Darys slid into the room, wearing all black, shielding the glow from a tiny penlight Johnny had given her in hopes of avoiding the booby-traps along the way. Her father was usually a meticulous man, one who found great beauty in order. She'd never seen him like this. She picked a careful path between the empty wine bottles, discarded dishes, soiled towels, and strewn papers.

Some remnants of his personality remained, however. In the midst of the mess, his clothing had been neatly laid across a chair and the belongings from his pockets lined up on the table nearest the window.

Wallet.

Comb.

Loose change

Pocket watch . . .

She snatched it, nearly upsetting the bottle of wine perched precariously on the edge of the table. Grabbing the teetering bottle, she pulled it close to her chest, not quite sure her fingers were up to the task of holding it by themselves. However, in her effort to steady the bottle, she managed to rake off a few coins from the table. They landed on the carpet, clinking as they hit each other.

Darys held her breath.

She was living her adolescence all over again, sneaking into his room, trying to get the control key for the family car. She pivoted soundlessly on the carpet, still carrying the bottle for fear that returning it would create even more noise.

Suddenly, Harvey released a loud snore. He rolled over in his bed, grumbled, struggled with the covering then spoke in a sleep-choked voice. "Honey, that you?"

CHAPTER 13

*D*arys froze, holding her breath. Then it hit her.

Her father sounded . . . normal. For the first time since this debacle began, he sounded like himself. Did she take a chance and answer him?

Her head and heart disagreed and even worse, her nervous stomach refused to converse with either one. She girded her strength and decided to take a chance.

"It's just me, Dad," she whispered.

"Ummm . . . yeah . . . 'Night, honey. . . ." His words trailed off into another snore.

Her heart rose into her throat and a quick sip of wine was the only thing that eased it back down to its rightful place. Gingerly returning the bottle to the table, she pivoted, heading for the door, weaving like a drunk around the piles of refuse in the floor.

She winced as she opened the door and a slice of blinding light poured into the dark room. Squinting against the glare, she stepped out into the hallway only to have someone grab her by both arms.

"Well?" Ford demanded.

"He called me 'honey!'" she managed between her clattering teeth. "He rolled over and called me 'honey.'"

Ford gaped at her. "He woke up?"

Johnny grabbed both of them and hauled them away from the door.

Darys tried to pull out of his grasp. "But I got his—"

He held a finger to mouth, gesturing for quiet, and then proceeded to drag them down the hallway to their room next door. Only after the door was safely closed behind them did he speak.

"You're telling us Harvey woke up and spoke to you?" He leaned down so that they were face to face. "He actually recognized you?"

"No." Her fingers tightened around the watch, as if gripping it would bring her closer to her father. "He rolled over and asked if it was me."

Johnny's gaze narrowed. "He said your name?"

She began to see the holes in her logic which had been fueled by exuberance rather than fact. She dropped into a large chair, feeling suddenly boneless and tired. "Not exactly."

Ford released an exasperated sigh and plopped down on the couch. He ran both hands through his hair. "Then exactly what *did* he say?"

She fought to cling to the last shreds of her fantasy. "He rolled over and said, 'Honey, that you?'"

Ford and Johnny performed identical shrugs and wore remarkably similar expressions.

"What?" she demanded. She didn't appreciate either expression of smug disappointment, even in the face of her faulty logic. "What?"

Johnny almost smirked as he crossed his arms. "'Honey' could have been anybody. Any woman."

Ford nodded. "Johnny's right. It certainly doesn't mean Harvey's memory is coming back."

"It could, too!" She sprang up from her chair. "He could be starting to remember me or maybe my mother or maybe—"

Darys glanced at herself in the large mirror on the opposite wall and stopped in mid-sentence.

There she stood—hands balanced on her hips, bottom lip thrust out in a pout grand enough to rival that of any ten-year-old child. Captured within the mirror's gilt frame, she was the very picture of a little girl, desperately looking for her father.

Darys drew a deep breath, trying to banish the fearful child back to the depths from which she spilled. "You're right," she said in a low voice as she sat back down again. "It didn't mean anything. All it succeeded doing was to make me even more nervous. I almost dropped . . ."

The watch.

In all the excitement, she'd almost forgotten her father's pocket watch.

She unclenched her hand to reveal the watch, sitting in a red-ridged circle impressed into her palm. Holding up the watch by its fob, she examined it closely for the first time. Suspended in mid-air, the crystal winked in the light as the watch rotated slowly.

Her stomach sunk farther than she dreamed anatomically possible. "Oh no . . ."

"What?" A concerned frown creased Ford's face.

How could she have been so stupid? So careless? She'd been so upset by her father's sleepy comment that she'd grabbed the watch without inspecting it first.

"It's—" she swallowed hard "—the wrong watch."

Johnny's face became a mask as he reached out and plucked the chain from between her pinched fingers. "It's

mine. At least, it was mine. Your dad won it from me today
—" Johnny flipped the watch open, displaying the time: a
quarter after one "—er . . . yesterday." He dropped to the
couch next to Ford and released his breath in a single
whoosh.

Darys stared at the timepiece cradled in Johnny's palm.
"Dad won it? How?"

He snapped the watch shut and placed it on the coffee
table between them. "It was a bet about the weather. A suck-
er's bet, I suspect. Never mind that. I thought we were
looking for some sort of electronic stabilizer gizmo." Johnny
offered her a small strained smile. "He must have really
rattled you badly if you grabbed my watch instead."

She toyed with the watch's chain, nudging it into the
shape of an "S". "I was rattled, all right, but it didn't make me
do something stupid." She paused for a moment, remembering the purloined sip of wine. "Dad's stabilizer looks like
a pocket watch. And you have to admit that in the dark, most
pocket watches look alike."

Ford balanced his elbows on his knees and perched his
chin on the point formed by his templed fingers. He stared
blankly across the room. "Maybe he used a different type of
stabilizer this time."

She nodded. "That's possible. I didn't see him before he
left on this latest trip, so he could have changed to something
else."

"Something else?" Johnny leaned forward in his seat.
"Like what?"

She pulled at the chain around her neck, exposing her
own temporal stabilizer. "A pendant like this, a bracelet, or a
belt buckle—something he'd keep close to him at all times."
She picked up the watch, hefting it in her hand. She should
have realized the moment she touched it that it wasn't a

stabilizer. It didn't weigh enough and lacked the telltale vibration of temporal electronic machinery. She closed her fingers into a fist around the watch. "You know what this means, don't you? I'll have to take this back and find—"

Johnny reached out and placed a restraining hand on her arm. "Let's not rush into things." He released a sigh as he settled back in his seat. "Your dad told me he'd had a watch like mine, but it'd been broken. Maybe that explains everything—why his memory is shot."

Ford shot her a sidelong glance. "But if it's broken, then why hasn't your father . . . uh—" he reddened "—disintegrated?"

Darys swallowed hard as emotion threatened to overwhelm her again. Time for logic to come to the rescue. "Normally, travelers go through a synchronization process which will allow their bodies to maintain themselves outside of their normal time stream. The stabilizer is used to shield their memories which are the only area of the body which can't be protected by a synch-process. I didn't have time to go through the process, so my stabilizer has an unusually wide range which protects my body as well as my memories. That's why it accepted your pattern when you came through the time door with me. And that's probably why Dad hasn't suffered physically because of a malfunction."

Ford looked a bit lost, but he persevered. "So what do we do now?" Ford asked. "Go back in and try to find the broken watch?"

Darys nodded. "What other option do we have? Stay here forever?" She stood up, her knees rubbery. Ford braced her before one knee could buckle completely. Earlier, adrenaline had provided her strength and false courage, but now that it was receding from her system, she felt weak, bereft.

Ford's forehead wrinkled in concern. "You're in no condition to go skulking around in his room." He took a deep breath as if making an important decision. "I'll go."

God help her from unlikely heroes. She pulled herself out of his grasp, determined to stand on her own two feet, literally and figuratively. "You don't know what you're looking for."

"And you do?" he countered.

He had a point. She searched her memories for the right words of description. "I know what it feels like. It . . . it hums," she explained.

"Hums?" He arched a single eyebrow. "A discernible tune?"

She ignored his futile attempt at humor. A demonstration was far more effective than a long-drawn out explanation. She lifted her stabilizer by its chain and held it toward him.

Ford closed his hand around the pendant and a moment later, he closed his eyes. His head tilted down, his chin nearly dropping to his chest as if he was falling asleep. A look of pain crossed his face and then slowly faded away. He lifted his head, eyes still closed. An unusually serene expression dropped over his face and a smile twitched at his lips.

Darys felt a slight buzzing in her veins and then the sensation gradually grew stronger. She closed her eyes, but still retained an indelible mental image of his tranquil smile. A tangled jumble of his thoughts poured into her mind.

Images overlapped, memories flowed, thoughts became garbled by other thoughts.

It should have built into a frenzy, but instead, it faded away into the background. After a few moments, she opened her eyes and discovered Ford staring at her.

He raised a hand and brushed the hair out of her face. "I know what I'm looking for, now." He smiled then turned to Johnny who had been sitting there quietly, watching and waiting. "Let's do it again."

Since the limited stabilizer range gave her no other option, Darys followed them back to her father's room. She remained outside in the hallway with Johnny while Ford crept in, with the watch in hand. She strained to listen to the silence, hoping that a lack of noise signaled his success.

One minute stretched into two.

Two into three.

An uneasy feeling settled in the pit of her stomach. Something was wrong.

"Johnny, I think—" A wave of pain slammed her in the back of the head. She turned to scowl at whoever had hit her, but no one was there.

"What's wrong?" Johnny whispered.

She winced as she rubbed the back of her head. "Someone . . . something hit me."

"Who?" He scanned the hallway. "There's no one here but you and me."

Another flare of pain erupted behind her eyes, as if someone was using her head for target practice. "Again." She rubbed the bridge of her nose. "It feels like someone's punching me in the face."

Johnny gave her a puzzled once over. "There's no one here but you and me."

"Uh . . . Darys?" Ford stood in the darkened doorway, blinking as his eyes grew accustomed to the bright hallway. "We have a problem," he said in an unnaturally loud voice.

"Sshh . . ." Johnny gestured for him to lower his voice. "He'll hear you."

Another man spoke. "He already has."

Harvey slapped a hand on Ford's shoulder and pulled him back a stumbling half-step to reveal the gun he had pointed at Ford's back. "I think you'd all better step in here where we won't disturb anybody."

Johnny took a step forward. "But . . ."

"Now!"

Darys jumped out of long-established habit. Her father wasn't normally a loud or demanding man, but there had been several times in her childhood when he spoke in a commanding voice that meant instant conformity. No matter what you had been doing, you stopped and obeyed his instructions without question.

And he was using that same voice again, which made the child inside her react with total obedience. Darys stepped past Ford and into the room, doing everything she could to keep from adding the requisite "Yes, sir." As she passed him, she noticed his dazed expression and the angry lump forming on his forehead. This was one side effect of the stabilizer she'd just as soon not share.

Harvey gestured with the gun for Johnny to enter and, after a reluctant moment, the man followed instructions, stepping into the suite. After closing the door behind him, Harvey slapped the lock in place and flipped on the lights. Darys noted that he was wearing a white terry cloth robe over burgundy pajamas, indicating he'd been sitting up, waiting for them to return.

"Now . . . ," he drawled, as he lined up his three hostages in the middle of the room. "Now, why don't you tell me what you were looking for?"

The three of them shared glances and it fell to Darys to be the spokesperson for the group; she was the smallest, the least threatening of the three and the one Harvey might respond to the easiest.

"Quit stalling," he commanded, punctuating his words by jabbing the gun barrel in the air.

Darys tried to smile, hoping she could disarm his anger with a healthy dose of charm. She'd managed to defuse his temper in the past; she prayed she could do it again. "Mr. Marsh, I—"

"It's Dr. Marsh," he said with obvious venom.

Her smile faltered for a moment then she tried again. "Uh . . . Doctor, I knew that Johnny's watch held . . . great sentimentality for him, and all I wanted to do was get it back for him."

"So you felt free to sneak in here and rifle through my belongings until you found what you wanted?"

She nodded, then added a theatrically crestfallen face. "And then Ford—" she graced him with a simpering sigh "—showed me the error of my ways. It's wrong to steal, even if you think you're doing it for all the right reasons."

Harvey's gaze narrowed as he glanced from Darys to Ford and back to Darys again. "So your young gentleman was merely trying to return the watch before I knew it was missing?"

The breath which was caught in her lungs released itself in a rush. "Exactly! You understand."

The ironic laughter that spilled from him was the most uncomfortable response Darys had ever heard him make. "I understand much more than you give me credit, young lady. I understand you're a terribly liar—almost as bad a liar as you are a thief. You broke in here, aided by this crook of a hotel owner, then stole the watch. When you discovered it wasn't what you thought it was, you sent in your confederate to try his hand at rifling through my things." He openly sneered. "What exactly *are* you looking for?"

None of them could formulate a suitable answer and the silence seemed to anger him even more.

"Come now." He waved his gun around, making them all cringe. "It's my forecasting tricks you're after, right?"

"Tricks?" Johnny narrowed his gaze. "I thought you said you worked from charts and figures and algo-algo . . ."

"Algorithms—a recursive computational procedure for solving a problem in a finite number of steps," Ford supplied.

Harvey turned to him and shot him a look of surprise mixed with only a little admiration. "Bright boy. That's exactly correct. There's no trickery involved. Forecasting is ninety-nine percent computation and one percent inspiration. But—" he pivoted quickly, making Johnny turn his attempt to jump the man into a benign head-scratching gesture "—it's that one percent of inspiration that plays in heavily on occasions."

"How so?" Johnny asked with a look Darys could only describe as wide-eyed innocence.

Harvey smiled. "You don't expect me to give away information for free, do you? There's a little matter of—"

A tinny song suddenly invaded the room. Harvey's grip on the gun tightened, his knuckles whitening. "What's that noise?"

Johnny's hand automatically went to his waistband. "It's my iPhone. I've got a text."

Harvey winced, as if the mild noise was actually ear-shattering. "Turn the cursed thing off."

Johnny fumbled with the button, but it continued its rhythmic noise. "I'm trying. It's not supposed to keep on beeping."

"Stop it! Make it stop!" Harvey held one hand to his ear and after a moment's hesitation, used his gun hand to block the "intrusive" sound from the other ear.

Johnny and Ford shared a fleeting look and then both leaped toward Harvey, Johnny hitting high and Ford tackling low. They all landed against the bed and the mad scramble for the gun began in earnest.

Their frenzied struggles took them off the bed and onto the floor where Johnny and Ford, again, coordinated their efforts, allowing Ford to pin Harvey's arms and Johnny to disarm him. But once Harvey realized he'd lost control of the weapon, his fighting efforts turned from protective to aggressive. In a desperate attempt to regain the gun, Harvey reached up and gripped Ford's throat with one large hand and began to squeeze. Unfortunately, Harvey had chosen the wrong victim and Johnny extricated himself from the melee of arms and legs, holding the weapon up in victory.

"Stop, Dad!" Darys ordered. She would have joined the fray if Johnny hadn't pulled her back.

He pointed the gun at Harvey. "Release him. Now." His voice held the same "Obey now" qualities to it as her father's had.

"You—won't—shoot," Harvey said between gritted teeth as he slipped his grip from a one-handed, almost theatrical strangulation, to a much more efficient choke hold. Ford's face began to turn red, and he clawed at the arm clenched around his neck. Darys shuddered, knowing that forty years of wrestling wrenches had given her father an iron grip. Her own throat began to close, maybe out of sympathy, maybe out of their connection.

Johnny drew a bead on Harvey's forehead. "Don't be so sure. It may have been over a hundred years since I killed a man, but it's not a talent that grows rusty over the years."

Darys placed a gentle hand on his arm. "Don't kill him," she whispered, fighting the tightening in her throat. "He's my father."

"Put the gun down or this one's a goner," Harvey said between gritted teeth.

She turned to her father. "Dad . . . don't. Please don't hurt Ford. Don't you remember him? The last time you saw him, he was only a child. But you liked him, remember? And me, what about me? I'm your daughter."

"Daughter?" He snorted. "Hah! You'll say anything, won't you? Anything to make me stop." As if to prove his point, he flexed his arm, making Ford's eye bulge momentarily.

"Only the truth, Dad, only the truth." She tried valiantly

to stop her tears from collecting in the corners of her eyes. "Your name is Harvey Kirk and I'm your daughter, Darys. You came here through a time portal from the future. It was only supposed to be a temporal vacation, but something went wrong."

"Time travel? Temporal vacations?" He wrinkled his face in something akin to disgust. "Lady, you got some imagination. And some nerve . . . thinking I'd believe a wild story like that."

She was afraid to raise her arms, for fear he would interpret the movement as hostile. The tears started flowing down her cheeks. "If you can't remember me then maybe you can remember Mom. She died only a couple of years ago. That's when you started taking more vacations. You said it was because you had more free time to enjoy them, but I think it was because you were trying to get away from all the reminders of her in our world."

Darys could see a crack start in his uncaring facade. As much as it hurt her to continue, she did. "Mom was a pretty important person, and everywhere we turn, we still see something of hers to remind us that she's no longer with us."

Harvey's grip loosened somewhat and Ford's color improved.

She continued. "I lost Mom and I don't want to lose you, too. You must release Ford and let me help you. We need to find our way back home again."

Johnny's small box beeped again and this time, he managed to silence it a millisecond after the sound started.

Harvey stiffened at the sound. "Home?" he said in a cracking voice.

"Home. Your home. With all your antiques and treasures. Just let go, Dad. Let go and let me fix things."

Harvey's face grew blank. "Let go," he repeated numbly.

The swollen muscles of his arm relaxed and all physical signs of his aggression faded away.

Ford pulled out of the weakening grasp and fell to all fours on the floor, gasping for air. Darys dropped down beside him and touched him lightly on the shoulder. "Ford?"

He nodded and drew in a rattling gulp of air. "I'm . . . okay," he managed between ragged breaths. "What happened? Why did he change all of a sudden?"

Why indeed?

Darys zeroed in on the small box in Johnny's hand. She took it from him, examining it closely. "What does this thing do?"

He kept a close eye on Harvey, who stood like a statue. "It tells me that someone is trying to send me a message on my cell."

"No." She shook her head emphatically. "Not 'what is it?' but how does it work?"

His brow furrowed, as if trying to recall someone else's explanation of it. "I don't know the specifics. It simply signals me when someone sends me message. It's a specialized wireless signal, I guess."

Although Ford was still sitting on the floor, he kept a wary eye on Harvey. "How would something like that make him change his behavior quite so quickly?"

"I don't know." Darys turned the box over in her hand, wishing she could crack it open and see inside. "If it activates because of a wireless signal, then maybe Dad's reaction has to do with the alternating frequency modulation. The signal this box was picking up could have jammed the frequency of whatever was making my father act the way he was."

Johnny took the unit back from her and stared at the small letters that formed on its screen. "Good Lord . . . not now!"

"What?" Darys and Ford asked simultaneously.

Johnny shot them a panicked look. "It's Angela."

Darys locked arms with Ford and helped him to his feet. "What about Angela?" she asked.

Johnny, who had so calmly pointed a gun to a man's head and threatened to shoot, now wore a look of unadulterated fear. "Oh damn, damn, damn!" He pushed the gun in Darys's hand and plowed his shaking fingers through his hair. "It's time. She's in labor."

Ford and Darys shared a shocked glance. Ford shrugged and offered Johnny an if-you-got-to-go-then-you've-*got*-to-go face.

"What are you waiting for?" Darys gestured toward the door with the gun, realizing only a scant few seconds later how dangerous indiscriminate gun-waving could be.

"Excuse me." Ford gingerly removed the weapon from her grasp. "That's better." He turned to Johnny. "We'll take care of things here. We'll be okay. Go, now."

Johnny nodded anxiously then made a beeline for the hallway. He paused at the door and locked gazes with Darys. "Good luck," he said in a strangled voice.

"You, too." Darys turned back to her father who was now sitting on the floor in a sprawled position. It looked as if he was holding a conversation with himself, one side posing questions and the other trying to answer them. After pushing himself up so that he could sit on the edge of the bed, he spread his hands out in a questioning manner. "I'm confused."

Darys mimicked his movement, dropping to a chair. "Me, too. Do you know who I am?"

He gave her a critical once-over and then shook his head. "Sorry. No. Should I?"

She drew a deep breath. *One more time, with feeling.* "I'm your daughter."

His eyes widened, and he showed no signs of his prior belligerence. "No kidding?" He turned to Ford. "She's kidding, right?"

"No, it's the truth." Ford flexed his neck. "The painful truth."

Harvey ducked his head and actually blushed. "About our little set-to . . . you know . . ." He looked up wearing an expression of honest contrition. "I'm really sorry. I don't know why I did that to you." He scanned the room like he'd never seen it before. "I don't know a lot of things . . . like . . . where am I?"

Assured by some inner sense that he was no longer dangerous to her or anybody else, Darys stood up with the intent to sit next to her father. But Ford stopped her with a disapproving stare.

"But he's my father," she explained.

Ford hesitated for a moment then drew a deep breath. "I'll make you a deal. You stay in the chair and I'll put away the gun. But if you sit next to him, the gun stays out."

"Then for God's sake, put away the gun." She turned back toward Harvey. "He's right to be cautious. You haven't been yourself, lately."

A hint of a smile crossed Harvey's florid face. "And who might 'yourself' be?" At her look of confusion, he added, "What I'm trying to ask is—who am I?"

Darys drew her strength from Ford, using his sense of resolution to help her resist the urge to sit next to her father and throw her arms around him. "Your name is Harvey Kirk," she said in a soft voice.

"Harvey Kirk." He repeated the name as if trying to determine if fit who he thought he was. "Harvey . . ."

"Kirk," she supplied. "And I'm your daughter, Darys."

He repeated her name silently then turned his questioning gaze to Ford. "And you?"

Ford dipped his head in respect. "Ford Nolan, sir."

"Are you my . . ." Harvey's voice trailed off.

Ford seemed to intrinsically understand the unfinished question. "No, sir. I'm not your son. In fact, we're no kin at all."

Her father looked relieved as he scanned the room. "Where are we?"

"In a hotel room. In Margin, Colorado."

"Oh." He continued to scrutinize the room, taking an inordinate length of time to take in every piece of furniture, every picture hanging on the wall. "Margin, Colorado," he repeated. He thumbed toward the door. "And that gentleman who ran out?"

"Johnny Callaghan," Ford supplied, "the owner of the hotel. His wife is . . . you know . . ." He gestured with his hands, indicating a large stomach. "You know . . ."

Harvey's look of general confusion deepened. "She's fat?"

Darys glared at Ford. Why all the motions? Why didn't he just say the word? She turned to her father. "He means pregnant—about to have a baby."

"Oh." Harvey contemplated the word for a moment. Then his eyebrows lifted. "Oh! You mean . . . like right now?"

A red-faced Ford nodded. "Evidently."

Harvey sighed. "Uh . . . I hope everything goes well."

"Me, too."

The aimless chatter petered out to nothing and they stared at each other in silence. Although he no longer seemed arrogant or aloof, this still wasn't the Harvey Kirk they knew and loved. He was much too subdued, too quiet for her likes. She stared at him, trying to find the light of her father's true personality in his eyes, some sign of hope she could cling to.

After a moment, he tried to smile. "You're staring."

"Oh . . . sorry."

She turned away. There was no spark of recognition, no

gleam of irrepressible personality. Her father was, for all intents, still missing.

Ford pulled a straight chair out from behind the desk and swung one leg around it, straddling it backward. He propped his chin on its back and released a heavy sigh. "What do we do now?" he asked.

Darys held out Johnny's watch, dangling it by its fob. "You told Johnny you had a watch like this, but it was broken. Where is it now?"

Harvey shrugged. "I don't know. I guess I threw it away."

"But that doesn't make sense. Without the temporal stabilizer, you'd have . . ." She couldn't bear to say the word *vanished.*

Unless, she thought, *he's made so many trips in the past he's developed a temporal anchor that shields his basic internal structure, but not his mind.* It was rare but theoretically possible. But if so, it meant the man she knew as her father was essentially . . . gone.

Darys buried her face in her hands. "Oh, great . . ."

Ford felt her pained disappointment as strongly as if it was his own. A pervasive sense of hopelessness tried to fill him, but he refused to let it overwhelm him. He tipped the chair forward. "Think, Harvey. Maybe you took it somewhere for repair. A watchmaker, perhaps?"

"God, I hope not," Darys muttered from between her hands.

Ford ignored her. "Maybe you packed it in your suitcase. Or stuck it in a jacket pocket?"

The man's face knitted in honest concentration. "I don't really remember the watch. I don't remember much of anything."

Ford wouldn't let himself be easily dissuaded. "But you don't remember throwing it away."

Harvey brightened a bit. "No, I don't remember throwing

it away." His posture changed, growing more erect. "Maybe . .
."

Darys lifted her damp face, hope replacing some of the
hopelessness. "Then it *could* be here. Somewhere. Like in
your luggage." She popped out of her chair and made a
beeline for his suitcase which had been slung in the corner of
the room. She tore through the jumbled items in the suitcase,
discarding them over her shoulder as she systematically
every pocket, every possible hiding place.

Harvey winced at her enthusiasm. "Do you have to be so .
. . messy?"

I'm being thorough," she countered. A pair of men's briefs
sailed through the air and landed on the end of the bed.

Ford sighed, walked over to the closet and began to go
through the pockets of the clothing hung up there. Halfway
through his task, the telephone rang.

He looked at Darys, who looked at Harvey, who looked
totally bewildered by the noise.

"Answer it," she told Harvey.

He held up both hands. "Answer what?"

"The telephone." She pointed to the instrument. "The
thing on the bedside table. Just pick it up and say 'Hello.'"

To his credit, Harvey did not try to answer the lamp.
Instead, he picked up the telephone receiver and followed his
instructions. After an intense moment, he nodded and held
the phone out to Ford. "It's for you."

"Me?" Ford drew a deep breath then took the phone from
the man's hand. "Hello?" He heard someone calling his name
as if from a distance then realized he had the ends of the
instrument reversed. He turned the phone around. "Hello?"

"Ford?" Johnny was practically yelling. "I don't care how
you do it, but short of killing him, find a way to get Harvey
down here."

"But—" Ford heard an anguished scream in the background.

"I don't have time to talk. Just do it. And have him bring his forecasting stuff." Johnny paused then added in a leaden voice, "It's a matter of life or death."

CHAPTER 14

"*S*uch marvelous technology."

Harvey shifted his briefcase into his left hand and ran his right forefinger lightly down the row of buttons for each floor. Both Ford and Darys had wanted to take the stairs, but Harvey started panting for breath even before they reached the door to the staircase, so they opted for the elevator out of medical necessity.

Holding hands tightly, Ford and Darys didn't need to talk. All their worries and concerns flooded through the invisible connection strung between them. Up to now, they'd thought finding Harvey would provide the answer to all their questions. But now that they'd found him, the discovery only served to pose more questions, to create more blocks to keep them from returning to their rightful places in time.

Their places in time.

Two wildly divergent times.

Ford couldn't help but marvel at this world with its technological wonders and marvelous advances that outstripped his ability to dream. She looked at the same miracles and scoffed.

They had nothing in common.

Nothing but a great appreciation for each other, physically. And Ford wasn't sure whether he actually loved Darys. Perhaps the machinery that welded their bodies together was placing a similarly artificial bond on their hearts. And souls.

Darys's hand tightened on Ford's.

Was she experiencing the same doubts? The same skepticisms?

How could she not?

The unearthly silence continued when they arrived at the lobby floor. The doors slid open to an empty lobby. The fire that usually crackled in the fireplace had burned down to embers. The counter, which usually bustled with people, was empty.

They stepped out, the sound of their footfalls filling the quiet room.

Ford broke the silence. "Johnny?"

They heard a faint voice. "In here. My office."

As they walked to the office, they could hear a strange rhythmic noise in the background. As they grew closer, the sounds became words and the words grew clearer.

" . . . two, three, four. Breathe, two, three, four."

When they all walked into Johnny's office, the last thing Ford expected to see was the man, kneeling on the floor at the head of the leather couch, his head bobbing in rhythm.

"Good girl, now a deep cleansing breath," he commanded.

They heard a gasp and then a groan.

Ford craned his head, trying to get a good look at the man. "What's going on, Johnny?"

Johnny Callaghan glanced up, red-faced, flustered, looking more like a harried business executive than a former frontier sheriff. For the first time since their initial meeting, Ford was struck by Johnny's startling resemblance to Barrett.

When Emma had encountered some difficulties delivering John Junior, Barrett had worn the same look of panic, terror, and helplessness. Ford couldn't help but shudder at the recollection. He'd been old enough to be pressed into real service and even now, he couldn't forget the sound of Emma's screams when Johnny Junior had demanded with a vengeance to be born.

Johnny pushed up from his awkward position on the floor. "It's over for now, sweetheart. Just breathe normally."

As they all approached, they could see another man perched on the edge of the couch by her knees. He stared at his wristwatch. "The pains are four minutes apart and closing. We're going to need to transport her soon. I'll call the road crew and see what's going on." The man patted Angela's hand then headed for the desk.

Ford stared down at Angela, who looked as if this baby was just as demanding as John Junior. "The doctor's on the way, right?"

Johnny shook his head. "They don't make house calls any more, Ford. We have to get Angela to the hospital."

Johnny turned an impassioned face toward Harvey. "The problem is we can't get Angela to the hospital. We can't go anywhere until the blizzard stops." He leaned forward and spoke with more emphasis that usually necessary. "It would be nice to know when the storm might stop." He tilted his head as if to say *"Get the hint?"*

Harvey returned a blank stare.

"I said, *'It would be nice to know if this storm is going to stop any time soon'.*"

"Johnny." The other man held up the telephone receiver. "The landlines are dead and I can't get through on the cell or the radio. I'll have to run down there myself." He glanced at Ford, Darys, and Harvey. "Do you have enough help to spare me, J.B.?"

Johnny nodded. "Yeah. Go ahead."

They all waited until the man trotted out the door.

Darys nudged her father. "Well?"

He shot her a blank look. "Well . . . what?"

"Check your gizmo or your papers or whatever, Dad, and tell us when this storm is going to stop."

He held up both hands as if to gesture his lack of understanding, but then realized belatedly he'd brought his briefcase with him. Shrugging, he placed the leather case on the desk and sprang the locks. He pawed through its contents, confusion masking his features. Finally, he pulled out a section of newspaper and thumbed through it, settling on a colorful page.

"The forecast says light flurries, ending around midnight." He looked around expectantly. "Is it midnight yet?"

Ford's stomach lurched.

"Not that," Darys said between gritted teeth. "Your computer printouts. From your weather forecasting algorithm."

Harvey gaped at her. "My what?"

"He doesn't remember," she said to no one in particular. She sighed and slapped her palm against her forehead in frustration. "He doesn't remember at all," she complained to Ford. She spun back around, facing Harvey. "You don't remember telling Johnny exactly when yesterday's storm would end and the split second the sun would come out?"

Harvey reached over and gave her a paternal pat on the shoulder. "Young lady, it's nighttime. The sun's not coming out until morning."

She clenched her hands into fists and shot Ford at withering glare. "You talk to him." She stomped away a few steps.

It was time for a cooler head to preside. Ford placed both hands on Harvey's shoulders. "Harvey, I want you to think really hard. Think about weather. Try to remember everything you know about the weather."

Harvey closed his eyes. "'Everybody talks about the weather, but nobody does anything about it?'"

Ford tried not to sigh. "No, that was Mark Twain. Try harder."

"Every cloud has a silver lining?" Harvey opened one eye as if he wasn't totally sure he wanted to see Ford's reaction.

Ford tried not to clench his teeth. "No, try to remember everything you know about accurately forecasting the weather. Try to remember how you did it."

Harvey set his lips in a firm line and wrinkled his brow in concentration. He tapped his finger against the tip of his nose. "I'm thinking . . . I'm thinking . . . and . . ." Harvey's eyes sprang open.

"And?" Ford prompted.

Harvey's look of expectation fell. "And I have absolutely no idea what you're talking about. I don't know anything about forecasting weather because I don't need to know anything about it." He looked over at Darys. "Darys, honey, didn't you explain to them about Proximity Controllers?"

Darys pivoted slowly. "You called me Darys."

He smiled. "That's the name your mother and I gave you. Darys Elise." He blinked, then slowly pivoted toward Johnny. His mouth dropped open in surprise and he reached past her to clap the harried man on the shoulder. "Johnny? Johnny Callaghan? Is that you? I don't believe it! What are you doing here?"

Johnny stared at him, his expression of panic growing slack-jawed. "Trying hard not to have my first child be born on the couch."

Harvey glanced toward the couch at Angela who was digging her nails into the leather upholstery. "So I see. Ma'am, my congratulations on the impending arrival."

"Th-thank . . . you," she said between pants.

Ford stepped forward, knowing he was the only one

operating at full capacity at the moment; Johnny was wrapped up in his wife's delivery, and Darys was mesmerized by the apparent return of her father's true personality. It was up to Ford to get to the truth. "You mentioned something about a proximity controller. What's that?"

Harvey stared at him for a moment, then his face creased into a familiar grin. "Why as I live and breathe! You're Ford Nolan, aren't you? Emma's little brother? All grown up into a strapping young man. What a pleasant surprise!" He pounded Ford on the shoulder, wearing a good-hearted smile.

"Yes sir, I'm Ford. Now about the proximity controller? What is it?"

Harvey waved his hand in dismissal. "Sorry, son, it's way too technical for you. Twenty-second-century smoke and magic."

Darys recovered sufficiently from her shock to glare at her father. "You brought a proximity controller with you?"

The man reddened.

"Don't you know how much trouble you can get . . ." Her voice trailed off. "That's how you did it." She spun around to face Johnny. "That's how he did it. That's how he 'forecasted' the weather. He wasn't forecasting it—he was *controlling* it! We use proximity controllers to shield ourselves from rain, snow, whatever weather condition is threatening."

"I thought you said you couldn't control the weather in your time," Johnny said in an accusing voice.

"We can't. We use proximity controllers merely to change the area immediately around a person. Like a . . . a . . ." She gestured an arc over her head.

"Like a twenty-second-century umbrella?" Johnny asked.

Darys nodded with enthusiasm. "Exactly. It controls your personal space."

Johnny drummed his fingers against the leather couch.

"But we're not talking about protecting a single person. We're talking about shielding an entire mountain. Is that possible?"

Her brow wrinkled in thought. "Theoretically, you could boost the signal with a large power source which would widen the area it controls. Of course, that's illegal in our world," she added offhandedly. "But if you took one back in time with you to the twenty-first century and found a power source strong enough to . . ." Her voice trailed off. "But that type of power source doesn't exist . . . yet."

This world of the future? Lacking? Ford found it difficult to believe. Considering how upset Darys was, and how much she was sharing it thanks to the stabilizer, Ford was finding it difficult to even think. He closed his eyes and tried to sort through the maelstrom of thoughts that cycloned through his brain. A simple question surfaced. "Couldn't he have brought a power source with him?"

Darys shook her head. "The only equipment he should have brought was his temporal stabil—" She stopped suddenly. "Oh Dad . . . you didn't!"

"Didn't what?" Ford asked.

She held her head as if fearing it would split into two. "Oh great. Really great."

"What?" Ford and Johnny asked simultaneously.

"Don't you see?" A single tear rolled down her cheek. "He used the main power source from his temporal stabilizer to boost his proximity controller." She glared at her father. "How could you be so stupid, Dad?" Before he could answer, she turned to Ford. "It allowed him to control the weather, but he didn't leave himself enough juice to protect his mind."

She stood on her tiptoes and placed her hands on her father's shoulders, pulling him to her level so that they stood nose-to-nose. "Where is it, Dad?"

"Where is what?" He wore a look of wide-eyed innocence.

Her gaze contained daggers. "Harvey James Kirk, don't play dumb with—"

"Oh-h-h-h . . ." Angela released a groan, interrupting Darys's interrogation.

Johnny dropped to his knees beside his wife. "Okay, Angela, concentrate on the picture of the peacock and start your hee-breathing. Hee, two, three, four." He took in a theatrical gasp along with her then expelled it. "Two, three, four . . ."

Harvey pulled out of Darys's grasp to peer over the back of the couch. "My goodness, she looks as if she could blow any minute."

Angela paused long enough to actually growl at Harvey.

"Concentrate on the peacock, honey," Johnny admonished.

Harvey turned bright red and turn away. "Oh yes . . . the peacock." He pointed to the stained glass sign, the recipient of Angela's intense scrutiny. "That used to hang over the entrance to the Crystal Plume. I spent many a night listening to miners spinning their yarns, there. And the beer." He closed his eyes and smacked his lips. "The beer—"

A prolonged groan interrupted him. Angela gripped the back of the couch and began to pant. "It's . . . getting . . . worse . . ."

"Dad," Darys warned, clutching his arms and pleating his shirt between her clenched fingers. "The proximity controller. I need to know where it is. Now!"

Harvey opened his eyes. "Huh?"

Ford moved closer, trying to create a united front with Darys. "Sir, if you do have one of these controllers, then you can help us by using it to stop the snow so we can get Mrs. Callaghan to the—"

A beep interrupted Ford. Johnny snatched his tiny telephone from his pocket, but not before Harvey exploded into action.

One moment, he was the affable Harvey Kirk, good-natured, sheepishly admitting he'd brought a purloined piece of equipment on his jaunt back through time.

The next moment, he was a madman.

He reached around Ford, knocked him off balance, and grabbed the gun from his waistband. Then he seized a shocked Darys and held her like a shield in front of him.

An ugly sneer cross his face. "If you'd like the snow to end and for your wife to give birth in a nice comfortable hospital, we need to talk proper remuneration, Mr. Callaghan."

"Dad?" Darys managed in a strained voice.

His grip on her tightened. "Sorry, dear. You've mistaken me for another man, evidently one not quite as desperate as I am. The money, Mr. Callaghan?"

"Hee . . . one, two, are you insane? Four," Johnny said between gasps of breath. "Put that thing up before someone gets hurt, Harvey."

"Dr. Marsh, to you, my good man. And I'm afraid the gun must remain in my possession during these contract negotiations." He emitted a short bark of laughter. "We're at loggerheads, I suppose. I want to talk contracts and all you want to deal with are contractions."

"Harvey, the pains are less than two minutes apart. I don't have time to mess around."

"Make the snow stop, Dad," Darys commanded, trying to ignore the jab of the gun in her back. "Make it stop, now."

He laughed again. "Come, dear, no one can control the weather. All we can do is be very, very accurate when it comes to predicting it. And then we demand a very, very tidy sum for our services."

Ford took a step forward, holding his palms out to demonstrate his unarmed status. "We know about the proximity controller, Dr. Marsh. We know you've been controlling the weather, not predicting it." Ford drew a deep breath. "And if you think people will pay a lot for predicting the weather—" he allowed a sly grin to roll across his face "— think how much they'll pay to control it. You're sitting on a veritable gold mine, sir. Don't sell yourself and your technology short."

Darys's eyes opened wide. "Ford!" she said in a strangled voice.

Her father's gaze narrowed. "Don't worry, my dear. I don't believe he's made such a quick transformation that he's fallen for the darker allure of monetary gain. It's merely a ruse to gain my trust."

"Think about it," Ford continued. "It doesn't make sense to merely accept the highest bid for your services. Think how much the other ski resorts will pay to keep you *from* selling to Johnny."

A look of greed shone through Harvey's self-satisfied smile. "That's an interesting concept. I must admit I haven't considered the idea of others paying me to withhold the technology." Harvey nodded at Ford. "You may have some use after all. Why don't the three of us retire to a more private place to talk?" He tugged Darys toward the door.

Ford shook his head. "Not until you stop the snow and let Johnny take his wife to the hospital." He took a step toward Harvey and his hostage, giving way to the sudden burst of bravado that filled his chest. "When you let them go, then I'll share my ideas on how you can make millions."

"Come now, son." Harvey's smile lost its gleam. "Certainly you realize that ideas are a dime a dozen. I find you amusing, yes, but not indispensable." He tightened his grip on Darys and shifted so that he could point the gun at Ford. "Not another step closer."

Ford disregarded the man's warning and inched closer.

"I've been studying this world, watching its television. I see possibilities that you haven't even dreamed of. You do know who I am, don't you? Certainly you know the name of Dr. William Crawford Nolan, the world-renowned inventor."

A frown crossed Harvey's face. "Who doesn't know the name?"

Ford swallowed hard. "Well, that's me. At least, that's who I'm going to be. But I'm giving you first crack at all the marvelous ideas that I have up here." He tapped his head. "With my brains and your technology . . ."

Ford realized he had Harvey's undivided attention. He took another step forward, and stood only inches away from the gun. Unfortunately, his gaze strayed down to the weapon and Harvey followed his line of sight, evidently divining Ford's true intentions.

Harvey dragged Darys back a step. "Stop your lies. I'm warning you—I'll shoot." Harvey shifted the gun so that it was pointed in Ford's general direction.

"Dad, no!" Darys managed to twist herself halfway around in order to face him. "Don't shoot him . . . please."

Harvey tightened his grip on her. "He thinks he can worm his way into my good graces and then overpower me. He's sadly mistaken." Harvey cocked the gun and sited it at Ford's broad chest.

"No!"

Three voices blended as one, with Angela's screams becoming a discordant fourth. One moment, Darys was standing upright. The next, she was slammed to the floor, landing on top of her father and becoming sandwiched between him and his two single-minded attackers.

A struggle ensued. Hands grabbed, fists flew. Darys couldn't tell which grunted command came from which man, but she obeyed all of them.

"Get the gun."

"It's in his other hand!"

"—your elbow in my face—"

When she felt her father's gun hand press into her cheek, she knew she had no other option than to bite him, but when she did, it was Ford who bellowed in pain. The gun flew into the air and an anonymous hand reached out to catch it. But another equally anonymous hand rose from the tangled heap and clawed it away.

Darys rolled over to the right, trying to escape the main section of the brawl, in hopes of counterattacking from a better position. She ended up face-to-face to Ford.

"No biting," he warned.

She managed a mumbled apology before her face was pushed into the carpet and something heavy rolled across her back. Unable to escape the melee, Darys curled into a small ball, protecting herself from scrabbling arms and legs as the three men fought for control of the gun. Any moment, she expected a shot to ring out and for someone to fall back wearing a surprised look and a bloodied shirt.

Suddenly, the gun sailed a few feet from the main scrimmage and to her surprise, none of the men seemed to be aware of its new location. This was her chance to end the fight with no bloodshed. The three men were so fully embroiled in their fight, that she was able to crawl to the weapon without discovery or incident.

In every vid she'd ever seen, the hero aimed the gun at the ceiling and fired to signal the end of the struggle. But with the laboring Angela present, Darys decided it wasn't prudent to fire the weapon. However, she did hold it up, over her head, in firing position.

"I have the gun," she announced in a loud voice.

They ignored her.

"I have the gun!" she shouted.

They still ignored her. Punches were thrown. Bodies

recoiled. Expletives flew. She glanced at Angela, who stared red-faced at the peacock and panted, seemingly unaware of the fight. Maybe, just maybe with that sort of focus and concentration, Angela wouldn't even hear a gunshot.

Sorry, little baby, but here goes . . .

Darys pulled the trigger.

CHAPTER 15

*N*othing happened.

At least, there was no explosion. No bullet ricocheting around the room. No plaster dust filtering down through a fresh hole in the ceiling.

Instead, Darys heard a beeping noise.

Harvey, who had just cocked his arm back for a punch, suddenly grew still. The rage on his face faded to a blank stare as his arm dropped down to his side. Johnny and Ford stopped as well, both heaving great sighs of relief that their brawl had miraculously come to an end.

They helped each other up.

"Good," Angela said in a strained, breathy voice.

Everyone, except the near-comatose Harvey, turned their attention to the woman lying on the couch. She held up a small instrument in her pale, shaky hand.

"It landed by me," she said between gritted teeth. Then she winced, dropping the phone to spread both hands against her swollen belly.

"Angela!" Johnny skidded around the end of the couch and knelt beside his wife. "You were brilliant."

"Self-preservation," she said with a grimace. She began to pant again. "You told me—how he changed—the first time. I saw him—change the—second time. I figured—I'd take a—chance on—a third." Her face tightened, then she drew a deep breath which erased some of the pain from her face. "You suppose someone could get me to the hospital, now?"

Darys picked up the cell that Angela had dropped in her pain then deposited it on the desk. She eyed it with growing apprehension. One little beep and her father might become a raging monster again. She turned to study Harvey's blank face but addresses Johnny. "Can you turn it off?"

Johnny appeared too concerned with Angela to respond.

She turned to Ford. "How do we make sure it doesn't change Dad . . . again?"

Ford shrugged, grabbed the box and moved it to the floor. Lifting his foot, he solemnly ground his heel into the beeper, turning the neat black rectangle into a collection of broken components. He turned and smiled. "Ta-da. Now there's no question." He used his foot to nudge the remains under Johnny's desk.

The smile fell from his face. "I'm more worried about the gun. What are we going to do to make sure it won't go off again?"

She looked down, realizing that she still held the gun. "It didn't go off in the first place." She held it up, pinching the grip between her thumb and forefinger, and staying well away from the trigger. "I wonder why?"

"Maybe it has a safety." He stepped closer, leaning down to peer at the weapon. Perhaps in concession to its deadly nature, Ford didn't act nearly as cavalierly with the gun as he did with the cell.

Still, she played to the side of caution. "You do know how one of these things work, don't you?"

He glanced up long enough to shoot her a dirty look. "Guns have been around for a lot longer than either of us." He reached over and thumbed a button on its side. "There. Safety's on."

Suddenly, the gun grew warmer, vibrating in her hand with an electrical hum. Although her first urge was to drop it quickly, Darys moved with slow deliberation and placed the weapon on the desk.

They both watched the black grip turn glowing silver. A keypad wavered into sight and, above it, appeared the words: *Property of "This Time Around" Travel, Inc.*

"Is that what I think it is?" Ford asked in a hushed voice.

Darys's mouth hung open. The gun's barrel started to glow, turning a shade of greenish-gold. After a series of barely audible clicks, the two pieces separated.

"What's happening? Why is it . . . falling apart?"

She knelt in order to get a closer look at the separating components. "I'm not sure. I think it's . . ." She stared at it, trying to read the coding on the slender gold tube. Where had she seen something like this before? She closed her eyes, searching her memory. To her surprise, the answer came with surprising clarity and speed.

"Damn it, Dad!" She grabbed the shining tube and shook it in his face. "This is why your stabilizer malfunctioned and didn't shield your memories. Just as I thought. You used *all* of its power source to boost your proximity controller. Do you realize what could have happened if you'd accidentally reversed the polarities?"

Something animated crept into his blank stare. His mouth twitched. "I had a fifty-fifty chance of getting it right," he whispered.

The blood boiled in her veins, making her head throb with every accelerated heartbeat. Indignation rose like bile in her throat. Her knuckles whitened as she shoved the golden tube at him. "Turn off the snow. Now!" she ordered, her body trembling in rage.

Her father took the tube, twisted it a half turn then solemnly handed it back. "There." He tried to look properly chastised, but a ghost of a smile haunted his face. "You know what? You look so much like your mother, right now."

Unable to cope any longer with the fierce intensity of her anger, she allowed the emotion to degenerate into its component parts: fear, worry, love and relief. Tremors rocked her.

"Oh Dad . . ." She fell into his arms, muffling her sobs on his shoulder.

Ford watched the two of them, overtly aware that every emotion Darys felt was rocketing through his body as well. Would she realize his thoughts, his fervent desire to see father and child reunite were what helped pushed her out of the path of righteous indignation and into her father's arms? The father-child reunion would be the one encounter Ford would never have a chance to experience, except vicariously.

And unfortunately, it wasn't quite the same.

A scream pierced the air.

Belatedly, Ford realized he'd narrowed his scope and attention to Darys and Harvey, and that there were others who needed help as well. He turned around and saw Johnny straddling the couch at his wife's feet.

"Hang in there, Angela. Just hang in there," he ordered.

Darys spun around as well. "Dad has stopped the snow, but there's nothing any of us can do about roads."

"It's too late," Johnny said hoarsely. "The baby's coming."

"There's something I can do." Harvey grabbed the gun-grip-keypad and punched in some numbers. A shimmery arched door wavered into sight to the right of Johnny's desk. Ford realized that it was a time door, similar to the one that he and Darys had stepped through.

"No, Dad. I'm not going to take a chance on losing you again." She shifted over so that she stood in front of him, blocking his path to the time portal. She held out her open hand. "Give me the controls. I'll go, instead."

Ford reached past Harvey and placed a hand on her shoulder. "You mean, *we'll* go. You can't go anywhere without me."

Harvey narrowed his gaze. "Why can't she go without you? Unless . . ." The light of discovery flared in his eyes. "Oh . . . is that why you're here? You're both traveling on her stabilizer?"

Angela moaned again.

Ford nodded. "There was an accident. It couldn't be avoided."

To his surprise, Harvey demanded no further explanation. He turned to Darys. "Your stabilizer doesn't have the capacity to carry a third load. Mine does. I'll go."

She held her hand out insistently. "Your stabilizer hasn't been working all that well lately, either. Considering—"

Angela changed from a moan to a full-throated scream.

"We don't have time to argue. I'll take my chances." Harvey sidestepped his daughter and leaped into the silvery door frame. He closed his eyes for a moment, as if trying to recall something, then punched in a sequence on the keypad on the door arch.

Darys lunged toward her father, but Ford grabbed her by the arm. "He's right. There's no time."

As both Harvey and the doorway began to fade from sight, he mouthed "Love you" to his shocked daughter and "Be right back" to Ford. A moment later, in a rush of air and the whistle of escaping time, he was gone.

Darys stood silently, hands clenched in fists at her side. Ford came up behind her and put his arms around her. She remained ramrod straight.

"He makes me so mad."

"I know." He sighed. "I know everything about how you feel."

She pivoted to say something then closed her mouth.

"Everything," he repeated, kissing her softly on the forehead.

She closed her eyes and rested her head on his shoulder. He held her tightly, wishing that for a moment, the world and its troubles would cease to exist for both of them.

But the world refused to cooperate.

They both became aware of the unpleasant noises originating from behind them.

"I . . . want . . . to . . . push . . ." Angela gritted out between gasps of air.

"Not yet, sweetheart, not until we get someone here. Just keep panting. Remember, they told you you'd want to push before it was really the right time to do it. Just pant."

"I don't want to pant," she screamed. "I want to push. Now!"

Ford leaned over Johnny, like an umpire peering over a catcher's shoulder. "Can you see the baby's head?"

Johnny nudged him away. "Would you mind, Ford? This is my wife."

"Have you ever delivered a baby before?" Ford challenged.

"No. Have you?" Johnny countered.

Ford raised an eyebrow. "Don't forget—my sister is a doctor. I've observed births before. I even helped, once. Sort of."

Johnny jumped up, waving to his spot on the couch. "Then by all means." He moved over to kneel on the floor by Angela's head. When the woman shifted her grip from the couch to her husband's hand, they could all see the half-moon cuts her long nails had made in the leather upholstery.

However, Johnny didn't appear as if he noticed how her

claws dug into him. He gently wiped her brow with a hand-kerchief. "Just hang in there, baby. Harvey's gone for help. He'll bring back someone from the future who knows all about delivering babies. It'll be just like on . . . on . . . *Star Trek*," he babbled senselessly. "Futuristic medicine, no pain. Just hang in there, Angie."

Once settled into the proper receiving position, Ford closed his eyes, trying to remember the steps the midwife had gone through when Emma delivered Johnny, Jr. The baby had been breech and that had posed several difficulties that Ford prayed he wouldn't have to face with this birth.

A quiet voice buzzed in his ear.

"You could manage better if you opened your eyes." Darys touched his shoulder and he complied, opening his eyes. "This connection works both ways, you know. I can feel what you feel, too." She placed a gentle kiss on his temple. "You'll do fine. Don't worry."

"I have to worry," he croaked, "I'm delivering my great-great-grand-nephew."

Angela released a window-rattling bellow.

"I think you left a 'great' out of there." Darys graced him with a half smile. "And it could be a girl, you know."

He bobbed his head nervously. "Duly noted. Now could you find me some clean sheets or towels?"

Darys ran off, following Johnny's harried instructions on how to locate the necessary linens.

Although gracious in her usual state, Angela had revealed a tendency to scream some interesting expletives as the pain grew more unbearable. There were even one or two Ford hadn't heard and Johnny promised to explain later.

Darys returned only seven screams later, skidding into the room with an armload of sheets and towels. "Will these do?" she asked breathlessly.

"Yes." With Johnny's help. Ford pushed the edge of one

sheet under Angela to give them a clean birthing area. He used the other sheet to tent across her knees, giving them a modicum of privacy. "Uh . . . now, we need warm water and something we can use to create a mild suction."

Darys ran to the small bar tucked between two bookcases and started running the water. "I wish Daddy would hurry. It may take him weeks to get someone to listen to him and come back here."

"Weeks?" Johnny howled.

"Don't worry." She gulped. "It doesn't matter how long it takes in the future. He'll still arrange to come back here within a few minutes of leaving. He just has to make sure he doesn't encounter himself along the way. He'll be back in five minutes . . . six minutes, tops."

Johnny used a towel to mop the sweat from Angela's forehead. "She may not last five minutes."

"The head's crowning," Ford shouted.

"Want . . . to . . . push . . ." Angela closed her eyes, leaned forward and started grunting.

"Not yet!" Ford shouted.

Darys watched Ford's face; it was a mask of indecision. As her father would have put it, he knew enough to be dangerous. She placed a hand on his forearm and gave him a small squeeze. "She's in good hands."

"My hands . . ." Ford stared at them, then something flared in his eyes. "Got to wash my hands." He stood up, pulling Darys into the place he'd just vacated. Shoving a clean towel in her hands, he pointed at Angela. "If anything happens . . ."

She nodded. "Be prepared to catch." She stared beneath the sheet, her face growing suddenly pale. "Just hurry," she croaked.

While Ford scrubbed his hands, Johnny offered his

support. "Now Angela, hold off for one more minute. Try not to push for one more minute."

Angela nodded, unable to speak.

Seconds ticked off like hours. Ford kept up a running commentary as he continued to scrub his hands thoroughly, talking about the other births he'd witnessed. Darys found herself holding her breath for fear of falling into Angela's frenzied pace and hyperventilating.

Ford returned quickly. "Ready."

She stood, and he slid back into place.

He peered under the sheet and his eyes widened. "Okay Angela, I think it's time. I want you to start pushing on the count of three. One, two, thr—"

"Wait!"

Darys watched the time door began to form in the same place as before. It pulsed with a metallic glow, fading in and out several times before finally materializing. A moment later, two forms began to appear, first as vague shapes in the metallic haze and eventually gaining form and mass.

She recognized her father's face first. Used to time travel, he held onto a handle and calmly waited for his transformation to complete. His companion huddled against the portal's frame, as if terrified of the whole process. The silvery fog lifted, revealing the identity of the medical expert he'd gone forward to retrieve.

Ford was the first to react.

"Emma?"

CHAPTER 16

*E*mma Nolan Callaghan stepped forward, shaking her head as if trying to regain her lost balance. She shot her brother a look which flared for an instant with shock and excitement. But a split second later, Emma reverted to her usual, professional air. "I understand there's a baby on the way?"

Darys shifted so Emma could better see the patient and her predicament. "It's coming—right *now*."

Setting down her medical bag, Emma tugged off her traveling cloak, depositing it into Darys's hands, then quickly scanned the office. "I need to wash my hands."

"No need," Harvey called out from the portal. "Your skin and clothes were automatically sterilized during the travel process." From the way he was holding the portal's handle, she knew he must be dizzy. A quick round trip in time tended to affect even a seasoned traveler like him.

Emma glanced at her hands then shrugged. "That being so . . ." Emma motioned to her brother. "Move aside, Ford."

He jumped out of her way. Blind obedience was the best course of action when his sister was in charge.

"You'll be in charge of my instruments," Emma ordered. "I suggest you lay them out on a flat surface, on top of a clean towel."

"Yes, ma'am." He started to pull her medical equipment out of her black bag.

Emma looked up and caught sight Johnny, sitting at his wife's side. If she was surprised to see him, she didn't show it. "Good to see you again, Sheriff."

Johnny tilted his head. "You too, Miss Emma."

Angela evidently forgot about her impending delivery for a brief moment. "You know her? Then that means she's from the past. The past . . ." She began to squirm as if to pull away from Emma's care. "I don't want a doctor from the past. I want a modern doctor, one from the future, even." Her face puckered in pain, in fear and in grave disappointment. "You promised me *Star Trek*. I want Dr. McCoy!" She tried to rise up from her position.

"Hold on, sweetheart." Johnny patted his wife on the shoulder, subtly applying enough pressure to pin her gently to the couch. "Miss Emma . . . er, Doc Callaghan, is the best doctor I've ever seen in this or any other century."

Before Ford could say anything, Emma jumped to her own defense. "I'm sure Mr. Kirk will tell you that little has changed, even in the future, when it comes to birthing children."

Angela started to say something, but Emma cut her off.

"Miz Callaghan, I've delivered many children as a doctor and three of them as a mother." She looked the woman in the eyes, using one of her most valuable medical skills: her well-placed confidence in her own abilities. "Trust me."

Angela met Emma's solemn gaze and slowly nodded. "Yes. I trust—" Any additional comment Angela might have made was lost as she reacted with a shriek to a demanding contraction.

Emma lifted the sheet, made a quick examination of the woman then nodded at Johnny. "It's time. Mrs. Callaghan?" She didn't wait for a response. "I want you to push. Push like you've never pushed before."

Darys turned her back to the proceedings. Sure, it was supposed to be beautiful, witnessing the birth of a new life. But Darys's nerves were shot. Her stomach was permanently snarled into a big knot. Her ability to string more than one thought together was . . . was . . . what was she thinking?

Warm arms closed around her.

"I've never been so glad to see my sister. I thought I was going to have to deliver that baby by myself. She's a good physchitan . . . physi . . . a good doctor." He blinked. "I must be more tired than I thought. My tang is tongling. I mean . . . my tongue is tangling."

She stared at him. "You feel . . . weird?"

He nodded. "Really . . . odd."

When his grip loosened, Darys belatedly realized how much support he was giving her. She sagged toward the desk.

"Darys . . ."

Harvey and Ford's voices blended together, but both sounded as if they were miles away. As she sagged, someone grabbed her. She looked up, expecting to see Ford as her rescuer, but she realized it was her father who was supporting her. Craning her neck, she saw Ford, bracing against the desk, arms unnaturally stiff and head hanging.

"What's happening?" she asked in a thick voice.

"Darys, sweetheart, tell me how you feel," her father commanded.

She allowed him to prop her in a chair. "All mixed down . . . up. It hurts. To think."

Ford was able to express himself better. "It feels like I'm drunk. Room's spinning." He managed to prop himself on one hand and hold the other in front of his face. "Fingers don't want to work." There was a moment of silence then he spoke in a slurred voice. "Oh damn . . . my hand . . ."

Although it was difficult, she focused on his hand. His fingers twitched, then for a very brief moment, they faded away. His arm simply ceased to exist past the cuff of his sweater. Then as quickly as it disappeared, it winked back into existence.

Darys drew a deep lung of air, suddenly able to breathe easier. "It's . . . passing." Her strength began to return. Rubbery knees grew stronger. Deadened nerves sang with renewed electricity.

Ford straightened, evidently able to stand again. "What was that?" he demanded of Harvey.

Her father shook his head. "I have no idea. It could have been a temporary glitch in your stabilizer." He shot Darys a tight-lipped expression. "They're not designed to carry two people, you know."

"They're not supposed to power a proximity controller, either," she countered.

He shrugged. "Okay, so you caught me on a technicality. I want you to explain just how you two got hooked up in the first place."

Darys opened her mouth to speak, but a scream drowned out her answer.

"Just one more push," Emma urged. She turned to her brother. "Ford, I need you, *now*."

Ford lurched toward her, but Harvey held out a restraining hand. "No. You're in no condition. Let me."

Despite her first instinct not to watch, Darys shifted in order to see some of the proceedings. The sheet blocked what was probably the most explicit view and allowed her to see the expression of determination on Emma's face, Harvey's fascination, and the look of pain, fear, and expectation on Angela's face. Johnny looked downright scared, but he continued to hold his wife's hand, helping to support her when she pushed.

Emma ducked back down into position. "I have the head. One more push . . . and here comes a shoulder and . . ."

Ford and Darys stood together, watching a smile of achievement cross Emma's face. "Here we are, little one," she spoke softly.

A plaintive squall filled the room.

"It's a—"

The baby's second cry drowned out Emma's pronouncement and her subsequent instructions.

But luckily, Harvey seemed to understand exactly what to do. After he handed Emma a pair of scissors, he placed a towel over his arms and gleefully accepted the howling baby from her. While he held the squirming bundle, Emma cleaned the baby's face, suctioning out its mouth and nose. All Darys could see of the child itself was a tiny red fist, flailing in the air. Its cries filled the room.

Angela strained to sit up. "Is my baby all right? He's crying so hard. That's not normal, is it?"

Emma gave her a broad smile. "It's perfectly normal. *She's* perfect."

Johnny's face lit up. "A girl?" he whispered. "We have a girl?" He wrapped his arms around his wife's shoulders. "We have a daughter," he said in absolute shock mixed with unbridled joy.

Emma and Harvey worked together to wrap the baby in a clean towel then handed her to her very new but very proud parents. As Johnny and Angela marveled over their child, Emma clapped Harvey on the back. "You do good work, Mr. Kirk."

"So do you, Doc." He glanced out the window, evidently noticing someone or something outside. "But we'd better get you out of here before anybody sees you. I'd hate to have to explain who you are."

She nodded and started gathering her instruments. Ford joined her at the desk. He placed an arm around her waist and gave her a squeeze. "I'm surprised you came, Sis."

She punched him playfully in the arm, a gesture meant to remind him that although he was bigger than her, he was still her "little" brother. "Not nearly as surprised as I was when Harvey told me where you've been."

He reddened. "I didn't intend to come along. It just sort of . . . happened."

"So, what are you going to do now?"

He shrugged. "Figure out how to get weaned from Darys's machine that holds us together and then come home, I guess."

"Oh." She looked around the room, her gaze hopping from one technological marvel to the next. "I bet you're having a ball here, trying to figure out what makes all these machines tick."

Ford felt himself flush with color. "It's a challenge, all right. Some of it I don't understand." He withered under her doubtful glare. "Okay, *most* of it I don't understand. But I'll sure have some great ideas to work on when I get home."

She planted her hands on her hips. "Are you *really* coming home?"

It was an odd question which caught him off guard and he stuttered through his answer. "Well . . . uh . . . of course." He studied his sister's tired face. Had his brief disappearance caused her to stay up nights worrying? Thoughts of guilt made his chest hurt for a moment. "Where else would I go?"

She shrugged. "You tell me. I figured you'd get so caught up in the wonders of the future that you'd never come home. You've been gone for a long time, already."

Aha! So she has been worried about my disappearance. He

tried to adopt a nonchalant air. "Aw, Emma. Don't exaggerate. It's only been a couple of days."

She closed her black bag with a flourish. "Maybe to you, but back home, it's been four weeks."

His mouth dropped open and the pain of guilt flared one more time. "Four weeks? That long?" He managed to convert his surprise to a wincing half-smile. "Time flies, eh?"

This time, when she punched him again, she wore a forgiving smile, signaling that amnesty had been offered. "So I can expect you home, soon?"

"Yeah." He rubbed his arm, wishing she could find a better way to convey her unspoken thoughts. "But I'm learning that 'soon' may be only a relative term when you're hitching a ride with time travelers."

She nodded knowingly then stood on her tiptoes to kiss him on the cheek. "Be careful, little brother."

He wrapped his arms around her for a brief hug. "I will, Doc. Say hello to Barrett and the boys." Guilt flared once more as he realized he'd given little thought to the family left behind as he traipsed through time. He tried to plaster a smile in place. "I sure am going to have some great tales to tell them when I get home."

Emma glanced at Harvey and Darys. "I bet you will, Ford. I bet you will. Well . . ." She heaved a sigh. "I suppose it's *time* for me to head back. Right, Harvey?"

Harvey shot her a smile that could only be described as grateful. "Whatever you say, Doc. I know I wouldn't leave that youngest one alone for long. He's a corker."

Ford found her cloak on a chair and held it up for her to put on. "Harvey's right. John Jr. can get in more trouble by himself than his brothers combined. Tell that rascal to stay out of my laboratory."

She nodded, looking suddenly fatigued. "I'll make sure to tell him. Good-bye, Ford." She kissed him one more time, then turned to Darys, holding out a hand which she hesitantly took. "Miss Kirk . . . nice to see you again. Take good care of my brother. Very good care."

Darys ducked her head and muttered something which Ford didn't quite catch. Emma leaned forward then laughed.

"You're so right, Darys. So right." She turned and faced Johnny. " Sheriff? It's been good to see you again."

Johnny settled the baby in his wife's arms, made sure she was propped comfortably on the couch and stood. "Miss Emma . . . Doc, thank you. You don't know how much it meant to Angie and me that you were willing to leave your home, your own time, to come help us. I can't imagine any other doctor, past, present, or future that I'd rather deliver my daughter. With your permission—" he glanced back at Angela who nodded with enthusiasm "—we'd like to name her after you, if we may?"

Emma's face softened. "Oh Johnny . . ." She nodded at Angela, who was rocking their newborn. "Mrs. Callaghan, I'm very honored. Thank you."

Angela beamed at her. "No. Thank you, Dr. Callaghan."

Johnny reached out and shook Emma's hand warmly. "Yes, thank you for everything. Tell that great-great-great-grandson of mine that we're all fine, thanks to you."

"Barrett will be thrilled to get news of you and your family." She turned to Harvey and linked her arm in his. "Shall we go, now? Speaking of Barrett, he's probably wondering where his supper is."

Harvey tipped his head in respect. "No problem, ma'am. I can get you back five minutes after you left."

Arm in arm, Emma and Harvey stepped into the portal archway. Johnny, having returned to his wife and baby's side, lifted his hand in a farewell gesture. Emma returned it, then locked maternal glances with Angela whose smile outshined the brightest star. Harvey's fingers flew across the keypad and the portal faded away.

As they disappeared from view, Emma blew Ford a kiss. "I love you," she mouthed.

"I love you, too, Emma."

The door vanished.

Ford turned to ask Darys what she'd said to Emma, but before he could say anything, a high-pitched hum signaled the portal's return.

Darys crossed her arms. "That was fast."

"Too fast." Ford moved as close as he dared to the arriving time door. A lone figure loomed into existence. Like a Cheshire cat, the grin seemed to form ahead of the rest of him.

"One down and two to go." Harvey stepped out of the door, dusting his hands off. "The good doctor was safely returned into the arms of her loved ones. Now it's your turn." He faced Darys. "You do realize that you and I are in for a spot of trouble when we get home. Me for taking an unsanctioned trip. You, for picking up a hitchhiker."

Ford rushed to her defense. "But it was an accident!"

"Sure." Harvey patted him on the arm. "Sure it was."

"Honest, Dad. The door was beginning to collapse and I was half knocked out of it. If Ford hadn't acted when he did —" she couldn't hide her expression of distaste "—only half of me would have arrived here."

"Collapse?" Harvey paled visibly.

Ford nodded. "The ground shook, but it wasn't a natural tremor."

"How would you know?" Harvey challenged.

Darys dismissed her father's question with a wave of her hand. "Believe me, Dad. He knows."

Harvey wore a dubious expression. "Tell me anyway."

Ford took sudden interest in his shoes, feeling silly about

explaining to a man of the future about his rustic attempts to study science in the past. "I keep . . . kept track of any signs of seismic activity in Margin, and each week, sent my results to the Jesuit Brothers in St. Louis. They're compiling seismic data from across the United States and are allowing me to contribute my findings." He felt his face flush hot. "I bet they're none too thrilled about me missing four weeks in a row."

"But why Margin?" Harvey asked. "Why you?"

Ford brightened a little. Evidently, Harvey knew nothing about seismology and for once in this world, Ford could be the teacher rather than the pupil. "This is a very stable region of the U.S., so any activity I pick up is likely an echo of shift movement somewhere else in the world. With data from all parts of the country, they can compare the figures and triangulate the actual epicenter of a quake. From that, they hope to someday be able to predict earthquakes before they happen. Think how many lives could have been saved in San Francisco if they'd had more warning."

Harvey dipped his head in thought. "So if the tremor wasn't due to natural causes, it must have been . . ."

"A temporal shock wave," Darys supplied.

"Damn." Harvey groaned. "I was afraid of that. It must have been dumb luck that allowed me to pick up and return Emma with no trouble. I must have hit it just right between waves."

Darys lowered her voice to a conspiratorial level. "Then you think it's going to get worse?"

Harvey nodded. "Unfortunately." He templed his fingers and tapped them on his chin. "You know what that means, don't you?"

Darys drew in a deep breath and expelled it in a whoosh. "The big one."

Ford cocked his head. "The what?"

"A temporal tsunami," she said in a solemn voice.

"A what?"

"A tsunami is a tidal wave caused by a—"

Ford interrupted her by holding up his hand. "Believe me, I know all about tidal waves. What I want to know is what in the world is a temporal tidal wave?"

Darys scanned the room as if looking for inspiration. Her gaze settled on the door. "Every time you create a time portal, there's some . . . leakage into the surrounding area. If you have to travel frequently into the area, the agency controlling your trip establishes a semi-permanent door that they keep . . . locked when no one's using it. It's not the opening of the door that causes the problems, it's the creation of those doors."

She glanced ruefully at her father. "Neither Dad or I were taking sanctioned trips, so we spilled a lot of temporal energy into this area, creating our time portals. Then there's also the damage that his proximity controller might have caused."

"Damage," Ford repeated. "Then what you and I felt earlier . . ." He swallowed hard.

". . . wasn't a glitch in the stabilizer, but an advance shock wave, a preview of what's to come. We've spilled too much energy in this area, and it's become saturated. If anybody else arrives in this time period, there's nowhere for the energy to go. It'll blast across here like flood waters in a dry creek bank." She nodded at her father. "Thank heavens you left the door up when you returned Emma. Who knows what could have happened if you hadn't."

Ford spun around to stare at Johnny and Angela who were more engrossed in their new child than eavesdropping on time travelers' secrets. "Then we have to get them to safety. We can't let anything happen to—"

Darys placed her hand on Ford's arm. "Don't worry.

They're safe—they're permanently anchored here. Even Johnny. We're the ones in trouble. We have to get back home before anybody else shows up."

She turned to her father, her expression darkening. "Like the time cops."

Harvey's face twitched, then he turned his attention to his keypad grip. "You'd better hurry and say your good-byes. We'll be heading out as soon as I complete the computations."

Johnny glanced up, his face registering surprise. "You're not leaving so soon . . ."

Darys tucked her hand in Ford's and led the way to the couch. "I'm afraid we have to. Johnny. We accomplished what we set out to do: to find Dad. And we have to get him back before he gets in even bigger trouble."

"I used to lock him up every Saturday night. I can't imagine what you'll have to do." Johnny laughed, then turned to Ford. "What about you? Are you headed back to your own time?"

"I guess so." Ford felt his chest tighten again. He never thought he and Darys would remain together forever, even in spite of their dalliance. But he didn't think they'd be separated quite so soon.

Darys squeezed his hand. "He's not going home quite yet. We have to make a stopover into my time first, where the temporal engineers can separate our signals from the stabilizer."

Ford's heart quickened. "The future? I mean even further into the future?"

She smirked. "Don't sound so excited. Twenty-one-oh-six may be the distant future to you, but it means immediate trouble for me and Dad."

"Trouble?"

She slipped her hand out of his, stuffing it into her pocket instead. "I thought I would sneak back here, grab Dad, and slip both of us into the proper time stream without raising any alarms. But even if we're able to sneak you through because you and I are using only one stabilizer signal for the both of us, I'm going to need professional help to separate us."

Separate us. "Separation" sounded so drastic to Ford. So final. So . . . lonely. He rather liked having another half to his whole. A spare yin to his yang.

She pushed him forward. "Hurry up and say your good-byes. I'm going to help Dad."

Ford stared down at the red-faced infant who slept peacefully in her mother's arms. "You know, I almost thought I was going to be the one to deliver my own great-great-great-grand-niece."

Johnny followed his glance and heaved a satisfied sigh. "So did I. She's a miracle, one way or the other. There haven't been any women born in the Callaghan family in a very long time. I know history has truly been changed, now."

"Changed?"

Johnny smiled. "It's hard to explain. Just know that this is the life I want to live. The life I would have chosen for myself if the decision had been mine to make."

"It wasn't your choice?"

Johnny slowly shook his head. "You'll find there's something, someone higher up than us who is controlling all this. Letting one man substitute for another. It's a grand plan that is far beyond our understanding."

Ford thought for a moment then hesitantly pointed up.

Johnny adopted a beatific smile. "That's my theory." He looked over Ford's shoulder. "Ah . . . Harvey. Ready?"

"Just about." Harvey motioned to Ford. "I need to talk to Johnny for a moment." Ford excused himself and Harvey waited until he was out of earshot before speaking. "Sheriff,

I just wanted to apologize for causing all these problems. You know—" he grew bright red "—the snow and everything."

Johnny held out his hand. "Water under the bridge, Harvey. I owe you a bigger debt for bringing Emma here to help with the delivery. We couldn't have asked for a better doctor. Or a better friend."

Harvey squatted down and stroked the baby's cheek with the tip of his forefinger. "I remember when Darys was this little. And it's awfully easy to want to keep them children forever so you can shield them."

Angela reached over to cup Harvey's cheek in her warm hand. "But they grow up. Into individuals with their own dreams. Their own way of doing things. It must be hard letting go."

"Indeed it is. But—" Harvey rose stiffly, his knees not cooperating quite as well as they did when he was a young man "—you still have a while before this little one goes zigzagging off, following her own mind."

"And her own heart."

Harvey held out his hand. "Take care, old friend. Take care of this Margin. I probably won't have a chance to come back to it again."

"This is a final good-bye then?"

Tears began to prickle his eyes and he blinked them back. "It is." They clasped forearms, then pulled together for a quick embrace. Harvey turned toward the time portal where Ford and Darys waited with veiled impatience. He spun back around. "One question before I go."

"Anything."

"Where's Crawford James?"

Johnny's brow furrowed. "Who?"

"Crawford James, your assistant."

Johnny glanced at Angela who returned his puzzled stare.

"I have no assistant. I've never heard of anybody by that name."

Harvey nodded. "And Tucker James. You don't know that name either, right?"

"No." Angela stared at him blankly. "Should we know them?"

A rush of emotion filled Harvey—equal portions of happiness and sadness. "I guess you shouldn't . . . now." He raised his hand for a curt wave. "So long."

A few seconds later, Harvey held his daughter's hand tight. "Ready, sweetheart?"

"Yes, Dad."

"You, Ford?"

"Yes sir—*wait* . . ." Ford hopped out of the portal archway, reaching into his pants pocket to pull out something shiny. He held it in a clenched fist out toward Johnny. "The night before I . . . left Margin, Barrett gave me this." He uncurled his fingers to reveal a large silver coin. "He said it was *your* lucky piece, not his."

Johnny picked up the coin, holding it to the light to inspect it. "I'll be hornswaggled. It is mine, all right." He flipped the coin in the air and caught it. "I haven't seen the ladies Liberty here in quite some time."

Ford stepped back. "Then you should keep it. After all, it's yours."

Johnny shook his head. "Nah. I've been plenty lucky without it. You keep it." He flipped the coin to Ford who caught it in midair.

"You sure . . . Sheriff?"

The man grinned. "Lady Liberty is more woman than I need now. Take a good look at her."

Ford turned the coin over in his hand. "I . . . see what you mean." He slipped the coin back into his pocket. "Thanks. For everything, Johnny."

"We have to go . . . now," Harvey ordered, "before the wave hits."

"Yes sir." Ford nodded, grabbing Darys's hand. "I'm ready."

Harvey punched the last button. "Here we go . . ."

CHAPTER 17

*W*hen Ford opened his eyes, he found himself in a blindingly white room, surrounded by people also dressed in white. When he tried to move, he realized he'd been strapped down like some laboratory animal. Every tawdry dime novel he'd ever read concerning creatures from outer space or faceless futuristic societies began to haunt him. His imagination, something which had been his staunchest ally when it came to invention and technology, suddenly became his worst enemy.

He struggled, fighting against the invisible bonds that held him to the bed. He would have continued to fight if Harvey's smiling face hadn't loomed into view. His mouth moved, but Ford heard nothing. A second later, Harvey held up some sort of electronic slate with precisely formed letters.

"It's okay. You're safe."

"Where's Darys?"

Harvey pointed to his right.

Ford stiffly turned his head, seeing Darys stretched out on a bed next to him. They still held hands. In fact, someone had wrapped some sort of adhesive paper around their fingers so that their hands couldn't be separated.

The smile she gave him banished the worst of the fantastical horrors he imagined. The wink she gave him vanquished the rest.

They were safe. They were being care for.

He closed his eyes.

When he opened them again, he was curled up on a different bed, this one soft, sweet-smelling, but still all white. Nothing held him down except for a familiar, warm pressure on his left shoulder.

"Good morning, sleepyhead."

He turned toward the sound of the soft voice. Darys lay beside him, her head accounting for the weight on his upper arm. She brushed an errant lock of hair from his eyes.

"I was hoping you weren't going to sleep away our forty-eight hours of quarantine."

"Quarantine?" His heart quickened its pace. "What's wrong?"

"Sshh. Nothing's wrong. They're just being cautious. The scientists want to make sure you're not suffering from diseases for which we have no cure. We've eradicated a number of them, but in some cases, their cures have been destroyed as well to prevent accidental outbreaks."

"What sort of diseases?"

She rolled over on her back. "The usual. Smallpox, influenza . . ."

He nodded. "That makes sense. They don't want to relive the influenza epidemic of nineteen-eighteen. I don't blame them. So many people died."

She shot up in bed. "What year did you say?"

Ford stretched his stiff neck from side to side. "Nineteen-eight—" The significance of the date made his throat close.

"How did I know that?" he croaked. "It's nineteen-twelve . . . I mean I left in nineteen-twelve."

"Did I mention something about it to you?"

"No . . . I don't think so. I don't remember anybody saying anything about influenza or any sickness. Wait . . ." He snapped his fingers. The temporal stabilizer. How foggy could he be? He grinned. "You told me."

"I did?"

"Sure." He gently tapped her head with his forefinger, indicating her brain. "Just then. It's because we're linked by the . . ." He reached over to flip back her collar, intending to expose the chain holding her stabilizer. She was unadorned. "It's . . . gone." He sat bolt upright in the bed, his heart threatening to burst. "Oh God, Darys, it's gone . . ."

She leaned up on one elbow and stroked his temple. "Calm down. It's okay. The specialists were able to isolate our signals and get us off the same stabilizer."

He held his hands in front of him, staring at them intently. They looked solid. He rotated them. Real. He reached inside his shirt, feeling his chest and the heart beating within. His rapid but steady pulse signified life. Something bumped his hand. He glanced down and saw a thin golden disk hanging on a chain suspended around his own neck.

"I have one, now. That must be why I know things I'm not supposed to. And I bet you're tied into it somehow." Without a moment's hesitation, he reached over and held his hand against Darys's neck. Her own heart thrummed at a decidedly different beat.

She pulled herself up to a sitting position. "We're not together."

There was a sense of finality to her words that Ford didn't like.

Darys reached over and straightened the chain so that the

disk lay flat against his skin. "It's for you, only. I'm in my natural place in time. You're almost two hundred years beyond yourself. The specialists weren't sure you could exist here long without some sort of power boost. They've never brought anybody forward like this."

"But your father did. He took Johnny from one century to the next."

"And no one is particularly happy about that. Luckily, the changes it made in our universe were mostly cosmetic."

"If we're not linked any longer, then how did I know something about nineteen-eighteen?"

She folded her hands in her lap. "I don't know. Maybe it's a ghost image left over from the stabilizer's previous user."

"If we're not linked, then how do I know it's nighttime, outside?"

She blinked, betraying his correct guess.

"If we're not linked, then how do I know that you want to . . ." he searched for her words, " . . . make love right now?"

She paled, becoming almost as white as her clothes.

"It's true, isn't it? You want to make love before you slap me in a machine and shoot me back to my world, right?" Something intense started building in him. He told himself it was anger, but he knew it was a lie. What he felt was desire. Deep burning, everlasting desire.

"Don't, Ford."

"Don't what? Tell you what I feel? What you feel?" He stood up, knowing if she touched him, he'd likely explode. "Don't tell you that I want you? Need you?" He stalked into the middle of the sterile room. "And that you want and need me?"

"Don't love me, Ford. You can't afford to. You have a life to go back to."

"Life? Sure. I'll spend the rest of my life in a barn that I insist everyone call a laboratory and pretend to invent things." He scanned the room, seeing no corners, no source of light, no shadows. "Who are we kidding? I'll never invent anything important, just gadgets and gizmos that look impressive but do little."

She shifted until her legs dangled from the side of the bed. "But you will invent things. Marvelous things that will benefit mankind. You'll live to a ripe old age and, during your life, you'll become a celebrated scientist." Her voice began to build in intensity. "People will know who you are long after you're gone. People like me will study you in school." She stood, almost shouting. "Dr. Crawford Nolan will be a shining example of what a person can become when they combine persistence, intelligence, and imagination."

Darys paused to draw a breath and to collect herself. She spoke again in a low voice while staring at the floor. "I can't claim you for myself because you're much too important for the people of the future."

He felt her pain—the pain of self-sacrifice. Although, in theory, it was noble and brave, in practice, it stunk.

Ford crossed the room and knelt on the floor beside her. He caught her hands between his, holding on when she tried to pull them away. "I can't stop loving you because it's inconvenient. I can't stop loving you because I have the potential to build something useful for the times beyond mine. No one has the right to ask us to stop. Not in my world or any of the worlds that come after it. I'm not leaving, Darys. I'm staying here with you."

She looked up at him, tears rolling down her cheeks. "You can't stay. They won't let you. They'll force you into the machine. Even worse, they'll call it magnanimity when they wipe your memory clean. You won't remember anything. Not Johnny, not his baby, not me."

Her tears sparked his indignation. How dared they? How dared they decide who and what he could remember? Even if he couldn't stay here, they had no right to attempt to eradicate his love by stripping him of his memories of Darys. The answer became obvious.

He stood, grabbing her arms and bending slightly at the knees so they were at the same eye level. "Then we leave. Together. Come back with me, and we'll hide in the past."

A spark of hope flared in her eyes. His fingertips registered it just as easily as they felt the heat of her skin. But hope flickered and died.

"I can't," she whispered. "The early twentieth century is too far back in time for me to exist without a stabilizer."

He tried to fan the dying embers of hope with optimism. "Nonsense. Barrett proved it could be done. He lost his memories of his own time, but he didn't forget his love for Emma."

Her pain was palpable. "But he only went back a hundred years. We're talking about almost twice that distance. Right now, it's twenty-one-oh-six. To exist in nineteen-twelve, I'd need a stabilizer just to keep my molecules intact. But then, time cops could trace the signal, find me, and take me back."

His mind raced ahead with calculations. If he couldn't live in her world and she couldn't live in his, then the only solution was a compromise.

"Johnny," he whispered. "What year was Johnny living in?"

Darys's brow furrowed. "2017."

Ford closed his eyes. "And Johnny came from when?"

"I'm not sure."

When did Barrett and Johnny change places? Although he'd been a child, certainly he'd noticed something—some change when one man stepped into the role of the other. Ford reached up and grabbed the stabilizer, as if holding it would clear his thoughts, sharpen his memories, help his to recall . . .

The disk pulsed in his hand.

A disk in his hand.

Not gold like the stabilizer but silver.

A silver coin—a lucky one, at that.

Ford saw twenty years ago as if it were yesterday, all at unnaturally slow speed. The coin had sparkled as Johnny held it between finger and thumb. All eyes followed its path as he flipped it, tracing a perfect arc through the air. It spun as it landed in Ford's hand, stopping only when his fingers closed around it.

Twenty years ago—eighteen-ninety-two. That was the first of many odd actions "Sheriff Johnny Callaghan" made. Only it wasn't Johnny Callaghan. It was his great-great-great-grandson, Barrett Callaghan, pretending to be the frontier sheriff.

Harvey was there. Good ol' Harvey. Watching. Leading. Giving orders that Johnny should have made. Covering for Barrett until he became more familiar with the requirements of his role.

CHAPTER 18

*J*ohnny sprang one hundred and twenty-three three years into the future, to twenty-fifteen. Barrett had leaped back the same number of years to the past. Both men prospered, molecules intact. Barrett may have forgotten his futuristic origins, but he certainly remembered his love for Emma; that was something to which Ford could attest.

He opened his eyes and locked gazes with Darys. Her face betrayed confusion then, after a moment, illumination.

Then dread. "Without a stabilizer, I'd forget. All about this world." She paled. "I'd forget my father."

Ford cradled her face in his hands, caressing her wet cheeks with his thumbs. "No one could forget your father. *I* won't let you forget. I'll grill you every day, keep your memories fresh." She tried to look away, but he wouldn't let her. "And Harvey can visit us. That'll help you retain your memories of him."

"But Johnny and Barrett exchanged places. There's a sense of temporal symmetry in that."

Ford grinned as an apt analogy sprang to mind. "Then we

rely on symmetry with what we're going to do, too. If time is like a seesaw, then Johnny and Barrett exchange weights from one end to the other and the balance of the universe was retained. What you and I are doing is shifting one person from either end of the seesaw to the middle."

A new light flared in her eyes. "Then, to maintain a perfect equilibrium, we need to split the difference exactly between twenty-one-forty-two and nineteen-twelve."

Ford threw the numbers on his mental chalkboard. "Two-thousand and twenty-seven. That's where we go, two-thousand and twenty-seven. Who would look for us there?"

She grinned. "No one." But the expression quickly faded to something much more serious in tone. Her face grew more solemn. "Arranging to run away. It'll cost every credit I have, bribing the right people."

"Credit?"

"Money," she explained. "Dollars. Lots of dollars."

"Dollars?" The word echoed through his mind. *Dollars . . . or perhaps all it would take would be just one lucky dollar.*

"My *clothes* . . ." Ford bounced up from the bed. "Where are my clothes?" He scanned the room.

"You're wearing them."

"No, not those. The ones I arrived in. My denim pants."

"They're here, somewhere." She stood up and scanned the room, finally stopping at what turned out to be an invisible door leading to a shallow closet.

He pounced on the trousers, and, to his relief, the coin was safely nestled next to his jackknife in his pocket. He pulled out the coin and offered it to her. "Consider this my contribution to the cost of our freedom."

"What is it?"

"A silver dollar."

A sad smile filled her face and she sighed. "One dollar

down and nine-hundred-ninety-nine thousand, nine-hundred and ninety-nine to go."

"I promise you; a coin made of pure silver from eighteen-seventy-eight must be worth more than one dollar, now."

Darys examined Lady Liberty's regal profile. *"Eighteen-seventy-eight,"* she read. "This is really quite old. But even today, I don't think it's worth a million dollars."

"Turn it over," he urged.

She complied, revealing Lady Liberty, yet again, in the identical pose. "A two-headed coin?" She tossed the coin at him and crossed her arms. "You think you're going to win a million dollars by making bets with a two-headed trick coin?"

He laughed, long and hard, the emotion almost as draining as a good romp in the bed. "No, silly. It's not a trick coin. It's an eighteen-seventy-eight Morgan silver dollar with an important misstrike. It has Lady Liberty on both sides."

Her face grew more animated with each passing word. "And someone . . . like a coin collector might want to get his hands on something like this—"

"Something *rare* like this," Ford corrected.

"Rare," she repeated. "How rare?"

"Rare enough to be worth a substantial amount of money in nineteen-twelve. But this is twenty-one-forty-two . . ."

"Oh, Ford!" She jumped at him, knocking him onto the bed where she landed on top of him. They became a tangle of bare arms, legs and assorted other body parts and the process to extract themselves became almost too provocative to bear.

"Not now," Ford said, more to himself as a reminder than as a reprimand to her. "We have to figure out how to get out of here, first."

She shot him a smile that could have charmed honey from a hungry bear. "That's my job."

❧

As Ford stepped into the workshop, he realized that the young man leaning over the workbench hadn't seen him. Ford wasn't sure how to announce himself, whether to cough or say "Hello" or what. He took a step closer, evidently making a noise which alerted his companion.

"John Junior, I thought I told you to get lost," the young man said, without looking behind him.

"Uh . . . it's not John," Ford said quietly.

When the young man turned around, he looked perturbed at first. Then his irritation faded away. "Uncle Ford?" His mouth dropped open and the screwdriver he held landed perilously close to his right shoe. "Is it you?"

Ford nodded. "Yeah, Nick, it's me."

Four very short years had turned Nick Callaghan from a devilish scamp to a strapping, handsome young man with his father's build, but with Emma's storm-colored eyes.

He stepped forward, tentative at first, and then building courage as he approached. He launched himself into Ford's arms as if he was still a fourteen-year-old terror. "Mom said you'd be back some day. She told us all about the time machine and going to the future to see you and everything. I thought she'd gone crazy, but Dad said it was all true."

"It is true, Nick. Every word of it." Ford tried hard to match Nick's youthful enthusiasm, but he couldn't—not knowing what he had to do. "Nick, I can't talk long. The time cops . . . the officials from the future think I'm staying here, but I'm not."

"Not staying?" Nick looked panicked at first, but Ford could see the gears turning in the boy's rather remarkable brain. Nick realized that "not staying" meant "going somewhere else" and that was the sure sign of an adventure of the making.

If there was anything the boy loved, it was a good adventure.

Nick grabbed Ford's sleeve, pleating it between his fingers. "Take me with you," he said in a breathless voice. "I want to see the future."

Ford brushed away the boy's hand. "You will, Nick. You will see the future, one way or the other." *If I can help it*, Ford added silently. "But there's something you have to do, first."

"Anything," Nick promised. "Just tell me, I'll do anything."

Ford tried to keep his voice even and low. "Tomorrow . . . you're going swimming with your friends, right?"

Nick cocked his head. "How did you know?"

"I just know," Ford said, fully realizing that any other explanation would be unthinkable. "There's something very important that you have to swear to me that you'll do. Swear, Nick. Not promise, not try to remember, but swear on the Bible, that you'll do."

Nick raised his right hand, his face flushed with the excitement of such a conspiracy. "I swear," he said with every earnest fiber of his body. "I swear, Uncle Ford."

Ford tried to keep control of himself but it was growing increasingly difficult. "Tomorrow, before you go swimming, check the rope."

"The rope?"

Ford nodded. "The one tied to the pine tree that leans out over the lake. The one we always use to swing on." Suddenly, Ford needed to hold his nephew, to feel the boy's blood rushing through his veins, to feel his heart thundering even if spurred by the prospect of such clandestine excitement.

Nick Callaghan loved secrets.

And this secret just might keep him from swinging out over a lake on a faulty rope.

This secret might keep the rope from breaking.

This secret might keep his neck from breaking.

This secret might keep Emma's heart from breaking.

"Swear it," Ford commanded.

The flush of excitement faded from Nick's face. He was bright. He probably realized what he was being told.

When he looked up at Ford, with Emma's solemn eyes, there was no trace of a headstrong boy left in face. Instead, there stood a man.

"I swear."

Silence permeated every cubic inch of the room and threatened to overwhelm both of them. It wasn't often someone learned that the day of their death was near, and received instructions on how to avoid it, completely. Any topic they discussed after that had to be anti-climactic.

Ford drew a deep breath and point to the bench. "Whatcha working on?"

Nick glanced over his shoulder at the work area, littered with items that weren't there four years prior. "Uh . . . about your workshop. Mom said it would be okay if I . . . if I . . ." His voice trailed away as he turned bright red with guilt. He ducked his head. "I promise I haven't messed with any of your projects." He straightened a bit. "But I have decided I wanted to become an inventor . . . just like you."

Ford's heart took an extra beat. "I'm flattered. But I sincerely hope you'll become a better inventor than I was."

Nick kicked an imaginary rock in an "Aw shucks" manner. "Sure. Me better than you. That's a laugh."

"No it isn't, Nick." Ford knew that this was a flame that needed fanning, a small interest that needed to become a passion. "It's not a joke. You can be better than me. Far better than me. You can pick up where I left off and go so much farther, do so many more things."

Nick's laughter was a bit strained. "Pick up where you left off? Oh, sure. It's going to take me years to figure out what half of this stuff in here does." An honest grin broke free.

"But you're home, now. You can explain everything to me. Show me the ropes . . ." His voice trailed off and he grew suddenly silent.

"Nick, I—"

Nick gestured for him to be quiet and Ford complied.

"That's what this is all about, right? Showing me the ropes. Literally and figuratively."

Ford couldn't bring himself to answer. But Nick needed no confirmation.

"I die tomorrow, don't I? At least, I will if I swing on the rope without checking it first. But now I know to check. And I'll live . . . but why?"

Ford couldn't believe what he was hearing. "Why? Because you deserve a full life. You deserve a chance to grow up, to become a man, to love a woman, to live a full rich—"

"No, not that." Nick cocked his head and smiled. "I realize you want to save my life. And I know you want to do it because you love me." He paused then looked Ford straight in the eye. "I love you, too, Uncle Ford."

Ford tried to respond, but discovered that his throat refused to cooperate.

Nick scanned the room, a new light of maturity filling his eyes. "If my new life starts tomorrow, then it seems only right that I do something important with it. Something special. Something . . . meaningful." He suddenly stiffened and stared at Ford. "You won't be coming back, will you?"

Ford felt as if the air had been knocked from his lungs. What sort of magic had occurred in the past four years that could have wholly transformed Nick from an idealistic child to such an insightful young man?

Such wisdom deserved the truth.

"No, I'm not coming back. At least, not soon. I'm returning to the future to live there . . . permanently. Someone's coming for me in a little while."

"It's a woman." The way Nick put it, it was more of a statement than a question.

Ford's heart soared at the thought of his love for Darys. Even though she was safely hidden so many years in the future, he could feel her presence, feel her soul touching his.

"Yes," he said softly, "it's a woman."

Nick smiled. "I knew it. Only true love could make you give up all this." He glanced lovingly around the room at the half-completed projects, the bits and piece of Ford's dreams.

"It's all yours, if you want it, Nick."

"For me?" Nick scanned the room a second time.

"Every bit of it. Every concept, every invention, down to every last nut and bolt in the place. Take up where I've left off, Nick."

"But they're your inventions."

Ford shook his head. "That's the problem about going to the future. Everything I want to create has already been invented. It's going to take me a while to catch up on their sciences and technologies. But once I do, I start over again."

He spotted a tarp-covered object on a nearby work table and a plan suddenly formed in his mind. "But there's one project I want to explain to you so you can file the patent as soon as possible." He pointed to the seismograph which he knew lurked beneath the tarp.

Nick followed his gesture. "But that's yours. You did it, not me."

"Not anymore." Ford smiled. "It's going to be the Callaghan Variation of the Wiechert Inverted Pendulum Seismograph." He couldn't stop his smile from growing even bigger. "And it's going to be the start of a beautiful career. . . ."

CHAPTER 19

*T*en year-old Emma Callaghan watched as her sister placed her dolls in a circle around the tree stump, and pour pretend tea into the acorn cups. A warm breeze ruffled the aspen leaves, and they quaked accordingly. Emma had known this was where she'd find Charlotte. It had been her own special spot to spend a long summer when she was little, too. But now, at her advanced age of maturity, she didn't do such things.

She walked quietly behind Charlotte. "Whatcha doing, squirt?"

Charlotte jumped. "You scared me." Her face began to pucker and Emma knew a squall was on its way.

"I'm sorry, I'm sorry. I didn't mean to sneak up on you. Mom sent me to make sure the bogeyman hadn't run away with you".

Charlotte sniffed with derision, the squall diverted. "There ain't no such thing as the bogeyman."

"*Isn't,*" Emma corrected. "There *isn't* such thing as the bogeyman."

"See? Even you agree with me. I'm just having a tea party."

"So I see. Is Lady Jane here?" Emma glanced around as if looking for her sister's imaginary friend. Little kids could be so stupid, sometimes.

Charlotte picked up a flower and began to pull it apart, dividing the petals evenly between the dolls. Emma recognized the recipe for flower salad, a staple at pretend tea parties everywhere.

Charlotte affected an annoying accent. "No, Lady Jane is off visiting the Queen Mother for tea. She did say she'd be back soon and bring Lord Caruso and his valet back with her."

Cartoons, Emma thought in disgust. Constant exposure to cartoons must have rotted her sister's brain. Two hundred and fifty channels of programming available at all hours, and this seven-year-old nincompoop insisted on streaming the same moldy British show over and over again. *The Adventures of Lady Jane.* Emma had outgrown such drivel years ago. "Mom said that lunch will be in a half hour. Don't be late, Peanut-brain."

"I won't, dork-head." Charlotte turned to the nearest doll. "Why, Mrs. Rumplepuss, what a lovely hat. Wherever did you find it?"

A weird noise drowned "Mrs. Rumplepuss's" reply. The ground began to shake and the acorn cups toppled over.

"What's going on?" Charlotte whined.

Emma grabbed her little sister and held onto the tree stump for dear life. She knew it had to be an earthquake. Maybe this was the "big one" her parents were always talking about. Maybe California was sliding off into the ocean just like everyone was always predicting, and Colorado would be the new West Coast.

Suddenly, the shaking stopped, but the weird noise continued. It sounded almost like a television set that had lost its cable feed, sort of screechy and full of static.

The noise grew louder until it ended with a loud boom which echoed through the valley. Charlotte jumped at the sound and buried her face in Emma's shirt.

There was a long sliding whistle and then the ground shook as if something had sailed through the skies and landed hard. A meteor? Emma corrected herself. A *meteorite* . . . that was, if it had made it all the way through the earth's atmosphere and landed. They'd learned that last year in science class.

Judging by the jolt, whatever it was, it'd landed nearby.

She stood, hauling her sister up by her hand. "We're getting out of here!"

"But my dolls," Charlotte whined. She leaned down, trying to pick up Mrs. Rumplepuss.

"Stupid dolls," Emma muttered under her breath. She grabbed the other three, stuck them under her arm and started dragging Charlotte and Mrs. Rumplepuss down the path toward home. She only made it a few feet before she had to stop.

Something large and silver-colored sat square in the path, blocking their way.

"Bogeymen!" Charlotte declared.

"More like aliens from outer space," Emma corrected, pulling her little sister behind her.

A harsh metallic sound came from the silver . . . thing, sounding like a rusty door hinge that needed oiling. Steam leaked from the top of it.

She heard someone coughing.

Charlotte pulled on Emma's sleeve. "I bet they're *Alien Slave Masters from Planet Altros*."

Finally, her sister made some reference to a program other than that insipid *Lady Jane*. And what did she remember? Some gawd-awful science fiction show. Wasn't that always the way these things went?

They heard another cough and then a groan.

"Aliens don't cough," Emma declared softly.

A silvery hatch sprung open, and three lumps tumbled out of the thing.

"Are you all right, Darys?" one thing asked another.

The smallest lump nodded. "What about you, Dad?"

The fattest lump grabbed its eyeless face. "I can't see. I can't see!"

The first lump grabbed the second lump's head and twisted it around. "There. Your face shield got turned around. Can we get out of these things now?"

The smallest lump began to tug at its head. "You'd think that a million dollars would buy something other than a third-rate, antediluvian time portal."

"Who's Auntie Divulie?" Charlotte whispered.

"No, an-ti-di-lu-vi-ans. They're those blue guys from *Star Trek*," Emma explained. "The ones with the white horns."

Charlotte screamed before Emma could slap a hand over the brat's mouth.

The alien ripped its head off, revealing neither a blue face nor white horns; it was the face of an ordinary-looking woman. Maybe these were the type of aliens that were stealing body parts, one piece at a time. Emma inched backward.

"Ohmigod, is she hurt?" the woman's head asked. "Did we land too close to you? Are you both okay?"

Emma swallowed hard. "S-She's okay."

Charlotte buried her face in Emma's stomach. "Emma, make them go away."

The thing began to tear off the rest of its arms and legs, and Emma realized belatedly that it was some sort of blobby silver space suit. The lady who came out of it looked perfectly normal, as if all the body parts were originally hers to start with.

Aliens pulled tricks like that on television.

"My name is Darys." The woman alien tugged at the head of the silver blob next to her. "And this is my . . . friend, Ford." The head came off and inside was a nice-looking man's face which was almost familiar-looking. "And this is my father, Harvey." It took both of the aliens to pull his head off.

Emma stared at him, deciding he looked more like someone's granddaddy.

Darys Alien continued. "I'm really sorry we scared you. We didn't think anybody would be out here in the woods."

Charlotte held up Mrs. Rumplepuss. "We were having a tea party."

Darys Alien smiled. "Those are fun. I used to have them when I was a little girl with my brother, Darrell."

Emma shook her head. "Tea parties are for little kids. Not for me. I'm ten. I'm too old for those things." She added a shrug. "And I don't have a brother, only old sissy-pants, here."

Charlotte began to pout. "I'm not a sissy-pants."

"Are too."

"Are not."

Darys took a deep breath. "Uh, ten? Then that means you were born in what year?"

"2017." Emma slapped her palm against her head. Everyone knew you didn't volunteer information to people from outer space. What an idiot she was . . .

The one named Ford opened his eyes wide then grinned. Emma had to admit to herself that he was sorta cute . . . for an adult, that was.

"We did it! It's twenty-twenty-seven." He turned and clapped the other man on the shoulder. "It might not have been the most advanced technology available, but it worked, nonetheless." He stripped off the rest of his silver suit and Emma could see he was wearing blue jeans.

Aliens didn't wear blue jeans. Did they?

When he walked toward her, she knew she ought to be scared, but for some reason she wasn't. He smiled and stopped a few feet shy of them. "Will you do me a favor, Emma?"

She was about to ask how he knew her name then remembered her big-mouthed sister. "What?" she asked suspiciously.

"Go tell Johnny . . . your father, that his friend Ford Nolan is back and we're coming to meet him just as soon as we get Harvey out of his protector suit. Will you do that for me?"

"You're really a friend of my dad's?"

The man nodded and used his forefinger to cross his heart with an *X*. "I promise. I've known him for a *very* long time."

Emma Callaghan and her little sister ran away, needing no second invitation to flee to safety.

Little sister.

Ford sighed. Johnny and Angela probably had their hands full with those two. He turned back toward Harvey who was struggling with the seam closure on his suit. Once he and Darys freed the man, they all surveyed the damage to the travel unit.

Darys scowled. "You think it'll fly one more time?"

Harvey gave the power unit a kick. "Yeah, this old thing's got a couple hundred years left in her. I'll get home with no problem." They tossed their suits inside it and Harvey pulled out the controller that rendered the unit invisible.

As they followed the path out of the woods, they saw a welcoming party of one charging up the hill toward them.

When he reached them, Johnny changed Ford's proffered handshake into a manly embrace. "Back so soon?" he quipped, pounding Ford on the back with enthusiasm.

"It's been almost ten years, right?"

Johnny nodded. "Almost. And *you.*" Abandoning Ford, he pulled Darys into a hug. "You haven't changed a day. Just as beautiful as ever."

Darys grinned. "I'm only a week older than last time you saw me."

"And the leader of this merry band." Johnny turned to Harvey. "I knew you couldn't stay away."

Harvey shrugged. "I may have to stay away . . . for a while, at least. We may have some time cops on our tail and I need to lead them astray. We aren't on what you'd call a sanctioned trip."

Johnny snorted. "Do you *ever* take a sanctioned trip?" He didn't wait for an answer. "So you two are going to stay here with us?"

Ford reddened. "We were hoping you wouldn't mind." He laced his fingers in Darys's. "We want to stay together and this is exactly halfway between our two times."

Johnny evidently spotted the stabilizer hanging around Darys's neck. "Are you two still—" he made a gesture of hooking his forefingers together "—still locked together?"

It was her turn to blush. "No. They were able to separate us." She fiddled with the medallion that hung around her neck. "Hopefully, I won't need this at all." She glanced up at Ford, her eyes filled with hope and just a little fear. "Should we . . . go ahead?"

He shrugged. "Now is as good a time as any."

Johnny turned his puzzled stare from one to the other, finally settling on Harvey. "What are they talking about?"

"Their stabilizers. They're going to turn them off."

"But won't they start to . . ." Johnny shot Ford a panicked look.

"Disintegrate? No." Darys patted his arm. "We made sure that Ford and I went through all the proper preparations for travel this time. The only thing my stabilizer is shielding is my memories. Once I turn it off, I'll be just like Barrett. My memory of the past will start to fade away, gradually. He doesn't mind not remembering his previous life. I won't either."

"That's because you and I are going to fill all of her days with stories about her father. Plus we have this." Ford dug into his pocket and pulled out the tiny stick they'd brought with them. "They scanned Darys's mind and stored everything here."

Johnny gaped at the machine. "It's so . . . small."

Darys broke the somber mood by pretending to pout. "Hey, are you saying I'm a nano-brain?" She laughed as Johnny tried to extract his foot from his mouth. "It's compressed data," she explained. "Six hundred terabytes worth. We didn't have room for everything, so we tried to concentrate strictly on the memories of my family."

"And this will help you remember Harvey?" He managed a laugh. "I've always found him pretty unforgettable."

Ford realized Harvey's laughter was a bit strained, not because he took exception to Johnny's joke, but that he was going to say good-bye to his daughter, perhaps forever.

Harvey put his arm around his daughter. "I want you to go ahead and switch your stabilizer off while I'm still here. If anything goes wrong, you still have a way of getting home where we can fix the problem."

She nodded then looked at Ford with a gaze that cut right to the center of his soul. Her voice dropped to a whisper. "Ready?"

He nodded.

He lifted the chain from around his neck and Darys followed suit. They tapped out the disarming sequence together.

Three-six-two-zero-zero-four-seven-nine.

After they hit the last number, Darys slipped her hand in his.

Ford's stabilizer fell silent quickly, its slight glow fading away like a dying ember. He wasn't worried; he was in no real danger. Going forward in time was easy. The only difference was that he'd jumped a hundred and nine years ahead instead of doing it one day at a time like everyone else. It was going back in time that was complicated.

Darys's hand tightened in his, and he feared it signaled a problem. But when he looked at her, no desperation filled her eyes. What he saw was love.

Pure, simple, timeless.

They waited, not in silence, but with the sound of chattering birds, chirping crickets, and rustling leaves. Nature's music to accompany a highly unusual violation of nature's laws.

Harvey leaned over and kissed his daughter on the forehead. "You'll be fine."

She held out the stabilizer then glanced at Ford. "Yes, I will be."

He gathered her stabilizer as well as Ford's and stuffed them in his pocket. "I'll use these as decoys to put the time cops on a false trail. They'll never find you here. Ford?" Harvey held out his hand. "Take good care of my girl. I'm counting on you."

Ford shook it solemnly. "Yes sir. I won't let you down."

"Sweetheart?" Harvey turned to Darys. "This isn't goodbye. I'll be back to visit as often as I can. And I'll make sure the time cops leave you alone."

She sniffed, trying desperately to maintain control of her emotions. But Ford could feel everything—her apprehension, her fear for herself, for her father. The connection they shared outlived any machine, penetrated all barriers, exceeded the hands of time itself. He had a piece of her soul and she, his.

"B-be careful, Dad," was all she could say.

"I will, Darys. I will." He kissed her one more time and she threw herself into his arms. After a few moments, Ford knew instinctively that she needed his strength to help let go of her father. He closed his eyes and concentrated, giving her access to all she needed from him.

He heard her release a shuddering sigh. "I love you, Dad."

"I love you, too, sweetheart."

Darys reached for Ford's hand, again. He opened his eyes, realizing that they were shedding her tears.

Harvey offered him a shaky salute. "Ford? Thanks. See you . . . soon." As soon as he turned his back, they could hear him draw in an emotion-filled gasp of air. Johnny silently motioned for them to remain back, and he fell in step with Harvey.

As soon as they got out of range, Johnny put his arm around him. "Buck up, old friend. I'll take good care of them."

Harvey merely nodded, unable to speak.

After a while, Johnny sighed. "You knew they would end up coming back together, didn't you?"

Harvey nodded again. "When you told me you'd never heard of either Crawford or Tucker James, I realized what was in store for them."

"I remember you asking about these James fellows. Who are they? Or were they?"

Harvey stopped and gave Johnny a watery smile. "Crawford and Tucker James should have been Ford's great-great-grandsons. In the original time line, Crawford was continuing a family vendetta, plotting to destroy the Callaghan family in 2015 because of something you did as sheriff of Margin in 1892. But Barrett changed history, and everything was rewritten. There was no blood feud between the families and, instead of being an enemy, Crawford James became your very trusted assistant. Tucker worked for you as well. When I came back and realized neither man even existed, it meant only one thing; Ford Nolan never returns to his time period to marry and have a child."

Johnny glanced behind him. "No, I suspect he'll stay here and do that, with your daughter."

Harvey swiped his sleeve across his eyes. "I expect you're right. Well . . . here we are. You don't need to go all the way with me. I . . . I'd rather do this by myself."

Johnny understood. It was hard to leave behind the people you loved. He was one of the lucky ones, though. He'd had a chance to return to the woman he loved.

"Until we meet again, Harvey."

"Until . . . ," he echoed.

Johnny turned and headed back down the path. By the time he reached Darys and Ford, he'd already made his decision.

"Ford? I have a proposal to make."

Ford and Darys shared a curious glance.

"What type of proposal?"

"How would you like to become my assistant?"

"A job? Here?"

Johnny smiled. This was all going to work out just fine. "A job. You see I'm going to need to be able to take off some time, soon."

"Time?" Darys and Ford pronounced the word as if it was coated in something bitter.

"No, no, not that kind of time." He led the way around the empty porch. "We're off season right now so the place is quiet. This is an ideal—" he couldn't help smiling "—time . . . for you to learn all about the way we run things here."

They rounded the corner and saw Angela and the two children huddled together in deep conversation.

"He said his name was Ford Nolan?" Angela was saying.

Emma nodded. "Uh huh, and then Daddy went—"

"Daddy!" Charlotte squealed, interrupting her sister. She started toward him, but her very protective older sister grabbed her, pulling her back.

Emma stepped forward as if to shield her mother and sister. She wore a fierce, protective scowl. "Be careful. They're aliens from the planet Antediluvia. They *could* be holding Dad hostage."

Angela began to laugh, ruffling their oldest daughter's hair. "No sweetheart, they're not antediluvians. They're friends of ours. No . . . not just friends. They're family."

Johnny nodded in total agreement. Family. It was a beautiful word. "Girls, come meet some distant cousins of yours —Ford Nolan and Darys Kirk."

"Cousins?" Emma lost her defensive posture. "For real? From Daddy's side of the family?" she asked with incredulity.

Johnny traced an *X* on his chest. "Cross my heart." The girls ran toward them, their fears swallowed up by their new familial fascination.

Darys stared at Angela's protruding stomach then shot Johnny a knowing smile. "Now I understand why you're so anxious to hire an assistant." She turned to Emma. "Know what? I was there when you were born."

Emma's mouth dropped open. "No fooling?"

Johnny couldn't help but laugh. "No fooling." He hugged his eldest daughter; she looked so much like her mother. Same rosy cheeks, same mischievous twinkle in her eyes.

There Angela stood, a proud mother, a loving wife, a woman of the ages. . . .

Ford leaned over, Charlotte already attached to his leg in complete acceptance of his role of cousin. "So . . . when's Angela due?"

Johnny's smile widened. "In about three weeks."

EPILOGUE

$\mathcal{F}$rom the desk of William C. Nolan, Ph.D.,
January 1, 2040

New Year's Day is a solemn day for me as I take time to remember all the impossible things that have happened to me since I arrived in the future. In the past twelve, almost thirteen years, I've seen and accepted the impossible. Although I feared always being an antiquated man in a wondrous, futuristic world, I've managed to study enough of the past to catch up. I even managed to earn my doctoral degree in geophysics and am continuing my studies in seismology.

It was during my studies that I realized my first moment of unmitigated pride. It occurred when I learned there had never been such a thing as the Nolan variation on the Wiechert inverted pendulum. But there had been the Callaghan variation.

Nick managed to not only unscramble my notes, but make an improvement on my original design. I found his name attached to many somewhat familiar ideas I'd had, but in every case, the completed invention far exceeded the original scope of my designs. I may have provided some inspiration, but Dr. Nicholas Callaghan, American inventor, had turned them into reality.

I couldn't be prouder of him or my other two nephews. Tim took "T.J. Nolan" as a penname and is . . . was . . . known as one of the great early-twentieth century science fiction writers. John Junior, my incorrigible nephew, took a while to settle down to eventually manage the Margin Mining Consortium. Thanks to his position, he was able to capitalize on the US Government's decision in 1942 to build an encampment where soldiers learned how to ski in anticipation of war with Germany. Margin Mountain Skiing started shortly after the war and morphed into a resort in the late 1950s.

The restrictions on time travel have been tightened, but so far, no one has figured out that my origins go back to the late nineteenth century and that my wife, Darys, theoretically hasn't been born yet. It's a hard concept to explain to our two children, Lida and Wil, so we've refrained from doing so.

Yet.

Speaking of Darys, we spent many years working hard to maintain her memories, but after a while, she decided that she'd rather concentrate on the here and now rather than a distant future. So we continue to reload only those memories that she has of her father and other family members. Somehow, Harvey has found several different opportunities to thwart the temporal authorities and has been back to visit his grandchild several times. He even managed to bring his son, Darrell, along on several of the trips and it's been a pleasure to meet my brother-in-law and, even more, to see Darys and him interact as if there weren't so many miles and too many years distance between them.

I guess Lady Liberty's double-sided luck has stayed with us, despite using her for our means to escape to my future and Darys's past. All in all, life has been very good, here in the mid-twenty-first century. I have the companion of a lifetime—many lifetimes, in fact—and we have two healthy, smart children who keep us thoroughly engaged and sometimes guessing.

Each new year brings us new challenges and new successes and I wouldn't have it any other way.

Ford Nolan

a.k.a. Dr. William C. Nolan

READER LETTER

Dear Reader,

This story has been a long time coming. I promised it to my readers many years ago, but then the original publisher changed their publishing philosophy and no longer wanted time-travel romances. With the first book still under their contract, I was unable to do anything but wait. And wait we did.

But then again, time travel stories have an advantage over other genres; we know we can always go back and spin a new story, like this one. And if the stars line up right, we may end up visiting Margin a few more times. After all, we have several generations of characters who are fighting to have their stories told.

Email me at suspense@suspense.net and let me know which character you think deserves the next story!

Laura Hayden

ABOUT THE AUTHOR

As a kid, when Laura Hayden wasn't watching TV, she was reading. So, her eighteen books and short stories straddle multiple fiction genres and include vivid characters with action, suspense, and humor.

ALSO BY LAURA HAYDEN

A Margin in Time

A Margin of Error

Ghost of a Chance

The Hope Chest Series: *The Thief*

The Hope Chest Series Five-Book Boxed Set

Magick Rising (anthology)

America the Beautiful

Red, White and Blue

Double Exposure (with Susan Ford)

Sharp Focus (with Susan Ford)

Angel (with Nicole "Coco" Marrow)

Sweet Contemporary Romantic Comedies

(Dogwood Series)

A Match in Dogwood (anthology)

A Dogwood Christmas (anthology)

Science Fiction/Fantasy Short Stories

Steel Crazy

Guardian of the Peace

Twelve Days

Nine-Tenths